When Nights Were Cold

SUSANNA JONES

When Nights Were Cold

PICADOR

First published 2012 by Mantle

This paperback edition published in Great Britain 2013 by Picador
an imprint of Pan Macmillan, a division of Macmillan Publishers Limited
Pan Macmillan, 20 New Wharf Road, London N1 9RR
Basingstoke and Oxford
Associated companies throughout the world
www.panmacmillan.com

ISBN 978-0-330-54484-9

1 3 5 7 9 8 6 4 2

A CIP catalogue record for this book is available from
the British Library.

Typeset by CPI Typesetting
Printed and bound by CPI Group (UK) Ltd, Croydon, CR0 4YY

For Joe, Alice, Dylan and Evan

Tall Trees, Park Road,
Dulwich
London

25 October 1913

Dear Sir Ernest Shackleton,

We are three graduates of the sciences from the
University of London. Our research interests are in
the fields of Physics, Biology and Botany. We share a
profound interest in biological and geological features
of the polar regions and we followed your expedition to
Antarctica in the Nimrod with the greatest interest and
respect. We understand that you are looking for men for
your next journey and hereby offer our services. We are
all active in sports, having experience of mountaineering
at high altitude, crossing glaciers and camping out in
bivouacs.

We are strong and healthy and believe we would be an
asset to your expedition. We are ready to endure hardship
and physical sacrifice.

Yours sincerely,

L. Locke
C. Parr
G. Farringdon

Part One

Part One

Chapter One

Last night I tried to climb the Matterhorn again. It seemed, for the first time, quite within my reach. I began from the Hörnli ridge, with my lantern in my hand and the weight of a full pack on my back, a coil of rope over my shoulder. Quite soon I was jogging upward over rock and snow to the pyramid's chiselled top. How easy it was. This time there were no loose stones or rotten boulders and my climb was satisfying and sweet. Yet when I lifted my eyes to take in the view I saw that the sky was still black. I shone the lantern – I had not dropped it – but, beyond my own arm, nothing seemed to exist. There were no boots on my feet, just thin stockings, and I could not move. I called out for my guide, then my companions. No one answered and I knew that they were dead. My heart slumped. I peered over the ledge to the glacier far below and saw a woman's body, arms outstretched, incongruous, a flat grey fish on the ice. Ink spots crept through the ice, burst into flowers around her head. *Black vanilla orchids,* a voice whispered and I crumpled between the rocks. My lantern had gone. The sun was up.

The back door slammed and a shriek brought me to my senses. I threw the bedclothes aside, stumbled to the window and lifted a corner of the curtain. The housemaid was chasing a man across the lawn. He was a short, barrel-shaped creature, but he leaped over the back fence without a second glance. I dropped the curtain and stepped back lest he had hidden in the neighbours' bushes to watch the house. It has happened before. Mabel scurried around downstairs, drawing curtains and locking the doors. I shuddered, climbed back into bed and resolved that it was safest to spend the day under my covers. A little later Mabel appeared with a pot of tea and a plate of kippers.

'You should have seen him. What a fright he gave me. His nose was all squashed up to the pane like a snout. I don't know what he expected to see in the scullery. There's nothing in it but pots and the laundry.' She put the breakfast tray on my lap, but I waved it away.

'Just the tea, Mabel.'

She shook her head, a gesture of hers that always intrigues me since nothing else moves. Mabel's hairstyle is rigid, a crisp cottage loaf over a face of freshly expanded dough.

'Aren't you hungry?'

'I might have some bread later.'

'I should have gone for the police.'

'There was no need, Mabel. You did well to get rid of him so quickly. Could you pour the tea while it's nice and hot?'

Mabel filled my cup and set the pot on the bedside table.

'It's the anniversary tomorrow, isn't it? If you just gave an interview to a newspaper, or wrote about the business – even after all this time – well, it would make things easier. It would make it clearer for people who don't know you and who got the wrong end of the stick.'

'No, Mabel. It would make things worse and I have nothing to hide or deny. They've decided, and I can't change it. Fifteen years since she died, and still not long enough. Even if I could, to talk about it now would either remind the people who have forgotten or inform the ones who never knew. Mr Snout down there was the first to show an interest for a long time.'

I sipped my thick brown tea, imagined the stream finding its way into a cranky little wheel deep inside my body, to set the millstone grinding for a new day, as if I were an old, old woman. Mabel tucked the edges of my blankets under the mattress then went to the window, scouring the garden with eyes narrowed into a pillar-box slit.

'As you wish. What will you have for supper today, Miss Farringdon? The butcher has some nice chops at a very reasonable price.'

'A bit of porridge will be more than plenty.'

I wondered what the intruder had gleaned from his brief visit. If he had seen my face at the window and the curtain sweeping it away, what story might he read from it?

'Certainly. And remember that I shan't be sleeping here tonight. My mother wants me at hers so you'll be alone. Will you be all right?'

'Father's old rifle is somewhere. I'm joking, no need to

scowl like that. Now you're getting on my nerves, Mabel. I'll be fine. Miss Cankleton and Mr Blunt are here, after all.'

'For what use they are.'

Miss Cankleton has Mother's old room, across from mine, and Mr Blunt lives in the attic. I talk to them if I meet them, but sometimes all that passes across the hall is *hello* or a nod. Once a week I collect their rent and I ask them if their rooms are satisfactory. They pay up and express satisfaction. We all hear each other's noises – the squeak of a wardrobe door, the groan of a rotten floorboard, a cough or a sneeze – gossamer connections which are enough for people like us who don't like our bonds tight.

'I'll fetch the newspapers.'

'Stop making a fuss. I don't know what's happening in the world and I don't care about it. Whatever Mr Baldwin does—'

'Mr Chamberlain it is now. If things get worse on the continent, you will know.' She took the kippers and left.

I tiptoed to the window. Somehow another year has sloped by since Cicely Parr's death. There was an inquest at the time, all the necessary business, and it was quite settled, at least by the coroner if not by the press. But I am the last surviving member of the Society and this seems to give me a certain poisonous glamour, notoriety of a kind I never wanted. I did want to be known, once upon a time, but not in connection with the accursed Cicely Parr.

I stayed in bed all day, kept the curtains closed, and when the sun set and it seemed safe I ventured downstairs.

*

Now I am sitting in the drawing room and nothing will trouble me because everyone is asleep. My neighbours' windows are black. The Dulwich streets are quiet and I am cosy. I like it in my den. I have my things here, I am comfortable and at the end of the night I shall sit at the window and watch the sun rise. I have an abundance of coal to keep me warm. I have a servant still and the money to pay her for months, even years, to come. Perhaps tonight I shall write to my sister and invite her for a visit. It has been a long time since she left and I have missed her. Perhaps a letter is all it would take to bring her back. If I have to spend the rest of my life in here, hiding from intruders and spies, I would rather do it with Catherine at my side. I look around my den, my bits and bobs. On the mantelpiece there's a photograph of the Matterhorn's north face, taken, I suppose, from the Schönbiel Hut, but I don't remember. I hold it, for a better look, still feeling all off kilter, my mouth acrid with the taste of bad dream.

Mountains, like stars, come out at night. After a day's deep sleep, knees bent, arms twisted beneath rumpled sheets, dusk gathers and they shrug off the covers to take their proper form. They breathe out icy air, grow a little, shed a little, may crack and roar to one another or to the night. I have heard them. They know the tread and intrusion of the hobnail boot.

It was not so long ago that I tramped the rocks some twelve thousand feet in the sky, with my axe and compass, wearing a sturdy pair of Jaeger knickerbockers. My sister never even saw a mountain, of course, couldn't have cared less, and I know she will not have altered, at least on this point. As children and young ladies we spent much time in this room, but even then it was never the same for Catherine as it was for me. I let my eyes bounce around the den, suck it all in through my dilated pupils.

I call this my den but it is a vast, rectangular room, with plenty of ornaments and furnishings. I spend most of my time by the fireplace. I have two armchairs and a settee around the hearth with a couple of low tables and a lamp in between. Some distance away is the baby grand piano and duet stool and then, in the corner that gets a greenish light from the back window, my globe. It is a large old globe, almost the length of my arm in diameter, and it spins as smoothly as it always did. Above the fireplace is an oil portrait of my father in his Royal Navy uniform. He looks solemn and a little worried, as well he should, for he was to meet great strife on his next voyage. His dark hair rises from his narrow forehead in a handsome, devilish stroke. I do not know why I never put up a picture of my mother or my sister. Father seems to represent us all.

Dearest Catherine,

It has been such a long time since I saw you (is it really fifteen years?) and I wonder how you are. If you think of visiting London sometime, I would be most delighted if you would like to come to Dulwich one afternoon for tea.

Your Grace

No, that is not quite right. I shall have to say more than that. It will look as though I don't know her, that any stranger could have written it. We used to be such close sisters and knew each other's secrets. She fastened violets in my hair and took me to play in the woods on Sydenham Hill. We had darker times too, of course – which family has not? – but we shared them as sisters do. She may have children of her own now, new relatives that I have never met. It is unlikely, though. She was not young when she married and left.

The fire is dying and I am not ready to be cold. A faint music seems to waft from the piano, a chord that separates into two high notes a semitone apart, repeating alternately like the ghost of a siren. The room is no longer my den but our family drawing room and I am shivering in my memories.

Chapter Two

The blizzard thickened but I had reached eighty-two fifteen and would make it to the Pole. My stomach cramped with hunger and there was no food to look forward to but pemmican again. I groaned as I forced one frozen foot forward and then the other. Pemmican would be the death of me. In the whirling snowflakes I saw chocolates, roast turkey, giant hams, flying and dipping on the wind before they dropped into the snow and vanished. Scott and Wilson trudged silently, a few feet ahead of me, as the piano played on.

'Grace, do make up your mind. It's your turn and you are trying our patience.'

'I'm ready.' I moved my piece – a darning needle representing Ernest Shackleton – along the fold in the map.

'Jolly good,' said Father, and sat back in his chair. His button, Captain Scott, was just ahead of my darning needle and the thimble which represented Wilson. 'I think we may go no further for this evening. These conditions require proper consideration and I'm too tired. We'll have our cocoa now.'

That night I was about fourteen years old and Catherine was eighteen. It was 1904 or 1905. The drawing room ached with music from the piano. Catherine had just learned that she had won a place to study at the Royal College of Music and we were excited. Father had allowed her to audition, but now could not decide whether to let her go. He always said that Catherine's music was the heart of the family, for it pumped the blood through our veins and pushed air into our lungs. Catherine leaned over the keyboard with her eyes half-shut. She stretched back as her fingers pressed into the tinkling diminuendo. It was a dark, wet evening and the fire had burned all day. Perspiration jewelled her forehead.

I took lessons, too, but was only a competent pianist. My parents encouraged me to be outdoors all day for, when I was nine years old, I had contracted pneumonia and almost died like my brother Freddie. Mother's greatest fear was that she would find me, one day, cold and empty as she had found him. To keep my constitution strong and my lungs healthy, I spent hours playing hockey and tennis. I walked through London's parks in fog and wind, and bought hot potatoes to stick in my pockets and warm my hands.

In spite of Father's grumpiness that night, I loved our evenings in the drawing room. The play with the maps had begun recently after Father had been talking about Scott's expedition to the Antarctic in the *Discovery*. Scott, Shackleton and Wilson had left the main party to reach the Pole but had to turn back, partly owing to Shackleton's poor health. I had told Father that I could not see why they hadn't been able to reach the South Pole. It seemed to me that if they had gone within a few miles, it could not be so very hard to go all the way.

Father said that I was very naive and I could not possibly imagine the brutality of the conditions the explorers faced. One mile might take hours to cover. A few yards might make a man relive his entire life and have dark thoughts he never knew his brain could hold. Father's eyes seemed to blacken when he said this. In order to educate me, he took to unfolding great maps and newspaper articles in the evenings and we would throw a die across the hearth to make the journey ourselves, paying attention to physical health, the weather, food supplies and, as my father put it, the qualities of the hero from whom any schoolboy might learn.

I was a schoolgirl, of course, but I did my best. I didn't have any brothers, only Freddie, who died before I was even born so he was just a ghost.

It became a game we played often. We laid out pieces of paper, cotton reels, any odd thing we could find, in order to represent the seals and whales in the southern seas. We made a paper boat to represent the *Discovery*, and put thimbles and buttons inside it to represent the men. We sailed her to McMurdo Sound and Father marked the places where Scott and his men had been in 1902. We ventured to other parts of the world, places that Father had been with his ships, but none was so exciting as the South Pole, still out of reach to man, now only by a few degrees. Sometimes we played Nansen and Amundsen, racing in their ship, the *Fram*, against the British, to the ends of the Earth.

Mrs Horton, our elderly housekeeper, placed the cocoa tray on the table in the window, spilling a little as she set it down. We wished her goodnight and she left. I put away the huts and penguins and began to fold the map. It was very large and complicated. I almost disappeared underneath it, but Mother took the corner and helped me. Father, who always had to be Captain Scott but tired quickly, settled into his armchair. I, Ernest Shackleton, curled up by the fireplace with my book, *Unpleasant Tales for Girls*, or some such thing that I liked, but I didn't read it. I watched my older sister at the piano and I listened to her.

Frank Black, who had been playing Wilson in our game, retreated to the cosy corner at the other side of the fireplace with his cocoa. Handsome Frank, with dark eyes like raven's wings. He was our neighbour and had come for tea and to congratulate Catherine on her success, then stayed to hear her practise. Mother always said that he was in love with Catherine and the music was his excuse to be near her. He would be a very good catch, said Mother, though not yet because he was going up to Oxford in the autumn and would not want to marry before graduating, which was just as well because Catherine had no idea how to be a wife yet. Frank studied with the same piano tutor as Catherine and I but did not have her extraordinary talent. They played duets some afternoons and Catherine was always stopping for Frank to go over his part. She helped him when he got stuck, but gently and quietly so that he wouldn't feel ashamed. He was clever, though, and great fun when we played our games. I longed for him to marry Catherine so that I could have him as my older brother. I liked him to come exploring with Father and me for Catherine never joined in, and Mother was always in and out of the room so spoiled the progress of the expedition. Tonight, though, Frank was as bad as Mother. He seemed more interested in my sister than in the South Pole.

Catherine played Bach's Concerto no.7 in G minor.

Father slipped a bookmark into his atlas and let it close on his lap.

Mother's lips made a thin, tight line. Mother saw no point in so much piano playing. *It's unhealthy for the mind*, she used to say. *Catherine will become imaginative.* She insisted that Catherine accompanied her to the Waifs and Strays Needlework Society and on visits to our neighbours, though Catherine hated at-homes and fumed about the pointless and tedious conversations of silly wives. She was a dreamy girl, my mother used to say, but must learn to stay awake. I did not mind visiting at all and was always willing to hand round the cakes when we had guests at home. I enjoyed entering other people's homes, seeing their things, and listening to adult conversations, but because I was quite good at it I was rarely required to go. It was Catherine who needed the practice and routine lest she go the way of our neighbour's niece, Margaret Mott.

Poor Margaret Mott. I had forgotten her. Mother had found her wandering half-naked in our garden one afternoon and could not get any sense from her. Margaret had a beautiful singing voice and was trilling to the birds in the trees when Mother came out to see why the gate was open. Margaret was just a few years older than Catherine but, after Mother had wrapped a cape around her goose-pimpled body and taken her home, Dr Sowerby sent her to the asylum so that she could have a rest. We never heard of Margaret again, but the vague threat of the asylum was with us from that day. Mother taught Catherine practical things so that she wouldn't become like Miss Mott, infected in the imagination by too much music. Catherine had to learn how to knit pretty animals to sell for orphans and how to pour from the teapot in such a way that the tea streamed into the cup without making a vulgar sound.

I gazed at Frank's feet. Now that the expedition was over, he was quiet. His shoes appeared to be politely still and evenly placed but then I noticed that they sometimes twitched and shifted with the music. In the andante the toes leaned forward, just a little, as if to listen more intently.

'So it's up to Oxford then, young Frank, and then into the law like your father, I suppose?'

'Yes, I certainly hope so, Captain Farringdon. I'll go to the Bar if I can.'

'Now that will please him.'

Frank was not telling the truth to my father but trying to impress him. He had told Catherine and me that he was going to be an artist and the studying was just to keep everyone happy in the meantime.

Catherine reached the end of the movement and paused. Stray hairs caught the lamplight and glowed red, little wires lit up around her skull. Her long, freckled fingers rested on the keys like leggy insects, then skimmed away again to turn the page.

When the music reached the fifth or sixth line and I felt safe inside it, I turned to peek through the gap in the curtains at the garden and watched rain land in puddles on the gravel path. The music played around my ears like the patter of falling water. The wind grew high and the notes tumbled and sliced through the air to touch my skin. When my sister was at college, I would go to Kensington and visit her there.

'Catherine,' I blurted, 'when you are famous I shall come to hear you play at the Royal Albert Hall and shall take a box near the stage so that you'll hear me shout *encore*. I'll wear a red silk dress so that you will see me easily. It will be wonderful.'

'Grace, you have such an imagination.' She smiled at me, glanced down and the smile stayed in her eyes and on her lips. I was glad that I had made her happy. 'But I'm most likely to be a teacher or an accompanist. That's what musical ladies usually do.'

I jumped up and perched beside her on the piano stool.

'Has he made up his mind yet?' I whispered. 'Will you go even if he won't let you?'

'I'm playing as well I can, to persuade him. If he won't pay for me then I won't be able to go and the concert at the Albert Hall will certainly never happen.'

'No. Of course it will happen, Catherine. Of course he must pay.' *If it doesn't happen*, I thought, *what will?*

Catherine turned the page of her music and I returned to my corner as she resumed. Her hair came loose and a thick strand obscured the side of her face. She tossed her head to move it and more hair came down.

'Stop,' cried Father. 'That's enough.'

Catherine's fingers snapped back from the keyboard. She stared at my father, who appeared to be struggling for breath.

'Are you all right, Herbert?' Mother shut her book and lifted herself from the settee, ready to run for his medicine.

The final notes twisted in the air, then dissolved.

Frank's feet shot back behind the fireplace and disappeared.

'Yes. Yes, I am perfectly all right.'

'What is it then?'

He opened his mouth but only a wheeze came out.

'Should we send for the doctor?' asked Catherine.

'Perhaps it is the heat,' I said.

'It is not the heat,' my father replied, at last. 'It was the music.'

'I'm sorry,' said Catherine. 'I know I have played this much better. I shall be all right, though, if you'll just let me get to the end. Why—?'

My father stood, reached for the piano music and closed it.

'I'm sorry, my dear. You played beautifully. I couldn't fault a note or a phrase. You are perfect. You always are.'

'Then I must go on, Father. I don't like to leave a piece

incomplete. It's disrespectful to the composer and it leaves me feeling all wrong. Please.'

My father lowered himself to the piano stool and landed heavily beside Catherine. He adjusted the knees of his trousers, tweaked the tips of his moustache.

'And it's easier for me to play if you are not sitting just next to me.'

'But it isn't fair of me to do this to you. Whatever was I thinking to let things come so far? You're not going to the Royal College.'

Catherine stared at him. I thought she might cry. She put her hand to her cheek to hide her face from Frank.

'It isn't quite right, dear. You're such a charming, pretty girl. When you play in public, people will be – looking at you.'

'Of course they will, Father. I can't very well sit behind a curtain.'

'But we won't always know who they are or what they're thinking about you. You have dreams of playing to hundreds of people in grand concert halls, but your music is for us, your family.'

'But listen—'

'I've always said that I couldn't survive an evening without your music, and I mean it. That is why God gave you this talent and made you a woman.' Father's sentence ended with a snap.

'The Royal College didn't mind that I'm not a man. I showed them that I'm good enough.'

Father patted her hand. 'Catherine, we know that you

are the best young pianist in London. You have nothing to prove to us. There's no need for you to go to the college. You would hate it. You'll stay here and play for me and we'll be happy, as we have always been happy.'

Catherine wiped her handkerchief across her brow and shook her head.

At the prospect of tears, Frank rose to his feet. He gave a slight bow. 'Thank you for this evening. Catherine, thank you for playing so beautifully. I trust this will be resolved and you'll soon be on your way to college.'

No one answered him.

'Why can she not study music?' I asked. 'Even if she doesn't give concerts or work in music? At least she should go to college.'

'Of course she may study music, Grace. I'm not such an ogre as to stop a girl playing the piano. But she cannot study at a college where it is all about preparing to play in public. College is for people who are planning careers. That's the point of it, you see. It would just build the girl's hopes.' He looked around the room for support. I fixed my eyes on the ceiling. 'Does it not seem indecent to all of you? Grace and Catherine have tried to blind me, with their romantic ideas of colleges and concerts. The reality is not so pleasant, I'm afraid.'

'She will be a bird in a cage if you keep her here.' Frank spoke up from the doorway. His hands were clasped firmly in front of him and his expression was angry, but his eyes darted quickly from Father's to Catherine's to mine so I knew that he was frightening himself.

'Frank,' said my mother, quietly, 'it's not as though we would put our daughters on the stage in the theatre, and a concert is not such a different thing from a play, after all.'

'Precisely, Jane,' said Father. 'You're quite right. I should have listened to you from the beginning. Yes, Catherine will be a bird in a cage. A songbird lives happily in a cage since it has never known the wilderness. This house is safe and my daughters have everything they need. Let's put an end to this now before more harm is done. I'm sorry I ever allowed the audition to take place. It was unfair of me and for that, Catherine, I ask your forgiveness.'

Catherine should have told him that forgiveness was not forthcoming but strangely, I thought, she did not.

When Frank left, a great portcullis seemed to clank down over the front door. I put a cushion over my face to escape and sat for a few minutes in the dark. Nothing happened. When I lifted the cushion, Catherine was still at the piano, her red hairs reflecting the light as though to send a signal out somewhere. Her chest and shoulders heaved, but she didn't cry. She rose from the stool and clattered upstairs to her room. My parents rushed after her.

I was alone. I went to the piano and, very quietly, opened the music and picked it up where it had stopped. With clumsy fingers and uneven rhythm, I played to the end. It was bad but the music was complete.

'The evening is over, Grace.' From the doorway my mother spoke softly. 'Go to bed and don't talk to your sister on the way. She'll soon be fine.'

'She wants to go to college. She'll be bored if she stays here.'

'A bored person is a boring person, Grace. She'll find plenty to do. You should be pleased that she'll still be at home with you. It's nice for sisters to have each other close.'

My mother, with her light voice and the wide, blinking eyes of a doll. She was always able to make things right. She could patch up a torn dress in moments. Sometimes she waved a pretend magic wand over an injured bird or swollen ankle, and it would get better, but tonight she was wrong. As I passed her, she rested her hand on my arm but I wriggled away.

'It's for the best,' she said. 'You'll see.'

Father was talking to Catherine in her room. I crouched at the door to listen. I hoped that she would threaten to leave the house and never come back. I hoped that she would threaten to poison herself and that my father would repent, but her voice was a calm, steady murmur.

'My leg is not good tonight.' Father's voice came close to the door. I moved away. 'I must take my medicine before bed.'

'Poor Father,' said Catherine. 'It must be very painful. What can I do to help?'

I understood then that Catherine would not fight. She didn't have the strength. Father loved her too much. And if Catherine had to stay here then I would also have to stay.

Catherine was supposed to become a concert pianist and I had planned to follow my father's example and become an explorer, though not, of course, in the Navy.

I'm not sure why I had imagined that this would be palatable to my family since, in 1893, my father had been one of those who voted against women becoming fellows of the Royal Geographical Society. He had mentioned it many times and with pride but, because he was my father and seemed to love me, I took nothing personal from it. I was his favourite companion for trips to London Zoo and Kew Gardens. He liked to share his knowledge of plants, animals, insects and climate with me, but he never talked to Catherine or Mother about these things. When he referred to girls and ladies, I thought that he meant ones like Catherine and Mother and the ladies we knew in Dulwich, who liked to stay out of the sun and travel no further than each other's at-homes. I didn't think then that he included me.

Father had been a real traveller when he was a captain in the Navy but now he was an invalid. He went to China when we were small and his ship was caught in a storm on the Yellow Sea. He told this story many times, never quite the same way twice, but I kept some version of it that I understood as truth. A sudden roll of the ship tipped four men overboard and my father was one of them. Afterwards, all he recalled was that he had been thinking of my sister and me, how strange it was that we were there in the morning cutting the tops off our boiled eggs, while he was already at night, fighting sky and sea. The three who went down with him drowned, but Father emerged near some piece of debris from the ship, hauled himself atop it and wrapped his arms around wooden struts that felt like table legs.

At daybreak he was floating on a flat, emerald sea. His head was resting on his arms, which were blue from the cold, but he felt hot and tried to pull off his shirt. A small boat sailed towards him, and human voices screeched like herring gulls. A rope went round Father's middle, tightened and pulled. In his hallucination he thought his rescuers were the three drowned sailors, come to collect him for the journey to the next world, but they were four cheerful fishermen from near Weihaiwei who wrapped him in nets for warmth and took him to the edge of the naval base. He fell unconscious and woke up later to find that he had gangrene from hypothermia and the surgeon had cut off part of his left foot and three fingers. He began to cough and, though he did not know it then, the damage to his lungs meant that the cough would stay with him for the rest of his life. Father was invalided out of the Navy and he came home, a smaller, weaker man who never liked to see his seafaring friends any more.

He told me that he regretted clinging to the wreckage in the sea and that he only did so in the hope of rescuing his men.

'I let them perish, little Grace,' he said. 'And God made me survive in this hopeless state for my sins. He is just, you see, but He is cruel.' He held up the remains of his hands. 'Anyone can look at me and know that I failed.'

I didn't like Father to say such things. He believed that God would not forgive him and he hated going to church on Sundays. He still attended, once a month or so, for the family reputation, but he said that God could not welcome him and it was hard. Sometimes I imagined myself diving into the water to rescue the sailors, swooping deep, somehow holding the collars of three of them in one hand, then using my other arm to swim quickly away and deliver them to my father so that the world could call him a hero.

Father walked a little, but his left foot was no more than a stump and he had pains that shot up his legs and made him gasp. He sat in his study, reading journals and puffing on a clay pipe. Sometimes he rode up and down the streets in a hansom and stared out of the window, trying to find something to cheer him up, but he rarely came upon anything he liked because he did not like anything much any more except for being at home. When his lungs weren't bad and he could pass an evening without coughing too much, he would attend lectures at the Royal Geographical Society in Burlington Gardens. Sometimes our family physician, Dr Sowerby, would come to see him and stay for dinner or drinks and they would smoke their pipes and complain about the stupidity of politicians, suffragists and omnibus drivers.

On other nights he would read geographical journals by the fireside late into the night, turning the pages with stiff flicks of his fourth finger and sometimes, when he forgot himself, the tip of his nose. He liked to read about the journeys to the coldest ends of the world – the Alps, the

Poles, Himalayan summits – places, he said, where Heaven and Earth touched and anything was possible.

Catherine and Father were quiet now. I crept back to my room and opened the curtain. The street was empty. I could see over the rooftops of Dulwich and Sydenham. Just a mile or two away was Ernest Shackleton's childhood home. He had been to the Antarctic with Captain Scott but came home early because he'd fallen ill, a bit like Father. I strained my eyes to see if I could make out the roof of a house that might be his, but all the houses in all the streets looked the same.

I put my finger into the condensation on the window and wrote my name. Surely, I thought, if my father could travel through the tropics and into the Arctic Circle, if my neighbour could reach the Antarctic and walk on ice, if Frank Black was going to Oxford, Catherine and I could at least get out of Dulwich.

Chapter Three

We opened the tent flaps and screwed up our eyes to survey the scene. The cracks were vertical, black gashes in the snow. From a distance they resembled people and I stared for some time to be sure that they didn't move. I pulled my hood around my face and squinted harder. The sun hummed in a blue sky but the good weather would not last.

We had slept well the previous night, but the snowfall had shifted the landscape. When we began to move, frostbite gnawed our feet, yet we still had miles to travel. My skis slipped forward, one and then the other, and I was off. I was slicing through the soft whiteness, bridging crevasses, dodging plugs of snow and passing safely across the land. I was headed south.

'Grace, put out your light. I'm not made of money.'

I rolled over in bed. Father was such a gloomy cheese-parer. He wouldn't even let me have a new dress and all my old ones were too short now. We lived in a big house with servants but there was never money to spend.

Where was I?

My sleeping bag.

My tent.

Blubber burning on the primus stove.

Ponies and dogs.

A motor car.

A motor car?

It began to melt. I was almost asleep.

'Your light, Grace.'

'Mm. Yes, in a minute.'

When was this? Later. 1908. Ernest Shackleton had left New Zealand for his next attempt to reach the Pole. Father and I read about it in the newspapers. This time he was the leader of the expedition, which I was pleased about but, still, I worried for him. I had seen a diagram showing the layout of the *Nimrod* and I could not see how it could be large enough for all that it was said to carry. There were ponies, men, dogs added in at the last minute in New Zealand, vast stocks of food, animal fodder, scientific equipment, all sorts of daily supplies, and a motor car (possibly *two* motor cars). It seemed to me that the ship would need to be several times larger than it was. I often lay awake fretting that it would sink, that the men and ponies would freeze to death in the sea.

I pictured Ernest on the flooded, rolling deck, his face filmy and his hair wild in icy clumps. The ponies and dogs began to fight, biting necks and ears, tossing and yowling. The men cried out and the car rolled off the deck and fell through a hole in a slab of ice.

But the ship must be strong because Shackleton intended

to reach the Pole this time. My father, who had been speaking to his friends at the Royal Geographical Society, said that the route to the Pole belonged to Scott and that Shackleton would have to keep off Scott's turf. I said that I didn't think they would find much turf at the South Pole. He roared: *He's not a naval man. He'll never succeed, the wretched scoundrel, asking all and sundry to fund him on this hasty escapade.*

I could hear him now, in the drawing room with our neighbour Mr Kenny, shouting about the scandalous behaviour of a shopman from our street who had done something terrible, but I could not catch what it was.

'Disgraceful behaviour.' Mr Kenny relished the words. 'I hope there's a brother who can chase him and shoot him.'

'I've a good mind to write to *The Times* on this very point.'

He was always writing letters to the newspapers and sometimes they were published and he read them aloud to us at breakfast.

I shut my bedroom door and pulled my pillow around my ears. I wanted Shackleton to succeed but how would he afford it? Could one just write to people and ask them for hundreds of pounds? Wouldn't they think it rude? It seemed a terrible thing to have to do for such an important expedition. Yet people were giving him funds and expecting him to pay them back when he returned. How would they know that he had the money? What if, like Father, he was injured and wouldn't be able to work? Father was wealthy because he had money from his father. He never had to write and ask a stranger for help.

I was coming to the end of my school years. I was trying to accept the prospect of a life at home like Catherine's, then perhaps marriage. It depressed me, for I knew it was all wrong and not the life I felt sure I was supposed to have, but my parents would never change their minds about university and work. How could I learn anything from the explorers when they never had to contend with such nonsense?

It was three years since Catherine should have gone to college. She no longer took piano lessons. She played in the evenings, still, as Father demanded it, but with a different kind of fervour. Her music was less precise. She was careless in difficult technical passages. She rarely bothered to learn new music, not with the hours of work and pencil scratching of before, but made lazy, haphazard attempts at pieces she had already studied. During the daytime she helped Mother run the house and she spent hours on her needlework, making rag dolls in bright dresses for the church bazaars. She never complained but she hardly spoke to me nowadays. I had annoyed her by continuing to mention the Royal College and all the things she might still do, if only she would try. She told me she never wished to speak of it again and that I had better worry about my own life for a change for I was hardly doing anything so extraordinary.

I still worried about her.

For the first two years after leaving school, Catherine had received invitations to dances and parties. She always declined. Neighbours invited her to give recitals, but she said that she no longer had the nerve to play to an audience. She had one or two friends from her schooldays and, though they paid occasional visits, Catherine rarely left the house except to run errands. The friends and invitations stopped coming and Catherine seemed relieved. When he was well enough, Father took her to recitals at Bechstein Hall, but he was embarrassed by his cough and sometimes spent most of the concert waiting in the lobby while Catherine listened to the music alone.

'I don't know about life outside the house,' she said to Mother. 'It doesn't seem to suit me any more. It's much nicer to be at home and not have to worry about things. Whenever I go into town, I come back with a frightful headache.'

'That's because you're disappointed, Catherine,' I interrupted. 'But you needn't give up.'

'No, that's because life is this way. Here I am and here is my life.'

I switched off my light but lit a candle and crouched on the floor to write a letter. I wrote to my Aunt Edith, my father's sister, who lived in New York. Edith and her husband owned a paper mill and were very rich, but Catherine and I had never met them because my father didn't like his sister. Father never explained why, but said that it was fair since she couldn't stand him either. I sucked the end of my pencil and tried to imagine her from the few details I knew. She was a giant who towered over the city and its people, managing her factory with her tiny husband (I had not met him either). She gazed across the water at my family – somehow we were all visible to one another –

and she looked a little like the Statue of Liberty. I wrote my letter and posted it the following day.

My aunt's reply came several months later. By now Shackleton had arrived in the Antarctic, one thousand five hundred miles from the South Pole. The *Koonya*, which had towed the *Nimrod* all the way, had returned safely to New Zealand.

Mother opened the letter at breakfast. She and I were alone, eating toast and marmalade as Catherine and Father strolled in the garden.

'What a strange thing this is,' she said. 'Your father must have mentioned you in his Christmas letter to your aunt. She's a very headstrong lady and her husband is quite eccentric. Well, everyone must have an eccentric aunt or uncle, I suppose. I've never met anyone who didn't.'

'Who?'

'Your Aunt Edith in America.'

Their only contact was through politeness at Christmas, or a death in the family. It wasn't Christmas and the envelope had no black edging. She must have received my begging letter.

'Has she said something about me? What does she say?'

'That if you want to go to university, she and John will pay all the fees and living expenses. Ha ha. They must be made of money or very silly. My goodness me. And she doesn't know the first thing about you.'

'She'll pay for me?'

'They have made a fortune and now they've gone into property, too, she says. I suppose they don't know what to spend it on. I wonder why they even thought of such a thing. She came to our wedding, but caused an argument with your father about *the vote*, of all things. I was glad to see the back of her.'

Edith must have been careful enough not to mention my shameful request. Mother read the letter again then folded it neatly, slipped it back into its envelope and pinched it shut.

'It makes no difference and you don't want to go to university, you know. There's too much work to be done here.'

'I don't do much work here.'

It was true. Although I did a little sewing and a few chores in the house, I spent most of my days out of doors, meeting my schoolfriends and playing sports. Catherine and Mother left little for me to do and never complained about it.

'Grace, I still say you may get married soon. There's no point in waiting for Catherine to be first any more. You might be waiting for ever, and now I think that we couldn't do without her at home. Perhaps we need to think a little harder about your future. Your sports keep you healthy and strong and I'm glad of it, but you meet no one except other galumphing girls whose mothers are all *suffs*, and you're hardly likely to pick up a beau through any of them. I'll talk to some of the ladies at church and the sewing circle.'

She gave me a secret smile. 'I wonder how Frank Black is getting along at Oxford. He must come home from time to time.'

'Frank Black? But he was for Catherine. You're not seriously thinking of him for me?'

'Now, Grace, it's always worth—'

'He's not interested in us any more, not after what happened with Catherine and the audition. He thought we were ridiculous.'

'I'm sure that's not true. They weren't quite right for each other. We've all been very busy these last three years and Frank will have been absorbed in his studies and university life. You're too dramatic about this sort of thing. And as for your Aunt Edith, she doesn't mention any plans to visit us, just to patronize us with offers of money. It's an insult.'

But I had sometimes bumped into Frank Black on my way to school or the park during the holidays, and he never asked me about Catherine. I would find some reason to say her name so that I might give him the opportunity to ask a question or suggest a visit, but it was as if she had let him down by giving up her musical career. He was as disappointed in her as I was.

Once we roller-skated past each other at the Crystal Palace. He called me Shackleton and I called him Wilson in reply, but then we didn't know what to say and I skated on fast so as not to lose my balance in front of him and fall over. Catherine never skated, though I told her that Frank went. She sometimes came with me to watch a dancing display or a polo match, but she could not risk hurting her hands.

Catherine seemed to acknowledge that she had lost Frank, just as she had lost her dream to study music. I could no longer reach her. She was drowning and she knew it, but would not struggle, would not give me her hand to let me save her, and I'm ashamed to say that she made me impatient.

'Would Aunt Edith really pay for me to go to university, even though she doesn't know me?'

'If she says it here and she has the money then, yes, I suppose she would. I've told you, though, money has nothing to do with it. If we felt that it would be right for you to go to university, your father would pay for it himself. He's well off from his stocks and your grandfather's death, you know, so we don't need charity. He'd rather be sure that you're happy and comfortable when you marry. A good marriage is a much better investment for you'll never need to work. No, I'll write a polite letter to your aunt and thank her very much.' Mother sipped her tea and gave a small cough. 'I'll ask Mrs Black how Frank is getting along. Perhaps he'll pay us a visit in his next holiday.'

'Oh, Mother.' I tossed my head in the manner of young ladies I had seen in the park.

'It can't do any harm.'

'Do you not consider Catherine's feelings?'

'I don't think she felt much for Frank. Whatever was there didn't last long and I never saw any tears over him. They weren't terribly good for each other, both on about art and music all the time, which was so bad for Catherine's state of mind. But he's a bright young man with excellent prospects and he's certainly handsome. I don't know any other men of his age who are so tall and strong. He has such a good head of hair, too.' Mother gave me a playful nudge. 'You must have noticed how nice his hair is. There are other pretty young women in the neighbourhood, not to mention in Oxford. I expect he'll be graduating soon, so you don't want to dilly-dally.'

'Mother, really.' I laughed. 'The sort of hair he has is not important. Only character matters. And he was planning to be an artist so I can't believe you like him as much as you say.'

'He won't be planning that any more. He has been to Oxford now and his mother told me that they're expecting him to go into law like Mr Black.'

'No, he's going to be a famous painter. He is taking law for something to fall back on. I'd better write to Aunt Edith and thank her myself. It's very generous, after all.'

I took the letter from Mother's hand and went straight to my room.

Of course, I wrote and told Edith that I would, indeed, be grateful for her patronage and that I would pay her back afterwards, as soon as I had a salary of my own. With a university education, I was sure to be rich in the future. I told her that I looked forward to meeting her one day and that, if her generous offer were to stand, I should do my best to make her proud.

*

The headmistress of my school, Miss Ladbroke, encouraged all her pupils to better themselves through education and work. She was a spinster in her sixties, and conservative parents held her up as an example of what might befall their daughters if they were not careful. My mother had once sighed that it seemed terribly sad that such a thin, empty life was turning into such a long one, but Miss Ladbroke's manner was sweet and feminine so, though pitied, she was not considered dangerous. She hid her feminism beneath a piccolo laugh and a mild but unpredictable deafness.

Miss Ladbroke had taken me to see various colleges and I fell in love with Candlin College just outside London. No one from my school was there that year so I could make the place my own and, unlike many women's universities, it allowed its students to take degrees. The main building was a strange red-brick chateau, tucked away in the Berkshire countryside and surrounded by deep woodland. It seemed to exist quite separately from the nearby towns and villages, a tranquil world where I would immerse myself in study.

When I returned, Mother was busy stitching clothes for the Waifs and Strays Society and Father had become exercised about the planned railway up the Matterhorn. *We must protect the sublimity of the mountains. A railway is a mutilation of Nature.*

'The Gornergrat railway is one thing. It is already there and we may as well accept and use it. The Jungfrau is a step too far, but this—' He tossed aside a newspaper and coughed into his fist.

*

Nobody noticed what I was doing. I passed the entrance examinations and won a scholarship to study for a degree in science, all without telling my parents. Aunt Edith had agreed to pay my expenses for three years. When they found out that I had won a university place, Mother nearly knocked the school door off its hinges. *Such perfidy!* she cried. *Trust a woman to be so scheming and underhand.* Miss Ladbroke merely smiled and remarked that she was grateful to Mother for raising her voice as she found it so difficult to catch all the words nowadays.

Mother rushed home at such a speed she caught her shoe in her petticoat and almost fell over on the pavement. She picked herself up and fell over again in our hall. In a fervour she took her sewing scissors, a length of muslin, and began cutting a new dress for me. She pushed and pulled me around, with a measuring tape over her arm and pins between her lips. She spat them into her hand to speak.

'This is going to suit you so well, Grace.' The fabric was mauve and had been in the cupboard for months, waiting for Mother to decide its purpose. 'You're more unusual than Catherine and we just need to make a bit more out of what you've got so that we can see you grow into the lovely young woman you are going to be. Yes, see this colour against your complexion? It just brightens you up. Wait till gentlemen line up to meet you.' She gave a strange whinnying laugh that made me jump, and tucked my hair behind my ear. 'The charming and exquisite Grace Farringdon.'

I held one end of the fabric at my waist as Mother let

the rest fall to my ankles, and I caught sight of my face in the mirror, suddenly as bright and pretty as Mother saw it, but it was alone.

'Mother, I don't think I'll meet many gentlemen. It's a women's college.'

'But you're not going to the college now, are you?' She spat more pins, frowned, then scribbled my measurements in her sewing book. 'When the dress is ready, I'll give you my pearls and you'll feel like a princess. Remember the stories you used to tell me about princesses? Remember how you loved Catherine to put flowers in your hair? That's the sort of little girl you were. We'll have you as you were meant to be – a lovely bride – not what that Miss Ladbroke thinks you should be. How does that preposterous woman think she knows anything about you?'

She had the manservant remove all the books from my room and hide them in the attic so that they could do me no further harm. When I told her that I was going to college whatever she did, she even consulted Father's lawyer, Mr Sweetman, to see if I was breaking the law. The dress was unpicked and put away. We shouted up and down the stairs at each other until we were hoarse. My sister would pass between us with her nose in the air and lips together, not prepared to be an ally to either of us.

Father's method was different. He wept that he was too old and weak to fight a cruel opponent like me. He regretted the hours we had spent together at the maps, letting my imagination roam, and confessed that he had done me great damage, but it was only because his son had died and he had needed a companion in the lonely evenings. He pulled his seat close to the fire and stared, pink-eyed, into the flames. Mother and Catherine shook their heads, and glared at me for putting him into a mood.

'Those women – the suffragettes and suffragists – who marched in Hyde Park last year, thousands of them. I was coming back from a lecture and I saw them from my cab. Every face I saw was miserable or hysterical, Grace. They weren't happy women. Even the ones who were laughing looked as though something – some demon – had got into them and was making them laugh, forcing them. I felt sorry for them, being so so –' he shut his eyes to find the word – 'not themselves, not anyone's *daughter*. I don't want that to happen to you.'

One evening at dinner he lost his temper and threw the salt pot at the wall. While we waited for Sarah, our maid, to brush up the pieces, I did the only thing I could think of and I threw the pepper pot after it. We both shed tears but neither could change our position and mine was stronger. I had the money and I simply had to endure the arguments until I could escape. After the tears, Father had no ammunition.

'You can cut me out of your will,' I said, blowing my nose so that he wouldn't see that I was crying. 'I'll manage on my own.'

'I would never disinherit you,' he pleaded. 'No matter what you do to me, I'll never do that, but I do not consent and never shall.'

We had planned to go to Sandon Perkins's lecture on

Cook and Peary at the Hippodrome, but Father gave my ticket to Dr Sowerby and they went off together.

On my last evening at home Arthur carried Father's old trunk to my room and I unlocked it with a dusty key, lifted the lid. The wooden chest had not been touched for ten years or more. Cobweb strands curled and rose like seaweed in a rock pool. A crumpled brown shoe lay at the bottom, bent and turning up at the toe. I reached for it and found, inside, a pair of spectacles.

I peered at them, meaning to ask my father later if he remembered how they had come to be there. They must have belonged to him once. The arms were loose, the lenses scratched and, when I tried them, they gave a blurry view of my bedroom. I tucked them back into the shoe.

Sarah cleaned the trunk and I returned to sorting through my belongings, deciding which to take so that she could pack them. I would have liked new clothes, but I had no money so had mended my old dresses and made myself a new skirt and blouse. I had a few books to take and hoped to find the rest in the college library. It terrified me that I might arrive unprepared. I didn't want to get anything wrong. I didn't want to be different from the others.

Sarah stepped back from the trunk with the soapy cloth in her hand. She sneezed.

'There we are, nice and clean, Miss Grace. I'll pack your clothes now.'

She knelt at my dressing table, pulling out collars, stockings, handkerchiefs. Everything was neatly folded but she opened and shook each item, refolded and placed it on the bed.

I lifted a framed photograph of my family from the mantelpiece. We were standing on the back steps, peering uncertainly at the camera. Even my father looked caught out, uneasy on his own property. Memory added colours to the picture. Mother had been wearing a shawl of peacock blue, too bright for her dark blonde hair and pallid skin. Catherine and I stood between our parents. We were the same height and both bore the Farringdon look, reddish hair and a sort of dark-eyed sleepiness. In the background, the door to the coal cellar was open, as though caught by the wind.

I put the picture into my trunk, for I believed that we would all soon be friends again. I added my pressed wildflowers and a photograph of my sponsors, Aunt Edith and Uncle John. The items sank into the black and brown ripples of my clothes. Miss Ladbroke had given me an old school microscope to take. I opened its wooden box to check that it was intact, held it for a while, examined a bit of fluff from my blanket, then pushed the box into the corner of the trunk to nestle in my shawl. We pulled down the lid and Sarah locked the trunk. We dragged it to the wall.

Grace, stop banging around like an elephant up there and bring me my veronal.

The floorboards and carpet hardly dulled Father's shriek. It was my duty to fetch the bottle of medicine while he waited in his armchair, rubbing his bad leg with his good hand. I hurried downstairs scarcely able to believe that I should not have to do this again. I shook out a cachet of veronal. Father took and swallowed it.

'Ah.' He pressed his lips together and saliva bubbled around the corners of his mouth. His eyelids drooped. 'It does the trick. It eases the pain so that I can sleep. Catherine, let's have a little music to wash the evening away. It's a sad night indeed. Grace is abandoning us tomorrow. Somehow you will have to take her place as well as your own.'

'What place is that?' Catherine put down her sewing and went to the piano. 'Grace is hardly ever here. I'm not going to start playing cricket or shutting myself away to read adventure books. How would anything get done?'

Catherine shuffled into place on the piano stool, stretched her fingers.

I went to her side and spoke quietly to her.

'Catherine, if you wanted to go away, I'd give you the money from Aunt Edith. She may even be willing to help us both. You don't have to give up everything and be angry with me. I don't want you to—'

'How can I leave now? Father is so weak these days. And who would help Mother with the house?'

It was true that in leaving I was abandoning Catherine to our parents, but she seemed to want to stay and did not care about finding any solution for herself. I perched on the footstool beside Father and held his hand.

'Herbert, will you read from the Bible this evening, since

it is our last night together as a family?' Mother's hand rested lightly on his wrist.

Father shook himself free. 'What the devil would be the good in that? I'm reading *The Times*.' He picked up the newspaper and rattled the pages. 'What nonsense,' he muttered. 'Madame Tussaud's with a tableau of the South Pole. A life-sized Ernest Shackleton. People will make money out of anything.'

'It sounds rather good,' I said.

'Well, I'm not going.' Father scowled. 'And certainly not with you.'

Catherine's fingers pressed gently into the piano keys and she began to play a Telemann Fantasia she had learned years before.

Father let the newspaper fall to the rug. He stroked my fingers with his thumb. He let out a series of cracked, weary sighs and his head lolled. He was, as Mother always said, setting off to sea. When the music reached its final bars, he jumped, stared at me with round, pale eyes.

'I can see them again,' he whispered. 'They're here.'

'Can you? You can see them? Will you be all right, Father?'

In the evenings, after taking his medicine and dozing for a while, Father sometimes saw pictures in the air. They seemed to come from his days at sea. I imagined old sailors, singing sirens, his friends, my ancestors, all life-sized in the shadows on the walls and up by the ceiling. Father would talk to them, not in sentences, not even in words that we could understand. Sometimes he cried out and would lift his arm to shield himself from high waves. On bad nights he would beg them to carry him away.

Tonight he did not converse with them but gripped my hand until it shook.

His face turned pink, drops of sweat formed on his brow, and then his skin whitened again as he sank into his trance. Eventually his eyelids fell. A tear ran down my nose and I hurried upstairs so that I would not change my mind.

Chapter Four

Why should I write to Catherine when she has done nothing to find me? Fifteen years she has had to post me a letter and see whether or not I'm still here. Edinburgh is far, but I know that she has been in London sometimes and not written to say so. Mabel's sister cooks for our neighbours and she told me that they met her once for tea at Brown's, but no one invited me. And they said that her husband, George, had died a few months before that, so I know she must have been lonely.

Over the road a dog barks. The Kennys used to live in that house. While Mr Kenny was practising homeopathy in Holborn, dispensing nettle tea and poultices of ivy leaves, Mrs Kenny gave dance lessons in a room at the back of the house. Catherine and I learned how to waltz in that room, with our old nurse watching, upright on her chair in the corner, nodding her head to the music as Catherine and I whirled. Sometimes we hid in the garden to watch grown-up men and women trot and step around the room, always a little tentative in the too-small space, always self-conscious and, to us, so amusing that we would hold onto each other, collapse into the pansy bed and rock with laughter.

New people live there now, a young couple called the Tickells, who have a friendly black and white mongrel they call Pongo. Sometimes they cross the road to pay me a visit and Pongo jumps on and off my front step, panting and seeming to laugh, the way dogs with long noses do. I give him a biscuit if I have one. Mrs Tickell is a cheerful, intelligent woman and has invited me several times to join her luncheon group, but I have told her that I am not quite well enough to attend, and would not be good company. Perhaps in the future I might accept an invitation. She is very persistent, I must say. *You're always welcome, Grace. My friends have heard about you and are dying to meet you.* That puts the fear of God into me and so I make sure my curtains are always safely closed on luncheon day. Perhaps when Catherine is back, we shall go together to that sort of thing. We'll enjoy the conversation and exchange a glance every now and then when something amuses us. Afterwards we shall sit up late with cups of cocoa, having a gossip and a fine time, right here in the den, and be glad that we are safe again.

I kick off my slippers and give my feet a wiggle. There isn't much feeling in them so I rub them with my hands. I stretch my legs out almost into the fire and let my stockings smudge in the ashes on the hearth.

A bright autumn afternoon. Yes, I think it was. We had a bad summer and a sunless September, but then a big, blue day landed on us. Carriages lined the drive and servants lugged trunks into the Main Hall. The red brickwork flamed against the sky. Young women called out friends' names and chattered in pairs and clusters. Some wore elegant and colourful hats and gowns, far more fashionable than my dowdy brown dress. I felt a little forlorn and uncertain.

Mother and I walked under the clock tower and into the north quad. Mother seized my arm and walked slightly behind me as though I were accompanying her and not the other way round. Sarah was to have come with me – it was usual to bring a maid to help one settle in – but just as we were about to leave, Mother had ordered her into the kitchen and said that she would travel with me instead. It was not because she had changed her mind but that she might have a little longer to change mine.

Mother's fingers tightened around my arm. I shook them off and stomped ahead.

'You can come home again now. We don't have to stay.'

'*I* am staying.'

'Slow down, Grace. I'm talking to you.'

'Yes, and everybody will hear you.'

The quad was almost empty. Just a few students and their parents lingered at the opposite side, but windows were open and curtains fluttered.

'We'll think of other plans for your future. It doesn't need to be this way and you don't have to be proud about it. Look at your Ernest Shackleton. He knew when to turn back from the Pole, even though it wasn't what he wanted. It was the right thing to do and now he's a hero.'

'That's ridiculous. I'm not going home with you.'

In truth, I longed to be back in Dulwich with Catherine and Father, but I knew it was only nerves and I would somehow survive them. We followed the path alongside the neat lawn. Rows of dark windows lined each side. The space behind them seemed somehow forbidden and yet it was to be my new home.

A third-year student led us on a walk around the college. I imagined that Mother would see the grand buildings and facilities and fall in love with the place as I already had. Indeed, as we strolled around the grounds, her eyes widened at the neatly mown grass, the pretty walkways and balustrades. She admired the statues, the carvings, the chapel and picture gallery.

'Very nicely done,' she said of the library and museum. 'Though I wouldn't like to be the one to dust them. Some of the teachers are forbidding, don't you think?' She gave me a tentative look. 'Their clothes are very severe.'

'They are lecturers, not teachers.'

I had also noticed that the principal and some lecturers wore very sombre clothes and did not look as friendly as the mistresses at my school, but I considered this an appropriate sign of academic seriousness which my mother could never be expected to understand.

We strolled through the woodland to the swimming pool, then across the road to the botanical gardens, where a couple of students pulled up weeds and tended to the plants. One of them had caught an earthworm on the end of her pitchfork and waved it at the other. They were both laughing.

'Is it not pleasant, Mother?'

'It would suit some, I daresay. It must be a sweet inter-lude for those who have no future but to work like cart horses.'

'Can't you keep your voice down a little?'

We returned to the Main Hall and passed through the long corridors towards my rooms. Mother peered at the ceiling. 'And all electric lighting.' She nodded, impressed by the place.

She watched some students as they passed us in the corridor. They greeted us politely and resumed their con-versation about the summer holidays.

'Very confident young ladies. They have plenty to say for themselves.'

Each student had a bedroom and a sitting room. My sitting room overlooked the north quadrangle and my bedroom, on the other side of the corridor, looked out over hockey fields and tennis courts. There was a bed, a wardrobe, chairs and a gigantic mirror. The founder of the college, a wealthy industrialist who had made his money from sewing machines, believed in educating women but insisted that every room had a large, oval mirror. Next to the fire was a small kettle. I could not wait to use it.

As we stood in the doorway of my sitting room, I heard my name. We turned to see another version of ourselves, mother and daughter, coming along the passage.

'Grace Farringdon? How do you do? I'm Leonora Locke. I'm two doors away from you. I'm a fresher too. Biology.'

Miss Locke's mother smiled from under a swooping,

elegant hat. She had a kind, expressive face which was familiar to me.

'Hetty Locke. Delighted to meet you.'

Mother let out an *oh* before she could stop herself. She lifted her mouth into a smile but I saw the confusion behind it. Mrs Hetty Locke was a West End actress who played in popular farces. She was often in the newspapers, part of a theatrical set considered, by people like my mother, quite scandalous for their affairs and divorces. She was striking: tall and long-limbed with black hair and a smile that dipped into a deep V. Her daughter had the same dark hair and green eyes, but was small, springy on her feet, and pretty rather than beautiful.

'You do look quite tired, my dears,' said Mrs Locke.

My mother managed a weak nod.

'There's so much to take in,' I said, 'and my mother hasn't been here before.'

'It's such a very strange place,' said Mother. 'Isn't it? Is it a boarding school or a university? I can't make any sense of it.' She grimaced. 'Perhaps it will just take time.'

'But I'd have loved to study somewhere like this. I envy our daughters. I can't wait to read Leonora's letters and find out what adventures you've all been up to.'

'Yes, indeed,' said Mother. 'But I understand that the girls are closely chaperoned and there is a very clear schedule of study, with chapel every morning.'

Mrs Locke swallowed her smile and gave a serious, emphatic nod.

Her daughter looked at me with interest. Her eyes were

sharp but friendly. She exuded warmth and colour, made me think of fireflies.

'We'll enjoy ourselves though, won't we, Miss Farringdon?'

'Certainly,' I said, brightly, to annoy Mother.

I wanted to ask my new friend what it was like to have an actress for a mother, a mother who didn't care what the neighbours thought and who yearned to be in her daughter's place at university. I must have stared at her quite hard but she smiled back, with no trace of shyness or nerves.

'Come, Leonora,' said Mrs Locke. 'Let's see if we can find some flowers for your vases.'

Leonora Locke hurtled down the corridor and her mother followed, upright and graceful.

I shut my sitting-room door and Mother began to cry, not her usual silent weeping into a handkerchief but a series of sharp hiccoughs which grew faster and louder until she collapsed to her knees and sobbed. I had never seen her so wretched.

'And these are the sort of people you're going to live with. They're not like us. I tried to warn you and now you see for yourself.' Her sobs intensified until she seemed to be choking. I went to her but she pushed me away. 'What a supercilious woman. And as for the facilities – laboratories and classrooms, for goodness' sake. It's like a boys' boarding school. Did you notice that the students in the corridors called one another by their surnames? They don't even say *Miss*. Grace, it is all wrong for you. Why won't you see sense?'

I crouched down, placed my hand on her back, touched the soft rim of skin that bulged over her corset.

'You'll have to go home without me,' I said after some time. 'I'm sorry. I can do without your encouragement, but I would, at least, like you to stop crying. It isn't helping either of us. Mother, please.' I stroked her arm. 'There's no point to all this unhappiness.'

She balled a handkerchief into her eyes.

'You're very severe for a girl of eighteen.' She tried a brave smile and squeezed my hand. 'I'll go now – I know you want me to – but I shall say this first. You'll always have a bed in your own home and, if you've grown out of being a student by Christmas, we'll be pleased to have you back. Your father and I will always be good, compassion-ate parents, no matter what you do, I'm sure.' She shook her head and sat in silence waiting for her breathing to calm. 'And we shall always have Catherine.' She stood, straightening her hair and hat. 'I'm leaving now. Your father wants pork chops for supper and I didn't tell Mrs Horton to get any.'

Poor Catherine, I thought. She will be there until she's a dusty old skeleton perching at the piano or hunched over the sewing box.

I stared into the large mirror, watched my room as it was reflected back to me. I saw a small, scared face among large, unfamiliar furniture. My reflection looked empty, as if I weren't behind my own eyes. I wanted the excitement back but my mother's tears had ruined it all. I didn't want to go home but I no longer liked being here.

I placed a small painting of a ship sailing from Cardiff on my mantelpiece. Father had kept it on his study wall and when I was a child he had found me sitting on the floor staring at it. He took it from the wall and gave it to me. I touched it now and blew a little dust from the glass. The room looked just a little better.

Before dinner, I went to find Miss Locke. I knocked on her door but there was no reply. I knew that I would feel more lonely and nervous if I stayed in my rooms so I decided to take a walk around the building. I set off down the corridor, along the central walkway and into the other side of the hall. I soon became disorientated and could not remember which quad was which and whether I was in the east or west side. I hurried up and down corridors, onto another floor, and finally had to leave the building, follow the path around to the clock tower at the main entrance and begin again. When I arrived back at my room, now choking back tears and beginning to hate the place, Leonora Locke appeared from her room and bellowed my name. A couple of doors opened, faces poked out to see what the noise was about, but Locke seemed not to notice. She grinned and ran towards me.

'You're brave to go exploring alone. Could you just help me with my pictures and things? Then we can do yours, if you like.' She lowered her voice. 'I'm not sure where to hang the male nude.'

She shot me a sideways glint and looked for my response.

I started, tried to hide my surprise by adjusting a hairpin just above my ear, but I suspected she was testing me. Voices rose and babbled behind us in the corridor and, for safety, I reached for Leonora's arm.

'I'd love to help.'

'Splendid. Come on then.'

She led, chattering about her mother and their frightful journey from London in a crowded train compartment with a man who kept coughing over them. She told me that I had interesting hair and she liked it, that she already regretted choosing to study science because she wasn't much good at practical work, she was terribly afraid that everyone would be very clever and she had promised her mother that she would join the Suffrage Society straight away, but she wasn't sure that she wanted to join anything until she knew who was who and what was what.

'I'm a suffragist, of course, and I can already tell that you are, but all societies and clubs have people one likes and people one can't bear.'

As she spoke, her hands made quick, graceful gestures. I felt ungainly and awkward, found myself tongue-tied.

'You seem very calm,' she said. 'How do you do it?'

I did not know how I seemed or even quite how I felt, but I had managed something at last. I had got away from home and put myself into another place.

Chapter Five

I did not know it then, but Locke was indeed to become my closest friend, and a fellow member of the Society. Our names were destined to be spoken together for years. Now it doesn't seem enough that our rooms were close, that we shared a bench in the lab, that we met on the first day, giggled at college dances in the picture gallery when either of us had to waltz with Hester the Hippo, no, not enough to make sense of what followed. In another, wilder world we roped ourselves together, crossed crevasses, fought blizzards and we suffered our first mortal loss. How can I trace that back to the genteel surroundings of our student life, this pleasant nursery for grown women where the height of excitement was the evening cocoa party or a new fashion for pinning up one's hair? I wish that Locke and I could have seen each other one more time before she died, had an afternoon or so of mutual forgiveness, of agreeing to put things in the past, but there it is. We did not. The Society is no more. It is all gone. And yet – the face at the scullery window. I fear that some ghost from the Society will always be with me.

The cocoa parties were strange and spirited meetings where young women discussed politics, suffrage, religion and whatever in the world needed putting right. Each evening, after dinner, we gathered in sitting rooms up and down the corridors, to better ourselves and the world, and to nurture our burgeoning friendships. We talked of flower pressing, cooking, gardening, embroidery and many other things I am sure I have forgotten. We gossiped about friends and staff, of course, and our families. If a girl had an eligible brother or two, she faced regular interrogation and was certain to receive more than the average number of invitations for the holidays. Locke and I liked to make fun of our biology lecturer, Miss Doughty, a brisk and earnest Candlin alumnus whose age could have been anywhere between thirty and fifty. Locke was poor at practical work so I conducted most of her dissections and experiments while Miss Doughty seemed not to notice. She moved from bench to bench, seeing only the bones and muscles and blood, as I took my knife to a rabbit or a tortoise and Locke pretended to be searching for something in a cupboard.

Locke and I were sipping cocoa in her room after lights out one evening. Others had come and gone but we had not finished talking. She sat in her armchair with her knees up to her chest, her pea-green dress falling to the floor, her hair adorned with pretty fan-shaped combs of ivory, and I on the rug by the fire in a plain blouse and skirt, hair un-pinned, as it always began to come down by the evening of its own accord. I stuck pieces of bread on toasting forks and propped them against the fireguard. Locke had a lover in London, a young actor named Horace who was playing a pirate in a West End theatre and whom she missed. They had met in the summer at a party and fallen in love playing charades. They wrote to each other almost every day, yet she had no intention of marrying him.

'He's handsome and I'm sure he'll be famous one day, but I could not be the person I am with him, if I were his wife. Where would the passion go?' She shook her head as though this were both obvious and sad, as though she had learned through years of experience, though I suspected she had picked up the comment from somebody else, perhaps her mother. 'You must meet my family and friends in the holidays and you must meet Horace. I am sure that we could find a lover for you amongst his friends.'

'Goodness.' I fiddled with the hem of my blouse. Young men in the park had begun to pay me attention lately, but I always ignored them and went on my way. Locke seemed decades ahead of me. I admired her nonchalant confidence. 'That might be nice.' I had liked the butcher's boy once and used to wait in the garden to see him swing through the back gate with his bicycle, gently fending off the neighbourhood cats and dogs as he took out a parcel of sausages or beef suet. I would sit by the door and hope for a smile. I had no idea whether or not I wanted a lover now, or should want one.

Locke's sitting room was pretty with vases of flowers on every surface, elegant figurines on the shelves. The framed sketch of a male nude had hung beside her mirror but the maid reported her to the housekeeper and she was ordered to take it down or jeopardize her future at college.

She promised me that it was still hanging somewhere in the room but wouldn't tell me where. I wished I had a few secrets of my own. My notes and diaries about the Antarctic were carefully concealed so that no one would see them, but only because they would seem silly and boyish. I thought Locke the most glamorous and amusing person I had met.

We spoke in low voices so as not to disturb the student next door, Cicely Parr, a second-year and captain of the hockey team. Locke and I discussed our futures. Most Candlin students expected to teach or to marry, but Locke and I had dismissed these on our first evening at college.

'I write plays,' said Locke. 'All I'm doing now is a comedy, a light-hearted farce, just to practise my skills.'

'If I thought of working in the theatre, it would finish my parents off altogether. My mother would end up in an asylum, or try to put me in one. No, I want to see the world, places I could never get to on holiday, even if I were rich, go on ships to – as far as I can get.'

'Ah. A sailor girl. How exciting. Men adore a woman in a sailor's uniform and I do think it would suit you. I saw one in the theatre last year and she sang a very comical song—'

I laughed. 'I wasn't thinking of doing it in the music hall. I meant the sea, the real sea.'

'But it would be much easier, and you could make a living at the same time.'

There was a rap on the door. Before we could speak, it swung open and Cicely Parr stepped in. Her hand was pressed tight against her forehead in a gesture of pain and somewhat theatrical martyrdom. She wore a flouncing white nightgown with ruffles around her neck and an odd lace cap on her head that seemed too small and gripped the skin of her forehead. She was tall, pale, pimpled and cold-looking. When Locke first saw Parr she had remarked, unkindly, that Parr looked like a corpse. *There's no blood in her*, she said. *She drained it out of herself.*

If someone complained about noise after lights out, we had to write a letter of apology and deliver it before eight o'clock the next morning. Parr seemed uncommonly affected by noise and made regular complaints about raucous first-years. I knew her well from hockey practice and knew that she could not have cared less who liked her and who did not. She was a very separate sort of person, aloof and quite contained. She seemed not to need friends and was not always kind or friendly to her team. She ordered us around the pitch as though we were foot soldiers, screaming when we were too slow, and turning her back when we did well. Once or twice I saw her so worked up about some trivial mistake one of us had made that her eyes reddened and filled with tears. She would blink them away quickly rather than let us see her so weakened. Everything was a serious matter for Parr. I didn't dislike her – though most of the team did – but she was a little nicer to me than to the others. We had discovered that we had both been at the Olympic Games the previous year, in the stadium at the same time, watching Britain win the tug of war. It was hardly a strong connection but she treated me with a little more respect after that, would pass a comment at half-time, *Might win this one, Farringdon, I reckon*, which would not be worth noticing from anyone else but from Parr seemed like an offer of friendliness that never managed to go further.

'Why such a din?' She winced, fixed her eyes upon Locke.

'We were practically whispering.' Locke glared back.

'I'll go to bed now—' I moved to stand but Locke pushed me down again.

'Farringdon, we needn't hurry to please someone who has entered without knocking.'

'I knocked.'

'You didn't wait for an answer.'

'For goodness' sake. I don't expect better from you, Locke, but, you, Farringdon, I won't have you in my team if you can't be responsible. I have to get up early for my exercises and now I won't get enough sleep.' Her right hand rose to her clavicles and she rubbed at her skin. 'I'm too distressed.'

Each morning, from half past five precisely, rhythmic crashes and bumps came from behind Parr's bedroom door. In the first week of term, several of us had gathered in the corridor worried that she was having some sort of fit and wondering whether it would be all right to barge in. The door had opened and Parr's head popped out, red and boiled-looking, to tell us to clear off.

'Your exercises wake us before the bell,' I said now. 'And we don't complain that you seem intent on bringing the building down. Perhaps we ought to, since you are so enthusiastic about rules and regulations.' I should not have said this, of course. I should have apologized for the noise and let her leave satisfied, but her criticism that I was somehow unfit for the hockey team was cruel.

'What business is that of yours? When you're working as a governess for some grim family you found in the *Morning Star*, you'll wake up when you have to. I should think you'd want to prepare yourself for what's to come. Goodnight. If you disturb me again, I'll make a proper complaint.'

Parr left and slammed the door, being careful not to catch her nightgown. A framed photograph of Locke's brother fell from the dresser and the glass shattered.

'She's insufferable.' Locke took the coal brush from the fireplace and knelt to sweep up the glass. 'She'll never have to work in her life – or marry either – if she doesn't want to. She's an heiress, you know. I heard that she owns two houses in London and another in the countryside.'

'And perhaps I'll have to be a governess in the end, but I am going to fight it all I can.'

'What's that smell?'

Leonora jumped up and came to the fire.

The toast was burnt. I opened the window and waved the pieces around in the cold night until they stopped smoking. Then I dropped them into the bin. Locke cut more bread and put it on the forks.

'If one has money, one can probably do anything.' I pictured Parr sweeping through grand houses and gardens, in her nightgown and cap, with no one near but cowering servants.

'She can't vote, though.'

'No, so then we're all in the same boat after all.'

I knew nothing then of the tragedy in Parr's life or how she had come to be so wealthy. Poor Cicely Parr. A tragic beginning and a nasty end. In between she met Locke and me, which may or may not have been compensation. But we were eighteen or nineteen years old and not able to be much better than we were.

'Why should you care what she thinks?'

But I did care what Parr thought. I cared because she was the captain and, despite her strange manners and eccentric qualities, I looked up to her. It was what Father had taught me and what I had learned from all my reading about explorers and heroes. We must respect our leader, even in difficult times. I wanted her to think well of me but, of course, Locke was right and I should not care.

Chapter Six

The *Nimrod* had sailed from the East India Dock to Temple Pier for exhibition to the public. Admission was 2s 6d. I had the money in my hand before I reached the Embankment. It was a cool day in late October but the crowds were pink-faced and sticky-looking. A group of boys played at the river's edge, trying to get a dog to jump over sticks and into the water, laughing and cheering as it splashed and panted. I became distracted watching them, tripped over a man's foot and fell into a shoe-shine boy, sending him sprawling. The boy waved away my apology, set out his stall again with a stoical shrug. I fought through families, couples and groups of young men to reach the pier, wondered why so many had come to see what I wanted to believe was my own private interest, and then I stopped. The sky and river thickened and thinned as I stared. Sounds flattened until there was just the soft lapping of water.

The ship was as long and narrow as the pictures had suggested, striking with its black hull and high masts. It lay calmly in the water as though, after its turbulent voyage, it wanted sleep. I had heard that members of the expedition team might be here to explain things to visitors and I prayed that there might be the smallest possibility of meeting Shackleton.

When I stepped onto the ship, the spirits of the explorers were so thick in the air that, were the real men here, I would not have noticed them. I peered into the men's sleeping quarters – they called them Oyster Alley – and the areas for the ponies and dogs and sledges, the food stores. Everything was just as the newspapers had described it and almost as I had imagined, but the ship was not thousands of miles away at the bottom of the world. It was here and my feet were touching the deck and its dust and air were going into my nostrils and down into my lungs. I reached to touch the wall. My hand rested on the wood as crowds shoved past. I shut my eyes to feel the place better.

We were out on the ocean, sailing across the Weddell Sea, icebergs hunched and sleeping. The men shuffled in and out of their quarters, up and down the ship, some silent, some muttering, one shouting to another. Water sloshed around my feet and sprayed my hair. Salt seared my cheeks and pricked my eyes. Ernest called out to me, asking for my help.

Farringdon, make sure that the ponies are all right.

Aye, Captain.

Aye, Captain?

What a fool. If I did not try to keep a grip on reality, I might lose my mind and slip into the wrong world, just as my father always did, and wind up talking to ghosts and sea spirits when I needed to concentrate on studying and learning.

I crossed the Embankment to the Medical Examination Hall to see the exhibition of stores and equipment. Photographs lined the walls, windows to a crumbly white world where coal-eyed men huddled to light pipes with mittened hands, where ice made an atlas of the sea, and the ship tilted, tall and black against the sky, as birds wailed above the masts. Around the room were stuffed seals, penguins, skua gulls, positioned as though ready to jump or to fly. A dummy explorer stood by the door of a weather-beaten tent all prepared to set out onto the ice. He was dressed in the clothes of a real expedition member. He looked as though there was warmth in him, as though he might open his mouth and exhale a white ball of breath. I wanted to touch him and I lifted my hand but didn't dare reach out, lest I disturb or interrupt him. There were two sledges, one loaded and ready for its journey, and the smashed-up remains of another.

There were sleeping bags, finnesko boots, ski boots, oil lamps and cookers. There were scientific instruments: the theodolite, for surveying and taking observations for position; the aneroid barometer, for taking the altitude of mountains; the hypsometer, for ascertaining the altitude by the boiling point of water; and the thermometers which were carried on the sledge journeys. I catalogued each item in my notebook.

I saw a small printing machine and a copy of *Aurora Australis*, which the members of the party composed and printed. There were several cameras, a gramophone and a sewing machine. I examined every item carefully, then I returned to the figure at the tent and watched him for some time, as though I expected him to speak to me. What might he say? I tried to shut out the chatter so that there were just the explorer and me. How I would have liked to enter that room, at night, and stand alone with him.

'Splendid to see the public so excited. We must celebrate this and encourage it.'

The voice was rounded and carried a sense of its own importance. I twisted around to see whose it was. My knees softened and I put my hand to my mouth, then snatched it away and tried to appear composed. It was Ernest Shackleton. He was as tall and handsome as he seemed in photographs and was addressing a group of men and women near the door. I must speak, I thought, and ask him about the expedition, real questions that others wouldn't ask, about the feeling of boots on ice, of frozen hair, the smell of burning whale oil. Would he ever consider taking someone like me on his next expedition? There was too much in my head. If only these people would go away, I could think of my words. I moved closer until I was just behind him. He didn't notice. *It's me!* I wanted to say. *Don't we know each other so well by now?* The crowd swelled and shoved around the door and this gave me my chance to do something I didn't know I was going to do. A tan kid glove protruded from his pocket. I snapped it out and put it up my sleeve.

I committed the act of theft without much control,

but I held the glove firmly in the crook of my elbow and walked away. Yes, it was shameful, but Shackleton was a polar explorer and must have plenty of gloves. I might knit a pair myself and send them to him, so that this one, this very glove that had warmed the flesh and muscles and bone of the great explorer's hand, could stay with me.

I dawdled along the Embankment, turning sometimes for another glimpse of the *Nimrod*. I had three years at college in which to lay my plans. I would return to my room and work harder than ever, not only at my studies but at my research and preparations. Shackleton may have failed, again, to reach the Pole, but we were closer now and within the next few years someone would certainly make it. The glove would sit on my desk and keep me sure of my way.

And it was dark when I reached the college. Curtains were drawn in most rooms around Main, but a muted light shone through and made the college shimmer. Only the top floor, as yet uninhabited, was dark. I saw spectres of future students bustling and laughing behind the black panes. I passed under the clock tower and followed the edge of the lawn around the quad to my door. In the long windows of the dining room and kitchen, silhouettes of cooks and maids moved. We were passengers and workers together on an ocean liner. I thought of my mother and sister at home, keeping the fires going and tending to my father in his bed, sailing on a different sea.

I arrived in my corridor to see that students were already closing their doors and leaving for dinner. The hem of my skirt was damp and dirty so I went to my room and changed quickly into my best dress, cream and brown with stiff, fiddly buttons. I dashed through the building to join the others.

Staff and students processed each night in fine gowns and jewellery. We gathered at the east common room and found our dining partners, all chosen and approved at the beginning of term. There were about a hundred and fifty students that year. Miss Hobson, the principal, would then lead us to the dining hall. The selected student of the day would walk beside her, required to make interesting and erudite conversation. No one enjoyed this privilege and each dreaded her own turn.

The procession passed through the library and then into the museum, bright with grand candelabra. A few latecomers waited in the shadows each evening, ready to creep out and join the back of the line. Tonight I was the only one. I fell into place after the others, catching phrases of the conversations, something about a sick uncle in Littlehampton and a tiresome classics lecture that no one had understood. I shut my ears and remembered the exhibition. The picture that came to me now was not the ship itself, or any item on board, but the figure of the explorer, setting out with his sledge, in the middle of a noisy hall in London, exquisite in his peace and determination, oblivious to gaping crowds. This was my lesson. I must keep him in mind, must be like him. I lifted my hands slightly as I walked and let them find his, just inches away. *Where is my glove? I had two.* I smiled and touched his fingers with mine.

The dining hall crossed the width of Main, separating the two quads. The senior staff and two chosen students sat at high table as the rest of us took our seats.

I joined Locke, who was with Hester Morgan and Cicely Parr. She was relating a meeting she'd had that afternoon with Miss Hobson. Locke knew how to amuse her audience, had eyes that flicked easily from one listener to another, knowing just how long to rest with each person before pulling in the next. Her hands made quick, graceful gestures. Hester Morgan laughed as Locke spoke. Morgan was a pleasant, always smiling girl with a pink bulbous face, thick limbs and a voice that had the quality of a lowing cow. She was standing to be president of the Suffrage Society and always wore an ivory *Votes for Women* button on her lapel. She was friends with Edith Foot and, later on, the pair were to spend time in prison for suffragette activities. Morgan kicked a policeman in the face and Foot took to sleeping on the roof of a house belonging to a Tory MP. Neither ever married and they shared a house after the war, not far from Dulwich but I didn't keep in touch. Perhaps they are still there now.

'Are you all right, Farringdon?' asked Morgan. 'Noticed you weren't in the lab today.'

'I'm fine.' I wondered whether I should pretend to be unwell. In fact I was still quite tipsy on my adventure and was sure I glowed with good health.

'She has a cough,' said Locke, who knew where I had been. 'And the fumes from all the chemicals make it worse.'

'Oh dear,' said Parr. 'Will you be playing hockey tomorrow or should I drop you from the team?'

Parr regarded physical infirmity as a sign of mental weakness. If a player were ill or injured, she showed no sympathy but bossed them out of the way. We put up with it because so often she led us to victory, but we sometimes asked each other what Parr would do if she twisted an ankle or felt unwell. We suspected that it would never happen. I laughed with the team but I aspired to be as strong as Parr. I had even taken up her regime of daily exercise before chapel, only making sure not to make noise and wake the others.

'It's nothing.' I gave a pathetic cough.

As we ate, Locke told us about her play. It was almost finished and she hoped that the Drama Society might perform it.

'You've written a play?' asked Morgan. 'What's it about?'

Locke explained. It was a comedy. A gentleman – his name was Charles – had fallen asleep under an apple tree while listening to his friends talk about their offices in the city. When he woke – or thought he woke, for in fact he was in a strange dream – he found himself in a new world, a hundred years in the future, where people travelled in fast motor cars and families had their own hot-air balloons. And, although Charles was still a city banker, he was now a woman named Caroline. His friends were women too and they were doing the same work as before. A farcical series of events followed – I did not quite understand these – involving hot-air balloons, people in strange androgynous clothes and lions roaming through the parks of London. At the end, Charles woke up, back in 1909. He was delighted to be in a familiar world, but was no longer a complacent fool. He spent his evenings wandering between gentlemen's clubs on the Mall giving out copies of *Votes for Women*.

'Very interesting,' I said. 'And inventive.'

'It's not entirely my idea. I borrowed it from a play my father's friend produced. It's called *When Knights Were Bold* by Charles Marlowe – who is in fact a woman – but in that play the character wakes up and finds himself in the chivalrous past. I don't think it has a political message like mine, though.'

'Hot-air balloons?' Morgan looked uncertain. 'Do you think everyone will have one in a hundred years?'

'I'm not H.G. Wells. I'm not trying to tell the future. I'm just playing. I think a hot-air balloon would be the perfect stage device for taking Charles into the future. That's all.'

'Does your play have a title?'

'*Turn Back the Clocks!*'

'Marvellous,' said I.

'Preposterous,' said Parr. 'Women will not be voting in parliamentary elections a hundred years from now and neither will they be turning into men. Nor men into women.' She took her knife and fork and played bully-off with a garden pea.

'Do you have to have to be rude about everything, Parr? I told you that my play is just for fun. You need to

73

have an imagination. Well, I suppose that you don't.' For the first time since I had known her, Locke appeared upset. 'And besides, we *shall have* the vote a hundred years from now, otherwise there's not much point in any of us being here at all.'

'Your play could be a great campaigning tool,' said Morgan. 'All students would want to see it. If the political message is softened with the humour of a farce, you might even convert Celia Horsfield and her friends.'

Celia Horsfield had opposed the motion at a recent debate on votes for women. It was carried by a clear majority and Horsfield had threatened to invite well-known anti-suffrage campaigners to college to convert us. Horsfield was a vain, not very clever woman, so we found it easy to mock her.

'She wouldn't understand the point, even in a light comedy.'

'You're wrong,' said Parr, 'to assume that we're unanimous in supporting votes for women and that you're superior in your position to Celia Horsfield. I myself am absolutely opposed to women's suffrage. Every time I hear about it, my teeth are set on edge.'

'But why?' I took a small mouthful of pork and chewed it slowly. I had not eaten all day, but did not want to appear hungry when I was supposed to be unwell.

'Because women don't need the vote. It is not because I'm foolish or silly or haven't bothered listening to the arguments that I believe this. I'm not a goose like Celia

Horsfield. It's very simple. Almost all women live and work in the domestic sphere and are not concerned with politics.'

'That's nonsense—'

'Women aren't in public life in the way that men are and don't need political influence. It's dreary and depressing to see all this conflict for nothing when there are more important things to care about. None of you has ever been anywhere or done anything and you probably never will. You make far too much noise about things of which you know nothing.'

'How do you know what we have all done?' Locke's voice rose above all others in the dining hall and the place fell quiet. There were glances from high table, some of interest and some of disapproval. Locke blushed. When talk resumed and bubbled up around the hall, we continued our argument in low voices.

'Have you fought in wars?' asked Parr. 'Are you going to fight wars?'

'Our vote might prevent wars happening.' Morgan waved her fork. 'And we might find treatments for injuries and diseases. We are at the beginning and we can't say what we shall achieve.'

Parr shook her head with a smile and gazed into the distance. She generally did this when she disapproved of the conversation. She didn't speak again that evening. I watched as she sipped her coffee, glancing sometimes at the door, eyebrows slightly raised.

I wanted to say to her, 'But I don't believe you.' She

seemed to oppose us only because she could not bear to agree with us. Parr suffered my friends and me as though we were a penance she must endure. Her ideas were wrong – I was sure of that – but I admired her strength. I was sorry that she had lost her parents, but I could see the advantages in having no family and a lot of money.

Lightning snapped over the turrets and rain battered the window panes. The sea was high and crashed against the red-brick walls. I drew back the curtain and, instead of the sea, there was Queen Victoria, battered and darkened, on her plinth at the centre of the north quad. I sprawled on my bedroom floor and took a fresh pencil. More lightning. I waited for the thunder.

In my pocket book I had drawn a cross-section diagram of the *Nimrod* and, while it would have been onerous and beyond my skills to attempt to put everything required on board, I put representative crosses, circles and so on to make up the various people, objects and animals. Around it I sketched the Antarctic landscape and marked on it the known islands, mountains, inlets and bays. I added the huts and depots. I followed the routes with dotted lines and marked the places where the explorers had turned back.

In my sketchbook I worked on drawings of ice and snow. I took my impressions from the photographs I'd seen at the exhibition, from my imagination and from books and journals I had read. To try to feel it for myself, I spent free afternoons in the college picture gallery, staring at a painting of a shipwreck in the Arctic Circle, where polar bears crunched on the skeletons of sailors.

We took drawing lessons in the gallery and were allowed to copy parts of the great paintings in pencil, so I worked, not at recreating detail, but towards evoking some sense of the harrowing atmosphere, the bleak outcome which horrified and attracted me. I kept the sketches hidden in my wardrobe.

'But it is no use,' I said to a dot for a pony on the sketch. 'I can't know anything at all until I go there myself.'

And when would that be? I curled up in my chair and opened letters that I had not had time to look at during the day. There was a short, polite letter from my sister telling me that we had a new carpet at home and that the garden was looking very pretty in the morning frost. She said that, although Father still refused to write a letter to me himself, he liked to read mine over her shoulder. I had letters from old schoolfriends, one of whom had just married a school teacher and was living in Herne Hill. She hoped that I would visit her next time I went home.

I wonder, I thought, if I ever shall. Home was remote now, another continent, and sometimes I wasn't certain that I could remember the way back. I opened my pocket book to a fresh page. Five minutes later I was sitting there with my pen poised above the paper.

I have wasted enough time. What shall I do?

Then I scrawled out my message. It took several attempts as I put lines through words and sentences, starting again and again. After filling and discarding seven or eight sheets of paper, I was left with this:

THE CANDLIN COLLEGE ANTARCTIC
EXPLORATION SOCIETY

What are the qualities of a polar hero?

When will men reach the South Pole?

What will Science tell us next?

*The Society will hold its inaugural meeting
on . . . evening in room . . .*

*The Society is dedicated to learning about
South Polar exploration and Science with a view to
past, present and future expeditions.*

All are welcome!

A rap on my door, but I wasn't making any noise.

'Hello?' I whispered.

'Nightwatchman, Miss. Principal's instructions. I have to ask you to turn off your light.'

'Yes, of course.'

So I put out the light and climbed under my bed covers. I slept with the confused feeling that I was at the start of something overwhelming. The dummy explorer lay beside me but now he was human and breathing. I pulled my pillow between my arms to make his head, let his warm breath caress my neck and I cradled him.

*

A few days later I pinned my notices up around the college. I had permission to use a classroom on the fourth floor for the Society's weekly meetings. In the afternoon, a group of classics students and their lecturer filed quietly out of the room whispering of Priam and Antigone. I slipped in with my portraits of Captain Scott and Ernest Shackleton, and a map of the Antarctic.

As I pinned Shackleton to the wall and smoothed him with my fingertips, I tried to imagine myself addressing a meeting. I stood at the blackboard, gazed at the small, scratched desks. I took a step towards the map and pointed.

'And here,' I told the empty classroom, 'at eighty-two fifteen is the point where Scott, Wilson and Shackleton had to turn back in 1902, though Wilson and Scott did make it to eighty-two seventeen on a walk southwards from their tent. They could go no further towards the Pole on this expedition and it was a bitter disappointment.' I must find a proper pointer. My hand was unsteady and it was hard to show the precise coordinates with a wavering fingertip. 'Shackleton was so ill by now that he made most of the journey on ski. Fortunately, despite the blizzards, they were able to locate the depot they had laid and so had food and shelter to sustain them before the return to McMurdo Sound. As you can imagine, the shore party was astonished to see them with their wild beards, red faces and long hair. In the recent expedition, however, we see that Shackleton and his men went further, reaching eighty-eight twenty-three, at a longitude of one-hundred-and-sixty-two east. Next time we are bound to succeed, but who will be captain?'

It was possible that no one would come. I had never heard much discussion of Antarctic affairs over dinner or tea, and Locke, my loyal supporter, would be at Drama Soc that evening but, such was my excitement, I could almost imagine proceeding alone. On the classroom door I stuck a sign: The *Discovery*. No doubt it would be removed before the meeting but it gave me a thrill to see it. I looked both ways to be sure that I was alone in the corridor and I gave the sign a kiss for luck.

I returned to my bedroom and dressed for dinner. Catherine had sent me a blouse with a note to say that she had made two from the same pattern, one for each of us. She hoped that it would fit me, that my studies were going well and that I would soon write to Father, though he was still too stubborn to write to me. She also mentioned that Arthur, our manservant, had left as there was little need any more to have as many servants as people. She added: *well, servants are people, of course, but you know what I mean.*

It was a chilly evening, too cold to wear a thin blouse, but when I held it up and saw her neat little stitches, the fine cream buttons chosen with care and sewn tightly into place, I pressed the fabric against my face and imagined her putting on the identical version, fastening her pearls around her neck and checking herself in the mirror. I wore the blouse with a heavy skirt and hoped for the best.

*

I still have the glove. It is in the cellar with my axe, but I shall probably leave it there. To think of showing it to Catherine and explaining how I came about it makes me blush, even now. I have filled the kettle and placed it on the coals. I reach for the biscuit tin on the mantelpiece.

One for you, Father? I offer him a ginger nut. His countenance softens. I have noticed, over many years, that I can make his expression change. I can make him severe and stubborn, or wise and tender, just by wanting it. Now I have made him hungry and he tries to eat the biscuit with his eyes.

I shall ask Mabel to have the piano tuned, tomorrow if possible. We used to have a blind man from Gypsy Hill, but the last time he came was probably when Father was still alive and now the tuner must be dead too. I'll have Mabel dust the strings and give the wood a good polish. Not only is the piano more than a semitone out, but three keys are stuck and so it is irritating to play. I tinkle the notes a little most days, but the sound is shocking and I have to go at it for a long time to reach a state where I hardly notice. One of the bad keys is top B so it is of no consequence, but middle F sharp and the A below that are also stuck. I try to sing the missing notes into place when they are essential to the melody but, as I am never quite ready when the moment comes, it sounds frightful. It is for Catherine, not for me, that I want the piano working again.

I shall leave her old sheet music on the lid and let her notice it. If she does not, I shall only have to drop a hint or two while we talk of Mother and Father, our childhood, the war and all. I will offer her a bag of sherbet or some peppermint lumps – Mabel will go out in the morning and fetch them – and she'll soon play herself into the past. She'll begin with Bach. I smile as I see her hands working busily together, following the intricate patterns and stitch of the music, and she will knit her way through the evening until we and our house are all one fabric again and cannot be undone.

I have a photograph, a long, curled-up thing. I unroll it, grasp the corners. I move my arms back and forth to get it into a position where I can read the words on the back.

Candlin College Hockey Team, 1909–10
(left to right) C. Parr (captain), B. Bright, H. Grime,
E. Jones, E. Thomson, J. Vause, F. Mitchell, C. Halford,
G. Farringdon, L. Corkell, C. Nelson, K. Boddy

There are more names but too faded to read.

Catherine will not want to see this. She was never interested in hockey or anything to do with running around. I imagine that she and George had a quiet life together. I have the feeling that she is thinking about me at this very moment. If I shut my eyes and concentrate, I believe I can almost reach her thoughts and pull them to me. I want to believe that I can. We used to play at this sort of thing, reading minds and sending messages. Once I sat in my bedroom, Catherine in hers, and we imagined Freddie into the attic so that the three of us could have a conversation by telepathy. I thought I heard a lot of noise from both of them but nothing that sounded like voices and, though I wanted it to be true and longed to hear words from Freddie, I knew that it was nonsense.

Catherine. Catherine. Can you hear me? Where are you? Listen and you'll know I'm here and have something to tell you. Cicely Parr – she – you never met her but I'm trying to explain. I can't get rid of her. I need you at my side now.

Chapter Seven

The Antarctic Exploration Society held its first meeting. I woke early and spent an hour before chapel preparing my speech. I skipped tea in the afternoon to give myself another hour. By the evening I was in knots, unable to breathe without my ribs hurting, and had to spend some time at the mirror talking to myself. Perhaps, if it went well, I would write a letter to my father and tell him what I had done. He might yet forgive me for leaving home and be proud that I was continuing the journey we had begun together by the fireplace.

But when I put my nose through the classroom door and saw Cicely Parr sitting at the front, rolling a pencil back and forth on her desk, my courage seeped away. It had not occurred to me that Parr might be interested either in the Antarctic or in anything I had organized. She wore a grey skirt and a cream blouse that made her skin appear yellowish. Her chin jutted out as though she were already bored, even slightly disgusted, by the whole meeting, though it had not even begun.

There was one other attendee, Winifred Hooper, a quiet,

bespectacled botany student, who sat at the desk behind Parr's and gave me a shy smile as I entered. On fine days Hooper would perch on an upturned basket on one of the long balconies, making garlands of primroses to thread through the balustrade. She had a peaceful air and seemed absorbed as she worked away in the sunshine. I knew little more about her, except that she had a fiancé – a medical student at Cambridge – and was only at college to pass the time until he qualified as a doctor. If he succeeded before she took her finals, she would not bother to complete her degree. I had heard her say this quite happily to a friend one teatime and I was surprised and inclined not to like her for it, but now, in my gratitude, I forgot all that.

I took a seat beside Parr and suggested that we might wait for more people before I declared the meeting open and announced the agenda. We sat in uncomfortable silence for five or ten minutes. Parr stared out of the window, though there was nothing to see but sky. Hooper glanced at me a few times, still with a polite smile which I forgot to return, and drew breath once, as if to speak but not knowing what to say. My nerves were making her uneasy but I couldn't help myself. I was wringing my hands the way Mother did before guests came to tea.

The doorknob rattled.

'Here you are.' Locke put her head into the room. 'Drama Soc's cancelled. Miss Wheeler's gone to nurse her sick aunt and might not come back. You don't mind if I join you?'

She noticed Parr and opened her eyes wide at me. I smiled. I could do nothing else.

Locke pulled out the chair next to Parr's and behind
Hooper's. She gave me an encouraging smile then turned
to Parr.

'Hello. I didn't know this was an interest of yours. Scientific, is it?'

'Yes, more or less. I don't think anyone else will come
now, so shouldn't we make a start? Farringdon, I trust you
have a plan.' Meaning that she thought I did not.

'At the Tennyson Appreciation Club they read out his
poems,' offered Hooper. 'I'm not a member but I hear it
always goes very well.'

'That's an idea,' said Locke. 'We could—'

'No, no,' I said, anxious that they should not take over
my meeting. 'I don't think Tennyson wrote anything about
the South Pole. Let me make my opening speech. I've
given it considerable thought.'

I took to the lecturer's podium with my notes, planted
my feet evenly, rubbed my fingers together, for they were a
little damp, and addressed the Society.

'Welcome, ladies, to the inaugural meeting of the
Candlin College Antarctic Exploration Society. Let me
explain to you what our purpose shall be. In our regular
weekly meetings I propose that we acquaint ourselves with
the particulars of recent and current expeditions to the Antarctic. We'll read the accounts of the *Discovery* and *Nimrod*
expeditions in the *South Polar Times* – and whatever else
we can find – and we'll follow their routes along the map.
I'm sure there will be much to consider and enjoy. You'll see
that I have already marked the journey of the *Nimrod* from

Hobart to McMurdo Sound.' I went to the map and pointed out the line of the voyage. 'I have listed the equipment and men on board, so we may gain a picture of the expedition and from there we might imagine what our men endured. We may also examine the scientific studies conducted on this and on previous expeditions and think about what we can learn from them.' I held up the exercise books I had purchased the previous day. 'These will hold the records of our meetings so we can write all our notes and observations in them. If there are no objections from the Society, I shall keep these in my sitting room. However, all members will be at liberty to borrow and use them at any time.'

The members of the Antarctic Exploration Society nodded. I cleared my throat.

'Now,' I said, 'the intention of this Society is not simply to learn from books in an academic manner and accept all that we hear, but to engage and, most important of all, imagine. How can we understand everything that the explorers experience unless we consider what we would do in their situation? What is it like to live in the harshest conditions that Nature can unleash?'

'A real snorker, I'm sure,' said Hooper with a small frown. She wore a necklace, a dove of paste jewels on a silver chain, and she fiddled with the chain. 'But how can we ever know how it feels? I'm rather interested in studying flora and fauna. I've never thought much about what it's like to be an explorer.'

'We'll do that too,' I said. 'Flora and fauna. Penguins, lichens, fish and all that. It will be part of the journey.'

'We might try some play-acting,' said Locke.

'That doesn't mean anything,' said Hooper. 'We won't know what it is to experience frostbite, or scurvy. It's rather silly to think that we can.'

'And this is not Drama Society.' Parr laughed as she spoke, but could not hide her scorn.

I thought of my father's hands, the deformed foot that made him limp and twist across the room, his pain and sadness. *My fingertips were like people, Grace. Each had its own character. The same applies to my foot. I often wonder where these bits of me are, as though they have gone to live somewhere else. It hurt when they left me. The physical pain does not compare.*

'This is what it is to lose part of your own body to the elements,' I said. 'I shall describe it to you.'

I switched off the overhead light so that only a small lamp burned. The curtains were open and light from windows across the quad shone in.

'So. Imagine.' I settled in the professor's chair and clasped my hands. 'We are together in our tent. We have travelled for days in blizzards.'

'Are we in the Antarctic specifically?' asked Hooper.

'No, it doesn't matter. We could be anywhere in freezing conditions. I'm just explaining frostbite.'

Hooper sat back in her chair, unconvinced, but Locke and Parr leaned forward with glinting eyes.

'See your fingers in the dark.' I whispered this to make them fearful. 'You've been in the snow all day, perhaps in icy water, struggling to swim. Your gloves are hardened and you can no longer feel your fingers. They turn white, then blue. With your teeth you pull off your gloves. And – your fingertips are black.'

I glanced at the ceiling. My father huddled and shivered on a stretcher while men tended to his wounds. His face creased up in pain but he didn't cry out. A surgeon stitched up the rotten stubs of his fingers and toes. He lay flat on his bunk for the beginning of the journey home, the end of his life at sea. What did he think then? I wondered. Was he glad that he had travelled despite the accident or did he wish that he had stayed at home? Of course, he must be glad, but then it made no sense that he wanted to keep his daughters in a birdcage, never to see anything of the world except the streets they first travelled in their perambulator.

'Frostbite's avoidable if you take care and wear soft boots,' said Parr with the manner of a slightly impatient doctor. 'That's the best precaution. For the feet, anyway, in snow.'

I didn't know about this so I said nothing. I gave Parr a pleasant smile to show that I was grateful for her superior knowledge. Then I pressed the light switch and the tent disappeared.

Hooper twisted the necklace around her little finger, slid the dove up and down the chain.

'I'm not sure that four women can really understand.' Her voice was both timid and sanctimonious. 'We'll never go there or anywhere near. We wouldn't survive a minute in the blizzards.'

'What do you mean?' asked Parr. 'Do you think women get colder than men? Not as cold?'

'No. Well, perhaps, yes. We're not as strong.'

'I've climbed mountains and crossed glaciers,' said Parr. 'And I've done it just as well as men, sometimes better. I can assure you that our bodies don't disintegrate in bad weather. Well, no faster than men's bodies.'

'Where did you climb, Parr, in the Alps?' I wanted to clap and cheer at this extraordinary revelation.

'My aunt and uncle visit Switzerland every year and I usually go with them. It's what my family have always done and I've been climbing now since I was about twelve or thirteen years old.'

'And you've climbed on ice and snow?'

'Many times. It's rather fun, if you're good at it.' She smiled, a crack that opened across her face and sealed over almost as soon as it was there.

'How wonderful.'

'I can easily imagine you out in the wilderness.' Locke smiled, possibly with sarcasm, but I think that even Locke was impressed by Parr that evening.

'I can thrive both in the wilderness and in captivity.' Parr smiled back with a shrug. 'We all can.'

If, by captivity, Parr meant her rooms at college, then she could have no idea what stifling places many of us had left behind and to which we would return.

Cicely Parr could whack the hockey ball from one end of the pitch to the other, run faster than most of us and never slip or fall. Though tall, she seemed to take up little space as she moved. There was a toughness to her physique and manner which sometimes made me think that she was bred from some superior species, something more than human, and she always had her eye on some high, distant place. I shouldn't have been surprised to learn that she was a mountaineer. It was easy enough to picture and made perfect sense. And yet it made no sense at all, I thought, with her views on suffrage. A woman who climbed mountains with men must surely want the right to vote.

I felt admiration for Parr and a little envy. I wished she had mentioned the Alps before I started lecturing on frostbite and hypothermia.

'Will you go to the Alps next year?' I asked her.

'I expect so. I usually do.'

'I can't imagine any such thing in my family. We walked on the Downs but I've never been on a mountain, not with snow and ice . . .' My voice trailed off. It was too soon to invite myself to the Alps with Parr, but already I was thinking what a lucky friendship this might be.

'Indeed. Well, my parents were killed in an accident on the Titlis in Switzerland, you see. They were excellent climbers, quite famous in the mountaineering world, and my father was a member of the Alpine Club, but they got caught in a storm on their descent and fell from a cornice. My father went first and my mother wasn't quick enough to anchor the rope. She flew off the edge right after him and that was that. In the Alps you can't often change your mind if you make a mistake.'

Parr related this in a matter-of-fact tone. It sounded

like a joke, a wry comment on her parents' carelessness. I was horrified.

'And you were just a little girl?'

'I was seven years old. It's why I love the Alps.'

Why didn't she hate them? But her eyes hooded over and her lips were firmly together. She had nothing more to say.

Locke, Hooper and I adjourned to Locke's room for cocoa. 'She is much more than I thought,' I said to Locke.

'I expect glaciers form under her gaze, avalanches hear her hard voice and turn straight back up the mountain.'

'She's not as bad as you think. She wants to belong, but she doesn't know how. And we must all try to get along if this is to be a success.'

'Of course. For you, Farringdon, I shall like Cicely Parr. I'll do my best. It's just so difficult to feel comfortable while she's in the room and I don't really know why.'

Hooper leaned forward in her chair, both hands around her cup, tilted her head and smiled to herself. Her hair hung in ringlets over her forehead. Her face was so small and her glasses so thick that they obscured her features and gave one the feeling of trying to see behind a disguise.

'If there were some sort of magic tram that could take me to the South Pole, I'd go. I'd like to see the penguins and all the ice. Teddy would love it too. He's my fiancé.' She stroked the fingers of her left hand with her right, as though imagining her wedding night. 'Just a pleasure outing and then home again.'

'But that's not the point at all,' I said, perhaps unnecessarily.

'What I like about the Society is that we are all so different but our interest pulls us together.' Hooper gave an amiable smile, removed her glasses to wipe away steam from the cocoa. 'Why isn't Parr here?'

'She thinks we're narrow.' Locke rolled her eyes. 'And can't bear to waste her time with us.'

'I think she likes to be alone sometimes,' I offered. 'She doesn't mean to insult anyone, but her mind is always in another place.'

There was a short rap on the door and it seemed to open by itself. Parr loomed in the space then moved shyly to stand against the door frame. It must have been obvious from our silence that we had been discussing her.

'I'm here to speak to Farringdon. May I come in?'

Locke pulled out a chair and removed a pile of books. Parr sat opposite me, smoothed her skirt over her knees.

'I know that your ambition is to be part of some Antarctic expedition one day.'

'I don't think I've ever quite said that.'

'Which is ludicrous,' she continued. 'As we know.'

'Yes, well perhaps one day I'll be a professor of science. Not all the scientists who go on expeditions are professors anyway. Sometimes they have been students of science with little more knowledge than I have. All sorts of people go.'

'No, not all sorts of people. One sort of person. Nobody

SUSANNA JONES

would want a woman amongst all those men, not in such conditions.'

'Did you know that men's beards are very inconvenient in extreme cold? Breath freezes onto them and then trickles off down their necks and chests. It makes them colder.'

'The chasm between your dream and reality is not going to shrink and close because you want it to. If you were prepared to adapt a little, to think in another way, it might be possible to achieve something.'

'Parr, I'm grateful for your concern, but I don't under-stand what on earth you're talking about.'

'There is other ground you must cover first.'

'Is there?'

'Following Mr Shackleton around like a schoolgirl, talking of writing letters to him. What would he think of you if you did? Then you say that women should have the vote. It's nonsense. We get on with the things we *can* do and we do them well. Look at this.'

Parr plucked a flimsy map from her notebook. She unfolded it and spread it over a desk. It showed a moun-tainous landscape with tight round contours, ridges, small villages, lakes and few roads.

'Do you know where this is?'

'The Alps?'

'Peru,' offered Locke.

'Let me see,' said Hooper. 'No, it isn't high enough to be either. See the altitudes.'

'So you've failed the first test,' said Parr, 'by speaking too soon. It's North Wales. You're looking at the mountains of Snowdonia and we're going climbing there in the Easter vacation, all four members of the Society.'

'We are?'

'I'll teach you what you need to know: basic walking skills, how to read a map, how to climb on snow, use ropes and all the other things.'

'How exhilarating.' Locke stood quite suddenly as though it were an epiphany, and made us laugh. 'Who would accompany us?'

'Who needs to come with us? We are four. An even number is best for rope work.' Parr looked at us, one by one, smiling.

We are becoming friends, I thought. She has shared her story, her tragedy, and now she can trust us.

'As a chaperone, I meant.'

Parr shook her head. 'I'm an experienced mountaineer so we don't need a mountain guide or any such thing. We'll stay with my aunt and uncle near Cader Idris and they'll look after us. My aunt has climbed the Matterhorn, you know, and I'm going to do it when I've finished my degree.'

'She's climbed the Matterhorn? Good lord.'

I imagined Parr in a wide-brimmed hat, striding along a snowy ridge, impervious to danger.

'How do we know if we can do it?'

'It's only Wales. We'll be preparing for when we climb in the Alps.'

'Surely *we* are not going to attempt the Matterhorn?'

'Not to begin with, but who knows? Farringdon, are you afraid? It is no use sitting here telling schoolboy tales of polar expeditions as though you live in a storybook.'

'But the Alps are not Erebus.'

'No, indeed. Many of them are much harder to climb. It is all about the spirit of adventure and survival in the harshest conditions. If more Antarctic explorers took the time to train on mountains first they would be much better—'

'Yes, I see, but my only income is for fees and living. My father would never give me money to travel to such places, or anywhere else for that matter. It's impossible.'

'For now there's only your train fare to Wales and I'll pay for that.'

'I can't accept—'

'There should be four of us, as I said.'

Now only Hooper remained unsure. 'If Teddy doesn't mind, I'll come, but only to sketch. You are not getting me to the tops of mountains, thank you very much.'

The moment called for courage and clear leadership.

'Parr is right. As President of the Antarctic Exploration Society, I propose that we further our understanding of travelling in hostile environments by accepting her gener-ous invitation. No one need be forced to go up mountains if they prefer to stay below. There can be opportunities for sketching as well as climbing. All in favour?'

'Aye.' We spoke in one voice.

At last, an expedition into wilderness and harsh con-ditions. I looked around at my fellow explorers. In the bedroom light, their faces glowed but their expressions were solemn and dark. There we were: Hooper the doctor's wife; Locke the actress and writer; Parr the lone mountaineer. I bit my lip and, smiling, sank into my chair. And me, whatever I was.

Here we all are, fixed in sepia: cocoa parties where I was photographed talking to faces I no longer recognize; Locke crouching by her fire reading a book, the title obscured by her hand; Winifred Hooper emerging from a woodland path with a basket full of branches and leaves and an expression of happy surprise; the principal in her sombre skirt, jacket and tie, stalking across the quad with a young, fuzzy-haired lecturer scurrying a pace behind.

Here are Hooper, Locke, Parr and me on the steps in the south quad. The walkway above us is empty, but some-one has left flowerpots and a spade or gardening fork on the balustrade. I don't remember seeing this picture before so I am not sure that I can trust it. Yet here we all are and we look a fright. It is a windy day, evidently, and our hair streams from the misshapen buns on our heads. Our blouses have high collars and the effect is severe. Even jewellery doesn't soften this drab quartet of dressed dolly pegs but I don't think that we were ever vain enough to care. And it wasn't as though we expected attention from men. The rules around male visitors were strict, and quite tiresome. We had almost none.

I go back to the picture of the four of us. I never tire of

Winifred Hooper's image. It is always as though I have just met her and am trying to take a first impression but know that I am getting it wrong. She has twig-coloured curls, pinned up into an untidy bird's nest. She squints through her little spectacle lenses. Her nose is soft and quite flat, a cockle shell. She has a sweet, dimpled face with a crease between her eyebrows. She seems to be gazing at someone or something to her right so that her head is slanted away from the light. She was the reluctant adventurer in our group and yet she was brave.

Anybody picking up this picture would point to Leonora Locke and say that she is the pretty one. They would not be surprised to learn of her many affairs and admirers, her talent on stage and her passionate campaigning for the vote. You can see the strength, the intelligence in her eyes. Her features are delicate and even. She is blessed with dark eyes and clear, cream skin, but it is more than that. Of the four of us, she is the one who seems to be more real than photograph. She seems about to step forward and address the photographer, or perhaps me, and I can almost see her arm rise, almost hear her spirited *Hello. You'll never guess what I just heard.*

Cicely Parr is the one whose image makes me laugh aloud, despite myself. Tall and gawky with a spot on the side of her nose, she looks as though she barged into the photograph and has no idea what she is doing there or what anyone should want from her. Her hair was always scraped so tightly that the sight of it gave one the faint beginnings of a headache. There is a pendant round her neck. It's too small to see the detail, but it may be a gold locket she sometimes wore. I had forgotten it.

Between Locke and Parr, I am quite the average girl. I am taller than one, shorter than the other, and am more conventionally attractive than one, less so than the other. My reddish hair would distinguish me, but in black and white it is medium grey. My expression is without guile or fear and I think I am the most ordinary of the four. Even so, I can see now that I was rather a pretty girl. I had a long, slender neck and good, clear features, Mother's deep-set eyes. In spite of all the sport, I was never flat-chested and angular, or big and beefy, like other sporty girls, just trim and firm. I should have appreciated myself more when I was young.

I imagine my three friends getting together now, in some Edwardian bedroom or sitting room in the clouds, to conduct a Society meeting without me, their leader. It's childish to feel left out down here when I am the lucky one who has survived, and it is not as though they would ever have forgiven one another and been friends in any kind of afterlife. It's more likely that Parr is up there, in a room of her own with plain walls and few belongings, and the others are in theirs with all their pictures and trinkets.

The wind is high tonight. The letterbox rattles and bangs. It sounds as though my stranger is trying to get in, but I would never let him. It is just the night.

Chapter Eight

Locke and Parr never thought much of each other. I was
friends with both and neither could understand why I liked
the other. Parr thought Locke silly, talkative and dramatic.
Locke made fun of Parr's awkwardness, her tendency to
pour scorn on ideas she didn't share. Hooper and I had
to become adept at diverting tricky conversations, making
conciliatory remarks to keep the mood among us pleasant.
But an incident occurred which showed the deep distrust
between them and which I have often returned to when
I try to understand those days. I suspect that Locke and
Parr never forgave each other for this quarrel and that, years
later, it was still in their minds even if they did not realize it.

Locke had turned a scene from her play into a sketch
and sent it to her mother. An anti-suffrage husband, who
had travelled to the future and seen a better place, returned
to the present and became a campaigner for the vote and
distributor of *Votes for Women*. Hetty Locke was a member
of the Actresses' Franchise League and was performing at
a suffragist pageant in Chelsea. She found her daughter's
sketch amusing and agreed to include it in the pageant. The

performance was just two weeks away and on a Thursday evening, so Locke would not be able to attend it without missing lectures and dinner. Certain that everyone would appreciate the significance of her achievement – *I'm a professional playwright now!* – Locke asked Miss Hobson for the afternoon and evening off and even suggested that she might take a few friends with her. Miss Hobson was known to be a suffragist, and had written articles about it for the newspapers, but she waved Locke away saying that she had better finish her studies and then become a playwright when she had learned a few things. She shut her study door in Locke's face then opened it, seconds later, to say that she had changed her mind. Locke might have the afternoon off, if her parents agreed, and take Hester Morgan with her as Morgan was too far ahead in her studies. She had been admitted to the sanatorium after chewing bagfuls of raw coffee beans at night to avoid sleep and be able to study until morning. Miss Hobson thought that she might benefit from a brief excursion. They must, of course, have a chaperone and be back by evening bell.

Locke and Morgan took a favourite maid as their chaperone and dispatched her when they reached Waterloo. She could be bought for a shilling. They attended the pageant, then met Mrs Locke and her suffragist friends for dinner and enjoyed discussions about the power of theatre and non-violent action in promoting the cause and converting the ignorant. Some campaigners invited them to Parliament Square to sell copies of *Votes for Women* and they stayed out late, trudging the pavements in the cold.

Somehow the pair missed the last train back to college and spent the night at Locke's family home in Kensington. They reappeared after breakfast the following day. I found them in a corner of the common room, glittering with the thrill of their adventure. Morgan told me how the audience applauded Locke's sketch and a man at the back of the hall stood to shout, 'Hear, hear!'

'It's a matter of time now. The opposition will wither and die.'

'They're withered and dead already. Look at the sorts who represent them here, dry old corpses who should have stayed in the last century.'

Parr was at the fireside reading a letter. She glanced up, folded her letter and left the room.

'What's she up to?' Locke craned her neck.

'Perhaps it wasn't kind to call her a dry old corpse.'

Locke bit her lip, winced. 'I wasn't – I didn't mean Parr, specifically. I was thinking of some of the older lecturers and – do you think she's furious?'

'She might not have heard.'

'I'm sure she did. Probably went sneaking off to write her own anti-suffrage play in retaliation. But no – she hasn't got any imagination.'

'I didn't think she was sneaking,' I said, always ready to defend Parr, particularly as Locke had referred to her as a corpse before and I thought her remark was deliberate. 'She has a drawing lesson around now.'

But I was wrong. Parr had gone to see Miss Hobson. We learned later that she went to ask the principal what should be done when one knew that the student next door was not in her room after lights out. After all, while one did not want to intrude, there were serious questions pertaining to our safety and, if it were the middle of the night and the student had not returned, might it not be considered an emergency? Miss Hobson asked Parr to explain what exactly she meant. Parr was always vague about her reply. She denied that she had mentioned Locke by name, or even this specific incident, but said she had merely repeated her question.

Miss Hobson discovered that Locke and Morgan had not been at chapel or breakfast that morning and threatened to have them sent down. Locke had a quick mind and a talent for performance. She simply denied that they had not come back that evening and she paid the maid a few more shillings to back up her story. Morgan nodded meekly. Miss Hobson would not believe that any Candlin College student would have the audacity to lie about such a serious matter so agreed to take Locke at her word. She fined the pair for missing breakfast and chapel but decided not to investigate further, perhaps wishing to avoid a scandal. Instead she assured Locke and Morgan that they would be watched closely for the rest of their time at college.

At the next Society meeting, we did not even begin official proceedings. Locke arrived last, marched in and banged her fist on Parr's desk. Parr, who had been sitting with her hands clasped beneath her chin as Hooper and I chattered, jumped back with a cry.

'Why the devil did you say anything?' Locke banged the desk again. 'It was none of your business.'

A slight pinkness spread about the edges of Parr's face, just around her hairline.

'I – I merely asked for guidance in what might be a dangerous situation. I was careful not to say anything about you. It was really a criticism of the staff and the nightwatchman.'

'But to what purpose?'

'If someone is not in their bed all night and nobody knows about it, shouldn't we all worry about our safety? What if a madman had come into the building and taken you? My bed is in the next room.'

'I think you knew where I was and felt perfectly safe.'

'How could I have known?'

They argued the point for several minutes. I had planned for some study of oceanography and Nansen's important work on currents at the North Pole and had even prepared sketches of the *Fram*, frozen in pack ice, as it drifted across the Pole. I was anxious to begin but no one was interested. Hooper sat at the back of the small classroom and finished off a letter to Teddy. Locke glared at Parr, tapping her foot against a desk leg. Parr stared out of the window with red-rimmed eyes.

I declared the meeting utterly pointless and suggested a postponement until the following week.

Locke chased me down the corridor. 'I'm sorry we ruined it, but do you see what she did? I'm sure she knew I was in London.'

'Parr was worried. You didn't come back all night and could have been lost or murdered in the city. If she had

When Nights Were Cold

only wanted to cause trouble, she could have told the nightwatchman and had the whole college up looking for you.'

'But she is more subtle than that. Look, I don't care about her and it's my own fault anyway, but I don't understand why you like her so much. She has shown herself to be malicious. I expect she is jealous because she thought I was with a lover.'

'Try to see things from her point of view. She's lost both parents and is quite alone. It's easy to see why she might be afraid at night.' We crossed the quad and entered the cloister. The chapel windows were open and the choir were practising Bach's 'Wachet Auf'. 'It would be best to forgive her. And you did lie about it, which is rather terrible.'

My response was pious and sanctimonious. The soaring voices of the choir seemed to emphasize this and mock me for it. I was disappointed in Parr. Why on earth had she gone to the principal? But I preferred to believe that Locke was wrong than that Cicely Parr could have acted with spite. Perhaps it was also the case that I envied Locke and Morgan their adventure.

'We have to keep her happy,' I said. 'For the sake of our travels.'

'I'm not climbing any mountains with her. Why does she want us to come with her if she despises us so much? Why doesn't she go with all these extraordinary mountaineering friends she has?'

I thought about this. 'I'm not sure that she does have them.'

'Oh, I see. I assumed—'

'They're all aunts and uncles and their friends. I think she thinks that we're her friends.'

'Strange way she shows it.'

'Yes, it is and that's why she's lonely, but I think she'll change in time. Will you still come to Wales?'

'Cicely Parr doesn't own all the snow and all the mountains in the world, though she may think she does. I'll come, but I still say that she is treacherous.'

The Society continued to meet each week and when Shackleton's account of the *Nimrod* expedition, *The Heart of the Antarctic*, was published, I purchased it and used it to guide our role-play.

We sat beneath the Earth shadows, as though it were sunrise at McMurdo. The long, black bars, projected up into the sky from the Western Mountains, crossed the ceiling of our small classroom. We travelled over plains of white, saw giant sastrugi and nunataks and their beauty amazed us. I was in charge of meteorology and took the temperature at regular intervals, boiled the hypsometer. Locke was the cosmographer, taking angles and bearings of the new land. In the freezing winds she operated the tiny screws of the theodolite. At times it almost brought her to tears, but her tiny, nimble fingers made her the best man for the job. Hooper made notes of our experiences and impressions in her diary. Parr was our guide, crunching through snow and leading us onward.

We followed Mawson, Mackay and Professor David

on their journey up the white slopes of Mount Erebus. A depression marked the old crater and we passed it, travelled towards the active cone at its side, not sure how close we could safely go, wondered what sort of noise it would make, if any. Parr led us safely up and down, not quite sure of the way, but telling us when to put our crampons on, where to make camp for the night.

From below Erebus one can see a strange glow which waxes and wanes. Sometimes flame bursts across the crater. And when Shackleton looked out through Armytage's telescope to see how his party progressed, he saw the six members of the main and support parties combined and, a little further away, the four figures of the Candlin College Antarctic Exploration Society.

Though we were clearly pretending to be men when we played our Antarctic scenes, we couldn't help thinking as women, when lying in our tent at night, imagining our sweethearts at home.

Sometimes we got along fine. Hooper heated a tin of giblet soup over the coal fire one evening. We had decided that it would be better to conduct the imaginative part of our proceedings without electricity. In the flicker and glow of flames we sipped the soup from large enamel cups. Hooper was the first to address the meeting and she spoke about the emperor penguin, the largest of all penguin species and that which breeds the furthest south. She laid out sketches of penguins on pack ice sheltered by bergs and cliffs, but it was not easy to see them clearly without holding them close to the candles. We held a vote and agreed not to switch on the electric light until the end of the meeting so we would maintain our special atmosphere, but take extra care not to start a fire.

Locke read Scott's account of his journey south with Wilson and Shackleton. She read aloud so beautifully that I forgot that I had read the work many times before. Parr applauded her, then followed with an informative talk about skiing and sledging, not that she had done either but she had aunts and uncles who had. It seemed that the difficulty of skiing on the horizontal was the matter of balance and it could take much time to master this. I was pleased that Locke and Parr did not mention their argument again but appeared to have overcome their differences. They made a particular effort to laugh at one another's jokes and agree heartily with pertinent comments.

We had some discussion about current expedition plans. Scott was planning another assault on the South Pole, while Shackleton was hoping to take a scientific team to the Antarctic for research. Presumably if Scott didn't make it to the Pole, Shackleton would be ready to leave his research and make a run for it himself.

'That's what I'd do,' I said.

'Shackleton might take you with him,' said Locke. 'Perhaps you could have a role in the scientific research.'

'Imagine.'

There was silence for a few seconds and then we all laughed.

*

Catherine had written to say that Father was becoming increasingly agitated and confused. His strange spirits were always at his side and it was embarrassing to leave the house with him lest he begin to shout and curse at some apparition in the air. He frightened children and made the neighbours cross to the other side of the street. Mother could not bear to witness his humiliation but could not stop him going out, so she spent most days alone in her room. It fell to Catherine to care for them both. I had promised to return at Easter to help, but now I could not go. I tried to persuade myself that this was all right because Catherine had chosen to stay at home when she could have left, and that she was a better nurse to Father than I could ever be. But it was unfair and I knew it. I lay awake most of the night and in the end decided that I would go to Wales as planned and try to be a better sister when I returned.

I wriggled further into my bed in the dark and drew the blankets to my neck. The ceiling was mottled, became pliable and loose as I gazed up. I let the adventure unfold as though watching a play at the theatre. Mountains soared, white and ragged, to a painted blue sky. Four characters stood on soft brown foothills and took the first steps of their ascent. And I thought that, in a way, it would be easy. All we had to do was rehearse and know our parts, and we would reach the summit.

Now I see the four of us on the edge of a mountain, a balcony path with rocks and stones underfoot. Parr and Locke are arguing while Hooper and I trudge quietly behind. The hill falls steeply away and we go on. Rain and sleet drive into us and every few minutes I have to wipe my face and eyes with thick mittens. My vision is blurred but I know the look of the grass and rocks underfoot so well that even when I close my eyes my boots are moving on, left and right, left and right.

Chapter Nine

The manservant met us at Penmaenpool Station and took us by pony trap over the estuary bridge. The train from Paddington had been delayed and it was now evening. The mountains were dark bruises on the sky and the estuary a grey space which sometimes gave up a hint of a glimmer. A narrow lane led us up the mountain to the house. There was little light except for the servant's lantern. The way was steep and wound through trees, between cottages. We held tight to our things and spoke in small, staccato voices. We passed two or three houses set back from the lane, part hidden by fir trees. And we heard the rushing of a waterfall into a deep river.

The pony pulled slowly until the lane became so steep that we could go no further. We jumped down at the side of the track and shivered in the cold, grassy air. Parr led us up to her aunt and uncle's house, Ael y Bryn. We trudged along a slate-edged path, through long lawns, to the porch. Below us was an orchard and, high above the gardens, a deep forest. The wind ruffled the trees and crept over our hair and skin. We looked around, tried to make out shapes in the dark. The estuary was now a wide black gash far below, marked off by the lights of houses and the railway tracks.

Parr rang the doorbell, then left us in the porch as she went to give instructions to the manservant for our luggage. An owl hooted and Locke mimicked the sound in a whisper.

Parr pressed the bell again, peered through the window. 'Where's Ruth? She knew we'd be here by now.'

Locke stepped back to gaze at the house. She was wearing an opera coat in deep blue that seemed dramatic at college but incongruous here. It billowed and ballooned in the wind.

'All the windows are quite dark. Are you sure your aunt and uncle are home?'

Parr looked uneasy. Then she explained, as though she must have mentioned it many times before, if only we had paid attention, that in fact they were away, just for the first few days.

'But the servants are here.' She rapped on the door. 'We'll have a fine time by ourselves.'

Hooper turned and stared out at the forest. 'Parr,' she said after a few moments, 'you can't expect us to stay here without your aunt and uncle. My parents will never stand for it. Teddy will be terribly upset.'

'I don't really see how they'll know.'

'But I don't want to be in this situation. It's compromising. If anyone knew that we were here without your aunt and uncle—'

Parr attacked the doorbell with her whole fist. 'You could

probably catch the night train back to London. If I were you, though, I'd stay for something to eat first.'

Hooper sighed, marched away from us, then returned. Her hair was coming loose and, with all its wild curls, resembled a child's scribble around a too-small face.

'I can't think why I came with you. You are all completely mad with your expeditions and mountaineering. It was all right when we were sitting around a classroom, but now we're outside this house in the middle of the mountains with nobody—' Her voice caught in her throat.

Locke and I looked at each other. Hooper was about to cry and Parr seemed to have brought us to a deserted house.

'I've been coming here every year since I was born,' said Parr. 'The worst thing that ever happens is that sheep get into the garden once in a while and trample the hydrangeas.'

'Let's not argue.' I hurried to Hooper and took her arm. 'Of course you're nervous, but Parr says it will all be fine so it will. If there are difficulties then we must embrace them together. Parr, we're very grateful to be here.'

'If you think I have let you down, I apologize,' she said. 'You can't blame me entirely, you know. Am I wrong to think that a group of suffragists might have a little courage, some sense of independence?'

'We have plenty of courage and independence,' I said. 'This couldn't be better.'

'We shan't be here all the time anyway. We'll spend at least one night in Llanberis before we climb Snowdon. My aunt may be back here when we return and my uncle may even be with her, but it's difficult to say since they don't like to keep regular plans.' Parr gestured towards the house. 'Do you like it?'

'It's beautiful,' Locke whispered. 'The house, the garden, the scent, the sky. It's all magical. Thank you, Parr.'

Parr gave Locke a glance and half a smile, as though she were wrong-footed by Locke's gratitude.

'Snowdon?' Hooper shuffled to a low wall and perched on it. 'Do you think I'm climbing Mount Snowdon when there's a perfectly good train?'

The door creaked open then and a woman of about forty greeted us and led us into the dark vestibule. Beyond the hall, a dim light flickered. A grandfather clock chimed a quarter past the hour. We followed Ruth up carpeted stairs to our bedrooms. The house smelled of old apples.

I perched on the windowsill in my room and peered through the curtains for a few minutes. I could see nothing but the outline of a tree. I whispered, *Thank you.* I wasn't sure whom I was thanking. Perhaps it was my father for, though he had done his best to keep me trapped in his house, it was he, with his maps, tales and strange spirits, who had made my journey here inevitable. Parr would say, *It's only Wales*, but for me it might have been the other side of the Earth.

After dinner we changed into our outdoor clothes and carried glasses of brandy into the garden. How strange to dress in men's clothes. Some women mountaineers climbed in their skirts – short ones with breeches underneath, or long ones with hoops and strings that allowed the skirt to shorten when ascending – but Parr thought this silly and dangerous. Parr always wore bloomers when she climbed on the continent and had a pile of spare clothes for us.

'I look like a frog.' Hooper flexed her foot and frowned. 'I'm not wearing these preposterous things. You can wear them if you will, but I'll climb in my skirt. Don't tell me not to, for I know that lots of climbers do. Lucy Walker wore a skirt on all her Alpine ascents. I know that.'

'Whatever pleases you,' said Parr. 'The Matterhorn would have been climbed by Félicité Carrel before Lucy Walker's ascent, only her skirt blew up in the wind and she could not move. I'm sure women have been killed horribly by their own skirts.'

'I'm serious,' said Hooper. 'I had a mad aunt who used to cycle between her farm and the local shop wearing bloomers, and the villagers threw rotten eggs at her. When you look at us, it's easy to see why. Never tell Teddy you've seen me like this.'

Locke roared with laughter, danced around the lawn kicking her legs up, then lay back on the grass, panting, looking at the sky. 'Let them throw eggs at me.'

Hooper glared. 'You're making a spectacle of yourself.'

'There's no one here but us. Where are your aunt and uncle, Parr?'

'My Aunt Jane is with her friend in London, just until my uncle returns. He's in the mountains in Bolivia. I'm sure I told you all this.'

'Bolivia? You certainly didn't.'

'We're all here now, so it doesn't matter.'

'I agree.' I perched on a low stone wall, pressed my feet into the mossy grass, felt it spring back.

The garden had three or four lawns, on different levels, with stone steps leading from one to the next and flower-beds between. We sat under an oak tree on the highest lawn with our glasses. I inhaled the fumes from my brandy for a few moments before tasting it.

'Parr, did your aunt and uncle really climb Mont Blanc and the Matterhorn?' I wanted to know Parr better but she gave little away.

'They did. It was quite a long time ago.'

'And your uncle allowed her to go with him?' asked Hooper. 'I can't imagine that.'

'Some men in the Alpine Club won't even speak to her. But she doesn't care. It's reaching the peak that matters. It has nothing to do with being man or woman, only with being human. My uncle understands that.'

'I think she should care,' said Locke, 'even so.'

'People will change,' I said. 'It is 1910, after all. We are not in the dark ages.'

'No.' Parr took a sip of brandy, let it rest on her tongue before swallowing. 'We are not.'

'But you don't want any of us to have the vote. I'm persuaded by the suffragists,' said Hooper. 'And so is Teddy and he's a man. So why aren't you?'

'In the wilderness we are all the same,' said Parr. 'But when we come back to normal society, we take on our roles again and that is that and nobody can help it. So we need the wilderness.'

I did not understand her, but was tired of arguments so I said nothing. I breathed in the sweet, damp mossy scent. I was glad that Mr and Mrs Taylor were away. I could pretend it all belonged to us: the big house and gardens, the mountains and the jewelled sky.

It rained in the night and I woke in a shaft of tepid sunlight. Beneath my window, small apple trees quivered in the breeze. I dressed in an old skirt with my outdoor bloomers on underneath. The house was quiet and I sat on the windowsill for a while to watch the estuary far below. Boats bobbed on the cool surface, fishing boats and a pleasure boat on its way to Barmouth. I saw the bridge we had crossed in the dark and the mountains rising behind.

After breakfast we gathered our knapsacks, bags of bread, Thermos flasks of tea, two long ropes. The rainy, fertile scent had intensified. The landscape around Ael y Bryn was vivid greens and browns with patches of pink and white apple blossom. Higher mountains rose beyond the estuary and stretched towards the sea, rugged and lonely. I hoped that the weather would sometimes be as wild as Parr had promised but now the sky was pale and soft.

At the other side of Dolgelley, near the base of Cader Idris, we packed our skirts into our knapsacks – Hooper did not – and began our ascent.

*

It was much easier than I had imagined. On the first steep stretch I lost my breath and thought I could not go on but, after a short rest, I stopped wheezing and began to feel rather good. We met other trampers, mostly men but sometimes women accompanied them. On one occasion, Locke turned to see a pair of men who had just said hello walking backwards staring at us, muttering about our appearance. Locke began to walk backwards then waved at them till, shamed, they resumed their walk. Parr told her to stop provoking trouble.

'You just need attention all the time, don't you? You're scandalous.'

'We're getting it anyway.'

'As I told you,' said Hooper.

'But I don't care,' said Locke. 'And you shouldn't either.'

Hooper sometimes put up a hand to call us to a halt. She would take her notebook and make a rough sketch. Each time, Parr walked a few paces ahead, gazing into the distance until Hooper had finished. I knew that Hooper liked to sketch but I also saw that she struggled to move as quickly as the rest of us and it was her way of stopping to catch breath without losing dignity.

I remember a particular sketch from that day. Hooper showed me before slipping the paper into her knapsack. She had made a neat copy of a small patch of map lichen, about an inch across.

'This is how long we've been alive.' She put the tip of her little finger across two-thirds of it. 'The whole piece has been growing for about thirty years. It works so slowly you see.'

'Do you mind climbing with us, Hooper? Have we rather bullied you into it, when you'd be happier counting years in lichen?'

She laughed. 'Yes, you have rather bullied me. But I'm happy to be the fourth member and my legs are learning to do as they're told.' She put her pencil and paper into her pack, took a few small steps to get going again. 'Besides, I couldn't leave you alone with the cat and dog.'

I smiled. I thought Parr was the dog and Locke the cat but Hooper would not say which was which.

Parr had said that there would be no view from Cader, just a deep soup of mist. The good weather lasted though and, on the summit, we had clear views over Dolgelley, the peaks and the sea. A sharp wind whipped up and we huddled for warmth as Parr scrutinized the landscape. Soon we were heading towards a jagged ridge where Parr was going to teach us how to climb with ropes. We learned how to use the ropes, how to belay each other and to find holds in the rock. It took time to learn the basic things, so we climbed the same routes, feeling them become easier each time. By the end of the afternoon our arms and legs were heavy and our fingertips red and burnt as though caught on the stove. We had scratches and grazes on our hands, but we continued to climb and knew that we were learning well.

So we went higher. We took the train north to Llanberis, spent two nights in a hotel and climbed the peaks of the Ogwen Valley. We scrambled up the spine of Tryfan, getting our fingertips onto its knobbly bones, learning how to place our hands and feet, to twist around an exposed rock or haul ourselves up a sharp gully. We hardly spoke except to offer a hand or to discuss our route. The wind brought a spitting rain and the rocks became dark and slippery. Hooper panicked once or twice on exposed sections and we had to wait and speak calmly to her until she could go on. She blinked back tears, wiped her spectacles several times and laughed at herself, but she always forced herself to climb the next rock and the next one until we reached the summit. None of us mentioned that her skirt was an encumbrance to her, but it was, especially on the larger rocks. Locke, who did no sport at college but could dance like a professional, found the rocks easy. She gambolled up to the summit, looked around and laughed.

Parr and I checked our compasses to navigate our descent. I could see that Parr wanted to do this herself, without my assistance, but this was my first opportunity to help lead the team.

'Follow me,' said Parr. 'I know what we're doing. It's all right, Farringdon.'

'I just want to be sure I know it for myself,' I said. 'So that I learn and so that we're all safe.'

'I wouldn't have led you up here if I didn't believe that I could get you all down,' said Parr. 'Do you trust me or don't you?'

'Of course I do. I'm just trying—'

'Then off we go.'

She stepped into the mist and disappeared.

'I wish there were a man with us,' said Hooper. 'I would feel safer.' She stomped forward, lost her footing and skidded a few feet down a slope of scree. Locke and I waited for her, calling for Parr.

'Where are you all?' Her voice cut through the cloud. 'I told you to follow me. This is dangerous.'

But we made it safely down from the rocks and stones then descended on grass. The clouds dispersed to reveal the whole of the valley with its gullies, cwms and ridges. We took a rest near Lake Idwal and Parr pointed out the many peaks. She named them one by one, like friends.

The following day we traversed Crib Goch and continued to the summit of Snowdon. We sang songs and made up a strange ditty, which contained bits of 'Rule Britannia', some yodelling and music hall songs to which Locke knew all the words. Locke and I were the ones who talked and sang the most. Hooper stumbled quietly along behind us, listening and laughing at jokes, but seeming content in her own thoughts. Sometimes we had to help her over rocks or round an exposed path. Parr marched on, not rude or complaining but always with an edge of impatience.

On our final day of hiking, I caught up with Parr to talk. We were following a stream down into the valley. Hooper and Locke were behind us, playing some game where they had to jump from stone to rock and never touch grass. They laughed and fell, stood wobbling on stones. Echoes of their voices bounced around the valley.

'Has it been all right for you?' I asked Parr. 'Only we are perhaps not quite like your usual companions.'

'That's all right. I don't mind what people are like as long as they try hard.' She softened and smiled. 'Locke doesn't like me, I know, but she is getting better at hiding it.'

There seemed no point in contradicting her when we both knew it was true.

'I'm not good at conversations and knowing how to discuss trivial things. You know, the way you and Locke are always joking about something and you both talk faster and faster and it's like a frenetic song. Well, when I try to come in, it's as though I'm out of tune or the words are wrong. It's just something you're good at and I am not.'

'I suppose it doesn't much matter.'

'I don't know. Anyway, I do like to have people around.'

Hooper shrieked and fell into the stream. Only her feet got wet and she pulled herself out quickly but she continued to squeal until she'd got her boots off.

'What a baby.' Parr gazed at Hooper, baffled. 'Why does she make such a fuss?'

'She's enjoying herself,' I said.

'Then why does she scream? We are not children.' Parr's face creased into a frown as Locke and Hooper paddled in the stream. I ran to join them.

Locke crouched on a boulder at the water's edge and dangled her feet into the flow. I sat beside her and took off my boots. My feet were blistered and hot. I dipped them into the stream and let out a moan of relief as the cold water rushed round my ankles.

'Imagine,' said Locke, 'if you came up here all alone with just a tent and a few warm clothes, a bit of food. You could camp out on the hills for weeks and no one would know where you were. I wonder what it would be like at night.' Her eyes glistened as they roamed the landscape. She grabbed my wrist. 'Think of the wind and the darkness, no one in the world but you.'

'And the sheep.' I watched my feet whiten under the water's surface. Pink streaks marked the places where my boots had rubbed.

'I don't think I could spend a night out here alone, but a little part of me wants to try. I'd bring some paper and try writing under the stars. No, but I'd freeze.'

'You could if you had to, if you lost everything else and had nothing but your tent and boots. You'd just wander on and on through the hills, come down when you ran out of food.'

Locke swished her feet in the water, kicked them gently.

'I'd rather do it with friends at my side. Less likely to go mad.'

'Or we could all go mad in the mountains together.'

'This is good. It's like washing something away, some grubbiness or scum from normal life.'

Hooper was in her boots again, walking away with Parr.

'We'd better catch them up. Parr never waits.'

*

We were back at Ael y Bryn, but now the windows under the gables were open and cheerful voices called from the hall.

'Girls, welcome back. We've been looking forward to meeting you. Are you all right? Come in now out of the rain.'

A small, slender woman bounced down the porch steps. She was in her forties or fifties, I guessed, with the same heavy eyelids as her niece, but a softer countenance. She wore a pretty white blouse and a full skirt, which trailed in the shallow puddles and made her seem unsuited for the outdoors. She reminded me at first of my mother and the comparison made me wonder at the difference between them. This feminine figure who had stood on the summit of the Matterhorn was a mountaineer disguised as a housewife.

I hobbled in my stockings, boots in my hands, across the muddy front garden. The blisters on my heels were now torn and bleeding.

'We're just back. Mr Taylor has had a wonderful trip to Bolivia and then we spent a few days together in London while he took his research to the university. You must be Miss Farringdon.'

I was too tired to say more than *How d'you do* and smile.

Mr Taylor appeared behind her and bit on his pipe as we introduced ourselves. He was a wiry man of forty-five or fifty with hair that sprouted up from his head as though freshly blown in the wind. His eyes were intense and inter-ested. His eyebrows came almost to meet each other in the middle then curved up and away at the sides like fish tails. The couple welcomed us into the house and we tumbled through the door as though we were in our own homes.

As we washed and dressed, they kept up a friendly interrogation by calling upstairs.

'Was it all right on Tryfan? Not too much mist?'

'Did you see old Evan Jones with his sheep when you went down the lane?'

'Have you eaten well? Has Ruth looked after you? We have good meat and fish up here. You must tell us if you haven't had the best of everything.'

One by one, we went downstairs and gathered in the hall, where Mrs Taylor looked us up and down, smiling and nodding.

'Now, Mr Taylor has been in Bolivia collecting samples of weeds and all the way from London has been telling me how he wished he were at home in Wales all along.'

'No, I was delighted to be in Bolivia, my dear. I merely said how much I looked forward to being back in Wales. And I wasn't collecting weeds—'

'Ah, quite right. You did tell me, didn't you? Not weeds but ferns.'

'No, not ferns, dear, types of grass—'

'Dearest, have you told them about their visitors? Why don't you tell them now? We might go to Dolgelley to take tea, if the young ladies aren't too tired. Were they staying at the George, dear, or the Royal?'

'Visitors?' Parr looked up. 'We weren't expecting anyone.'

'Two young men. Now what were their names? They

were students. They said they'd written to tell you they'd be in the area so we thought you would know, but then we looked on the hall table and saw the letter. It must have arrived after you'd left for Llanberis.'

'One of them was Wilfred,' said Mr Taylor after some thought. 'And I don't remember his surname, not for the life of me. He was the shorter one, wasn't he?'

We stared at each other. Apparently, none of us knew a Wilfred.

'Are you sure they came to see us?' asked Parr.

'Oh yes. And the other was Frank something. They were from Oxford and so very polite. Aren't they your friends, Miss Farringdon? I thought that they were. I'll have Ruth bring the letter in.'

'I know a Frank who is at Oxford but not a Wilfred. I'm sure it's not the same Frank, though. I haven't seen him for a long time and he won't know I'm here.'

Then I realized. It must be Frank Black and it was no coincidence at all. Frank had talked to Mother and that was how he knew. Now he would find out, and might tell my family that this was not quite the gentle holiday I had described to them.

Mrs Taylor passed me the envelope. 'I don't see why we shouldn't all meet for tea.'

'I should like that.' I had better see Frank and talk to him directly. I opened the letter.

Dear Grace,

I trust you are keeping well and enjoying your studies.

*It must be a year or more since we last met but I hope you
have not forgotten me. I happened to see Catherine last
week and she told me about your trip to Snowdonia. By
extraordinary good fortune, my friend and I shall be in the
area at the same time for a spot of sketching and painting.
If you have time and it does not inconvenience you, we
would like to invite you and your friends to tea in Dolgelley
one afternoon. You can write to us at the hotel, or call in.*
    Yours,
        Frank

So my mother had had no hand in the matter and
hadn't sent him to find me. Still, it seemed an exceptional
coincidence and I suspected a deeper motive. Perhaps Frank
and Catherine had met but – I began to create the story
in my head – Catherine had been aloof and shy. He had
come to enlist my help and find out whether there was any
possibility that she still loved him. Or had she lost her sense
of decorum and was writing sad love letters to him which
he wanted her to stop? No – and this was better – they had
become close again, perhaps attended a piano recital or
two together, but Catherine refused to fall in love because
her duty was to take care of Father. Frank wanted me to
persuade her to change her mind.

'How exciting of you, Farringdon,' said Locke. 'I knew
that the wilderness would lead you to some passionate encounter.'

'But Frank is hardly of the wilderness. He's my neighbour in Dulwich.'

'And you are both in the wilderness now.'

'Stop it, Locke. It is not at all what you are thinking.'

It was agreed by the Society that, though tired and ragged, we were not altogether done in and would be delighted to take tea with Frank and Wilfred. We cleaned and bandaged our feet, buttoned and hooked ourselves into dresses, put combs in our hair and became ladies again.

I kick away a slipper, peel off a stocking to inspect my foot. It would wear me out to walk far now and the foot looks appropriately innocent. The skin is very white, soft around the toes, just a little cracked under the heel but I have no blisters or corns, no bunions. Who would suspect this long lily of a foot of having been anywhere but genteel, civilized places? I run my hand along the bone, rub my toes. But on the heel and inside the arch are darkened places, the faded stains of ancient blisters. They have a quality of rust. There's a tiny scar on the sole where I once trod barefoot on a blade of flint. I put my fingertip over the scar. It's just a little bump, a pimple, but I still remember the scream I let out.

The hotel burned bright on the edge of the estuary. Slate-roofed houses piled up on the hill behind, snagged up in pink strands of sky. I thought that Frank was lucky to be able to paint all this onto a canvas and take it home with him in his trunk. We walked onto the bridge and watched the Barmouth train as it pulled out of the station.

'A perfect evening,' sighed Hooper. 'Teddy would love this part, if not the climbing. I don't think he has been to Wales.'

Mr and Mrs Taylor led us to a cosy lounge with a large fire, thick carpets and deep chairs. Frank Black and a tubby dark-haired man were seated at a large table by the window. Frank was pointing to something outside. When he saw me, he jumped to his feet and said something to his friend, who looked at us all then settled his eyes on me as though he had been trying to guess. I gave Frank a smile that felt shy and uncomfortable.

I could not perceive any obvious change in Frank and yet, without Catherine nearby, or his parents either side of him, or Dulwich Park spread out behind him, he was not the Frank Black I knew. Perhaps he seemed taller than before, or his hair was darker. He had a small, rather modest moustache, which was new and very handsome. Perhaps my mother's enthusiasm for his physique had opened my eyes a little to his attractiveness.

It mattered little, for Mr and Mrs Taylor interrogated them over tea and scones. We learned that Frank and Wilfred had climbed Cader Idris that day and would have a few more days of walking and sightseeing before returning to Oxford. Frank and I were at the end of the table so were able to converse by ourselves for a few minutes as Wilfred attempted polite engagement with Parr and was met by her usual haughty indifference. Locke and Hooper rescued him by answering questions on Parr's behalf and regaling Wilfred with our adventures.

'And what have you been painting, Frank?' I asked.

'Landscapes, mainly. I've painted some scenes in Oxfordshire recently, but they're very poor. I'm not nearly ready to try selling them yet.' He garbled this sentence, a little uncertain of himself. 'You're all scientists, aren't you? Is that why you're friends?'

'We're in a Society together at university.'

'We're all members of the Antarctic Exploration Society. In fact we are the whole Society, we four.'

I wished that Hooper had not said this. I remembered evenings in Dulwich with Frank as Wilson and myself as Shackleton and I felt foolish.

'Ah.' A smile played around his eyes.

'The purpose of the Society is to conduct serious research,' I said. 'We're following Scott's preparation for his next expedition and learning from past ones.'

'But we have a lot of larks, really, don't we?' Locke elbowed me.

I smiled. 'Well, there'd be no point in doing it if there were no pleasure in it, would there? But we have serious intentions too.'

'For me there'd be no pleasure in that at all,' said Wilfred. 'It would give me nightmares, that landscape. North Wales is as wild as I like it and a little bit more. In fact, I like the world best like this, observed from a table in a hotel with hot tea.'

'Grace, your father must be – very – ' Frank looked at me and stopped. I knew that he was remembering the incident with Catherine and the piano. He widened his eyes into a question as though I was supposed to talk about my father's condition in front of everyone.

'He's very well indeed, thank you. And Catherine, she is enjoying—'

Locke clapped her hands. 'Why don't you gentlemen come with us tomorrow? It's our last day and we're only going to have some fun. They can come with us, can't they, Farringdon?'

Mrs Taylor took a bite of scone and waved her hand to indicate that she had a good idea.

'I thought it might be fun to take the train to Barmouth and have an easy day at the seaside all together,' she said. 'What do you say? If you two would like to accompany us, we'll have a fine time.'

We arranged to meet at the station the following day. Frank slipped out to wish me goodnight.

'Grace, I must tell you how good it is to see you again. I want you to know that I'm very sorry if I caused your family any distress with regards to Catherine. I wanted to be her friend still but we just – she just didn't seem to like me much that night. Anyway, I'm sorry for it, if there was any misunderstanding.'

'Catherine liked you, Frank. She used to tell me so.'

'But it was not to be.'

'None of it was her fault.'

'You know, if you're an artist you don't just say: very well then, I give up. The point is that you can't do anything else and I don't believe that Catherine *could have* done anything else. My father doesn't want me to be an artist, but I'm taking no notice of him and am all the more determined to succeed. I cared for Catherine, Grace, but it would never have worked. It was as though she just lost herself, and wanted to lose herself. She might have shown some courage.'

'Perhaps you didn't try hard enough to understand. Your father doesn't want you to be an artist but he didn't stop you going to Oxford. I believe he was rather enthusiastic about it.'

'Yes. And look at all the young women who are rebelling against their families and doing everything they can, Grace. The scientists and suffragettes and mountain climbers. Well, for goodness' sake, look at *you*. You've got so much more spirit than your sister.'

'Please don't talk about Catherine that way.'

He walked away, a little pale. As I kept my eyes on his face, I began to understand and thought myself very stupid for not seeing it sooner. I had not seen it in him and, more stupid still, I had not seen it in myself.

Frank turned. His overcoat rumpled slightly in the wind and the tips of his hair brushed across his forehead.

'I'm sorry, Grace,' he mumbled. 'I meant – it isn't to do with Catherine, my reason for coming here.'

'But to draw a comparison between my sister and me – I wish you hadn't.'

'You know how much respect I have for Catherine but, really, we were never more than friends. I loved her playing, of course, but I also liked to spend evenings with your family. It was all so eccentric and fun. Don't be angry. We're spending tomorrow together and – ' he slid his fingers under his scarf and tugged at it – 'and I want to talk to you.'

I called an official meeting of the Society. We took lanterns, a pocket book, our supper and followed the garden steps up to the highest of the lawns, then climbed over the stone wall to get up onto the hill behind. A steep path edged the forest and led past the overgrown entrance to a derelict gold mine. We trotted single file along a narrow trail into the heart of the forest and came to a small, ruined shepherd's cottage. The roof had fallen in and the walls were only partially intact. There was a fireplace and part of a chimney and we found slabs of stone and slate for seats. We hacked at overgrowth with our knives and collected a pile for fire. When it was flickering nicely, we heated Ruth's mutton stew which, in truth, was still quite warm from the kitchen stove.

'This is the most delicious food I have ever eaten.'

'Much better than seal or penguin.'

'But seal or penguin would be fine, if that were all we had. Nansen liked fox flesh, but I don't imagine that tastes good. Perhaps, after hundreds of miles on snow, it's delicious.'

I wanted to go further than this. I wanted to walk and walk. The gap between home and away was already wide and treacherous. There would have to be two of me now or I wouldn't be able to survive. I was splitting into two, becoming my own twin sister.

'Now we know we can climb mountains and that we're stronger than we were last week. That's our main achievement. Apart from you, Parr, of course,' I said. 'You could already climb.'

'No, I haven't learned anything this week,' said Parr, blunt and clear, 'but I never expected that I would.'

'Farringdon has had another success, I think.' Hooper poked me with her foot. 'Now, if you had a husband like Frank, you'd be able to go anywhere you liked and he would follow you. He seems very modern.'

'But he'll never be my husband.'

'A husband *like* Frank is all I said.'

Hooper placed her foot on something and jumped when it moved. She stood to see what it was.

'Ugh. Look at that.'

'What?'

Hooper picked up a ram's skull with the hem of her skirt, peered at it under the lantern light. The bone gleamed around black eye sockets.

Locke watched her with amusement. 'A week ago you wouldn't have touched that, even when it was alive and woolly.'

'I'm used to things now,' said Hooper, still gazing at the skull. 'And I've realized that there isn't time to be afraid of everything. I'm still not sure what to tell Teddy when we get back. He only likes books and cricket and tailors' shops, but I'd like to do some more of this. Well, he might be like Frank and Wilfred and give it a go, but I know he would never permit the Alps.'

'Then climb as much as you can before you get married,' said Parr. 'Or marry someone else.'

Locke laughed and shook her head at Parr. 'That's rather severe advice.'

I stirred the stew on my plate. Tiny globules of mutton fat glistened in the firelight and I chased them with my fork. I remembered my mother's remarks about Frank's appearance. How irritating that she should be right.

Flames twisted and lapped against the cottage walls. For miles around us there was nothing but thick forest. I imagined the shepherd who had once inhabited this place, living out of sight among the dark trees, lighting his fire under the big chimney, and listening alone to the sheep out on the hills.

Our day in Barmouth was all pleasure. Frank and Wilfred, Mr and Mrs Taylor, and the four members of the Society all went off together on the train. We walked on the beach and we strolled around the town. The four of us were tired and sore so we didn't walk far. After a week on the mountains your limbs are full of bent springs and dodgy hinges. But we had a lovely luncheon in a cafe with a view right out to the sparkling grey sea. In the afternoon, we stopped on the promenade for ices. Parr and Locke stood together and pointed at something on the horizon. I don't know what it was, but they were nodding at their shared observation, seeming quite friendly and pleased.

Frank and I became closer in Barmouth. The others watched us so I tried to keep apart from him and not show much interest, but it was such a pleasure to have him there that I could not help but talk to him sometimes. Don't ask me what we said because I cannot remember, and I have often tried. Then, at dinner, Mrs Taylor arranged things so that I was seated beside him. We hardly spoke, though, because Locke was quizzing Mrs Taylor on her Alpine climbs and I wanted to listen.

'And I suppose you didn't get mountain sickness or you wouldn't have been able to climb Mont Blanc.'

'I probably had a headache when we reached the summit, but I would hardly have noticed it by then. There was the view, and the pleasure of having done the job, and the soreness everywhere.'

'It's very romantic.' Locke's nose was pink and sore-looking from the wind. Her cheeks were pale and made her hair seem darker than usual. There was tiredness in her features but she chattered away, as lively and interested as ever.

'Yes, but one is always aware of the dangers,' said Mrs Taylor. 'We saw accidents and – well.'

There was a silence and I am sure that we were all thinking of Parr's parents. Parr reached for her water glass and took a sip. She seemed about to speak but changed her mind and, distracted, turned the glass between her fingers.

Frank and I had a moment alone near the station and he kissed me.

A kiss on my hand. That was all and it was over my glove,

my cream glove. It seems like nothing now, I know, but then—

Frank wanted to see me again, of course. I wrote to say that it would be difficult to receive him at college, but that the picture gallery was open to visitors on Thursday afternoons and had a notable collection of Victorian paintings. He might like to visit one day.

A kiss, on my left hand. Yes. The fingers inside the glove were rope-burned and scree-grazed. The nails were broken and scraggy. The hand belonged to me, but when I regard my hand now it has the look of another person's altogether. I am not sure where that leaves the kiss.

Chapter Ten

'Father, what happened to Edward Whymper after the Matterhorn accident?'

I knew the story but wanted to hear it from him. It was the end of the summer vacation. I sat beside him in the drawing room. King Edward had passed away in May and Father decided that he must follow shortly. *My life is nicely finished off now*, he would say. *I don't want to straggle on into somebody else's era. I'd be the unwelcome guest at the dinner party and I'd rather just go.* Catherine was in her position at the piano but not playing. She moved her fingers around above the keys as though thinking where to start, but she had been doing this for several minutes and I wondered if some music was playing in her head that she could not quite catch and tether. My father pushed tobacco into his pipe and patted it down with his finger stub. He lit it and sucked deeply.

'There was an inquest, of course, all that business about the rope breaking and whether he or Taugwalder cut it. Not possible, of course. The weight of four men already plummeting and pulling you down – how could you have time to pick up a sharp stone or find your knife to cut the rope? Whymper didn't even see what happened because he was last, still coming round the corner when the first one went. I have always felt a sort of connection with him because of the tragedy, not that it was the same thing as – well – of course, but you know. To see those men die and be too late to save them. It's a terrible thing to live with.' My father's eyelids pinkened. 'Don't know where the poor chap is now, but I think he's still alive. He's been all over the world. He's probably up a mountain somewhere, though nothing so high or dangerous as the Matterhorn again. You'd lose your nerve, wouldn't you?'

'The Matterhorn is not so difficult for modern climbers, is it?'

'Good God. Many have climbed it but some still die. It hasn't got any smaller, or less treacherous. Nobody has yet climbed the north face, of course. Look at a picture and you'll see why. Mind you, if they get away with building a railway to the top, that'll be the end of it as a proper mountain. You can take your wife up to the top and bring her down again half an hour later. Pah.'

'But some women have climbed Whymper's route, and from the Italian side, too.'

'Yes, a few obstinate female creatures who must spoil it for the climbers.'

I thought there was a glimmer in his eye and he might be teasing me so I ignored the comment.

'But it's not the highest peak in the Alps, is it?'

'No, of course not. There are several higher. Mont Blanc

and the Monte Rosa are the highest, but it's the shape of the Matterhorn that's the thing, the way it has been chopped and carved into a thing that cannot be climbed and yet must be. I'm glad I never saw it when I was a young man, or else I'd have probably wanted to give it a try. Damned silly way to break your neck, though. Or worse. They never found the body of Lord Francis Douglas, just shreds of his clothing. All that was left.' My father gazed into the fire, wiped his left eye. His hair was in tufts of white, which glistened at the roots. 'Still, at least Queen Victoria never managed to ban the sport. Men will always have to do it, schoolboys will dream of doing it, and that is that. I'll have my veronal now. This conversation has made me sad.'

'Do you suppose that he would have been strong enough to reach the South Pole?'

'Who, Whymper? He wasn't anywhere near the South Pole. What are you talking about? Don't suppose he was even interested in it. Greenland – he went there.'

'No, I meant his strength and technique on the mountains. Having learned those skills, he could use them to cross the Antarctic, if he had wanted to reach the South Pole.'

'Oh, yes. Well, I expect so then, but you've got to want to do it. You wouldn't succeed otherwise.'

Nothing ever changed in Dulwich. I returned each vacation but no longer considered it my home. In the evenings we gathered around the fireplace and Mrs Horton brought cocoa. Father read his journals, accompanied by the rattling and wheezing of his chest. Mother embroidered linen and offered unconnected remarks every so often.

Catherine sometimes played the piano and sometimes worked at her knitted dolls and animals for orphans. She had become accomplished at these and made little elephants with curving trunks and tusks, cats with long, fine whiskers. I sat sighing in the cosy corner and made a show of reading my largest and most difficult college textbooks.

Catherine and I sometimes strolled together around the neighbourhood. We visited our old schoolfriends, but she did not ask much about my new life and I probably showed no interest in her activities at home. Once she surprised me by saying she was expecting to get married, but when I questioned her she admitted that there was no suitor.

My last few days at home during that vacation were quiet. Father took to his bed and we nursed him. My parents begged me not to return to college but the doctor said that my father's condition was not dangerous, or no more so than usual, and so I shrugged and apologized, and said that I must go. The old arguments caught light and burned until my head ached. I longed for my friends, my place in the lab, the classroom where the Society met, and my room with my own furniture and kettle.

Catherine helped me pack.

'I wish I could be as strong as you and just do what I wanted regardless of everyone.'

'And what do you want?'

'To play the piano with Frank again.' She did not pause.

Her answer was simple and straight as though she could want nothing else.

'I'm sure you will.' I tried to smile.

'I'm too shy to ask him but perhaps he'll come one day.'

I hugged her and together we pushed my trunk to the door and down the stairs.

'I'm worried about you, Grace. I wish you wouldn't go away. I have a feeling about it.' She puffed for breath, leaned against the wall. Her arms, freckled and long, folded across her chest.

'What do you mean?'

'You should really stay here. It's going to be harder when you finish university and can't find anyone to marry you.'

'I'll do without marriage then,' I said, but I had no idea whether or not I should mean it. I often thought of Frank but, like Locke, did not want to imagine myself as a wife. 'It was never my ambition.'

I spent the last weekend with Locke's family in Kensington. There was a party to celebrate Mrs Locke's final performance in a new play. I wore a pink silk dress that had once belonged to Catherine and I fastened a band of tiny roses in my hair. We walked through a hall that smelled of lavender and almonds. And then we were in a drawing room. Jewels, bright gowns and dark suits blurred and merged into dancing shapes around the floor.

I drank champagne for the first time. The sudden, sharp fizz made me sneeze.

A door opened to a small courtyard. I breathed sweet air

that did not smell of London. In the centre, a small pond rippled in the night breeze. I shivered, smiling, and stepped towards the water. Two young men stood at its edge, intense in their conversation, gesticulating with cigars. Their smoke mingled and rose above their heads into a ribbon of satin. Locke introduced me to her lover, Horace, and her brother, Geoffrey.

Geoffrey resembled his older sister but was tall, a column with a puff of biscuit-coloured hair on top. He was a sweet, overgrown sort of boy who welcomed me cheerfully to their home, then teased Locke about her height. *Still not ready to grow up, my dear sister?* Horace was of medium height but stocky, dark-haired and dark-eyed. He had rough skin and a loud, full voice. It was no surprise that his most successful role so far had been as a pirate.

Locke sauntered to Horace, snatched his cigar from his hand, put it to her lips and took a deep drag, before putting it back in his mouth. Like an actress, she was aware of her appearance at each turn and from every angle, but there was humour in her affectations and she was never conceited. Horace kept his eyes on her, an almost-smile on his lips at everything she said.

The cigar smoke gave me a warm, exotic feeling and seemed to go pleasantly with the champagne. Locke's father told me that a friend of his, a theatre producer, had met Shackleton on a ship to Australia and they had put on a charity show for the other passengers. The producer was taking a production of *When Knights Were Bold* to Hobart, the play that had inspired his daughter's magnum opus.

And then we were in an upstairs room, white-walled and airy. The party murmured through the floorboards and I was still clutching my glass. Locke and Geoffrey disappeared into another room to find the costumes. There was much banging and cursing and after a few minutes they dragged a trunk into the room. It was filled with cloaks, shawls, fans, masks, jewels, wigs, swords and a gun. We were going to try out Locke's play, *Turn Back the Clocks!* I was eager to begin.

Horace played Charles and I played Caroline. Geoffrey took the role of Charles's best friend, and Locke played all the other parts. We followed the rough stage directions in Locke's script and we made up moves ourselves. It was comical and sometimes we couldn't speak for laughing. We added a shooting scene so that we could use the gun and this resulted in Caroline shooting Charles so that there was no possibility of returning to the old days as the play demanded. I thought this gave the story a satisfying conclusion, but Charles reversed the act by waking up from death, making the shooting part of his dream. He then shot Caroline and I enjoyed performing her violent death.

Locke came to my room at bedtime.

'My brother likes you. Did you notice how he laughed at everything you said? He isn't usually like that. I think you might get along well together.'

I smiled in the darkness. I didn't know whether or not I could fall in love with Geoffrey – though I liked him – but the knowledge that he liked me was unexpected and sweet.

Now I was thinking of the strange encounter between Shackleton and the theatre producer. I imagined them performing some play together, with the whiteness of Antarctica as their backdrop, the whole world their audience.

'Night then.'

'Night, Locke. I liked your play.'

'You shall be in it when it is performed, one day. You're a proper actress you know.'

'Oh, I'd be no good. I want to do things that are real, not make-believe.' I shut my eyes and boarded the ship to Tasmania.

If only my family could be like Locke's.

The following day Locke and I took the train back to college.

Chapter Eleven

Frank swayed slightly on his feet, a willow in the mildest breeze. He blinked and scratched his nose. His head moved from left to right and then back, as though he were not looking at the painting but watching it. I backed into my hiding place at the gallery's entrance, a gloomy corner between the outer and inner doors. The air seethed with floor polish and library-book dust and I stifled sneezes into my handkerchief. I had slipped out of the lab early, left Locke to clear up my bench and invent an excuse for my disappearance. Here was Frank, not quite real now, slight in his morning suit and heavy black shoes. I imagined him as a character from some secret painting, a thoughtful gentleman pretending to examine paintings in a gallery as he waited for his lover who, unbeknown to him, watched from a dark place.

But Frank had come all the way from Oxford to see me. It would not do to make him wait while I spied on him. I opened my journal, as though I might be making a few notes for my next drawing class, and crossed the room with the feeling that there was no floor and I was swimming from my side to his. I tried to banish the thought of myself as his secret lover in case it showed on my face and appalled him. A kiss on the glove is no kind of promise, after all.

'Grace.' In his nerves he gave me a smile that was too wide and looked odd on his narrow face, but I did just the same. 'How nice to see you. How are you?'

'I'm very well.' I grinned and nodded like a puppet.

'Extraordinary place this. What a collection.'

'Yes.'

He nodded too and his smile simmered down into something quite attractive. He gestured towards my journal and spoke in a low, secretive voice. 'You've brought work to do. Are you sketching out a masterpiece of your own?'

'Oh, no. It's just a – a prop to make it look as though I'm supposed to be here.' I snapped the book shut lest he see my inadequate efforts. 'How are you, Frank?'

'I'm well. Are you able to talk to me or is this awkward? It is awkward, isn't it?'

'Rather.' I fingered the edges of my notebook. 'We must just behave as though our meeting is a coincidence.'

'Right you are. Of course.' He stepped back, raised his voice. 'Goodness me. I hadn't realized that you studied here. Extraordinary.'

Two ladies in osprey-feathered hats glanced at us from the nearby still life of apples and pears.

'Perhaps not,' I whispered. 'We had better talk about the paintings. I'm not sure who might be listening. I mean, not that we're saying anything much but—' I gestured towards the painting. 'Was this the one that you particularly wanted to see? It's considered especially fine, though I must say I can't bear it.'

It was a sentimental portrait of a little golden-haired girl on a swing, bluebells in her hand and a long-eared dog at her feet.

Frank laughed. 'It was something to look at till you arrived but I was too conscious of myself to notice much about it. She's a smug little thing, isn't she? Let me guess your favourite. I've seen most of them now.'

'I'm sure you can't.'

'Oh, I think I can.'

He left me to make a quick circuit of the gallery, returned with a smile. 'Yes, I know your favourite and you mustn't deny it.'

'You seem very sure of yourself.'

Frank led me directly to a painting of a broken ship in Arctic ice. Polar bears prowled and surveyed the wreckage. It was a wild scene that provoked the deepest terror of Nature.

'I remember playing at explorers with you and your father. And then you told me about your Society when we were in Wales. But it's more than that. You like its violence. And the loneliness. It's the wrong Pole, of course. I'm aware of that.'

I looked around to see if anyone had heard. The two feathered ladies were now standing beside a Millais, discussing it with the art tutor. I lifted my journal and pretended to be looking at some detail in the painting, checking it with my notes.

'That's an odd thing to say, Frank. I do like it but that's because my father used to tell me about the Arctic Circle, about Captain Cook and Franklin. Polar bears are beautiful beasts, but because I like to look at them in a picture does not mean I'd like to get anywhere near them and be eaten by them. Or see anyone eaten by them. Great heavens. I didn't think that I was known as a person who likes violence and loneliness. Do you not look at this painting and see how bleak it is?'

Perhaps I sounded more indignant than I felt. In truth, I was merely embarrassed that he had exposed me so neatly.

'Yes, yes I do. I'm terribly sorry, Grace. I didn't mean to say – I expect that what I meant to say was that *I'm* attracted to the violence and loneliness in it and I was attributing my feelings to you. I thought that we shared something, you see. I do think of you as someone attracted to the elements. Well, it's just that, when I used to come to tea, you were always charging off into the rain, when the others wanted muffins at the fireside. You seemed rather wild and your clothes were always a bit dirty with mud and now I'm being rude again and I don't know what's the matter with me. I apologize. I didn't want to offend you and now I see by your expression that I have just made matters worse.' He drew a sharp breath. 'Grace, how is your father? Is he just as he always was?'

I liked to hear myself called Grace again. It was always Farringdon these days – Miss Farringdon from the lecturers – and it touched me to be called Grace. The North

Tower bell began to toll and my friends would be putting their study things away, scrubbing the benches and heading for tea.

'He's frail but, in the way that I think you mean it, he's the same. Actually, I haven't seen him for two months. I should visit but—'

'Quite. Grace, I say, it's awfully good to see you again. I used to enjoy our talks when you passed my house sometimes. You always seemed so cheerful and hopeful, despite – well – sorry, I'm being rude again. You must think I came all this way with the sole intention of making impolite remarks, but nothing could be further from the truth. I have enormous respect for you and for your family.'

A scene lit up in my head as though Frank had popped a slide into a magic lantern. My family, in the drawing room, all frozen in a moment. Catherine was at the fireside, head bent over knitting needles, hair falling around her neck in copper coils. My father hunched under the standard lamp, elevated somehow in the little yellow coin of light, finger stump on the corner of the page of his book, ready to flick it over. My mother floated an inch or two above the carpet in the doorway, mouth open as though bringing some message. I remembered Frank on his last visit to our house, in the same doorway, his vain attempt to rescue Catherine.

'So you're happy here at college. Good. And did you all enjoy your excursion to the mountains?'

The change of subject was a relief. With my family I was the stubborn, unhelpful younger daughter, but Frank saw me as an independent, adventurous young woman and it seemed quite easy to be the person that Frank admired.

'Yes, and we're planning our next, and the next.'

'Wilfred and I enjoyed ourselves magnificently. In Oxford we're usually in a room talking to each other, or waving our forks over dinner, and that is very well; but we found that in Wales we might walk for six or seven hours and not have passed a single word, and not realized it either. It's a good thing for friends to do, isn't it?'

'I think so. Now, Frank.' I leaned towards him for effect. 'Wouldn't you like to travel to such a place as this?' I nodded at the picture. 'Imagine. Not to be eaten by bears, of course, but to feel the terror of the landscape. You could paint it yourself.'

Frank shuddered, shook his head. 'If you would lead the way, Grace, I might follow but I would hesitate to make my own way there.'

I was about to suggest that I would be glad to lead, but the moment was spoiled when Celia Horsfield entered the gallery with her mother and father. Celia was a few paces ahead of her parents, bleating loudly about which pictures they must like and which they mustn't. Her black ringlets bobbed and bounced as she moved. She dictated a particular order for circulating the gallery and reprimanded her father for setting off in the wrong direction. I was reminded of a comment Locke once made – that the women who don't want the vote are invariably the same ones who expect the trees and stars to bow to their wishes. Horsfield glanced at me, nodded, then fixed her eyes on Frank. Her eyebrows rose into a sly question. 'Silly girl,' I muttered. 'How inconvenient.' And I hurried out to the vestibule. A few minutes later Frank followed me and found me in my hiding place.

'Grace, might we not find a chaperone so that we can continue this conversation over tea somewhere?'

'I didn't get the principal's permission to have a visitor, so if I admitted to having one now you would be sent packing. Even brothers are frowned upon, never mind friends.'

'It's a pity.'

'Besides, I have studying to do, letters to write. I am very busy today.'

Frank tipped his head to one side, grinned. 'Come down, O Maid, from yonder mountain height.'

I backed into the corner. Frank glanced behind him, saw someone coming and stepped away until they had passed.

'Tennyson,' he said, when we were alone again.

'What?'

'My quotation just then. It was Tennyson.'

'I know that.'

'Sorry.'

We made our separate ways to the woodland behind the college and met by the pond. It was early evening, still light, but in that dark spot it was midnight. Frogs croaked and insects whirred above the water's creased skin. Strange crackles and plops echoed around the pond and the trees. Frank reached for some bit of leaf caught up in my hair, pulled it carefully away and discarded it at my feet, like an unwanted garment.

'Won't do your reputation any good to go to dinner with the forest in your hair, Titania.'

I wanted to kiss him and almost did, but knew that I was supposed to wait for him to move first. Wind shook the trees and ran through my hair like soft fingers. It made me uneasy and a vague kind of anxiety made me stiffen slightly. He took my face in his hands, which was what I had wanted, but when he leaned to kiss me, I pulled back.

'What?'

'Catherine,' I blurted, before I could stop. And I meant it, but I didn't want to mean it.

Frank tried to mask his irritation with a smile. I wanted him to say that he would make it all right because, of course, I didn't want to stop at all, but he said nothing. I had got it all wrong. I turned and stumbled over the rough ground, through the trees to Main.

The corridors were so long that if someone were crossing at the other end you could not recognize who it was. I have often dreamed of these corridors since, the wide staircases, the doors on either side to bedrooms, study rooms, classrooms, the many empty rooms on the corridors above, all with their fireplaces, windows, huge mirrors, waiting for future students to arrive and move in. Sometimes, when I have not been entirely happy, I have dreamed that I could go secretly to one of those empty rooms, light a fire in the hearth and curl up under a silky eiderdown. I wanted my bed now but, before reaching my room, Locke came from her study, snatched my arm and pulled me in.

'Was it Frank Black?'

'Horsfield told you?'

'She's telling everyone.'

I fell onto Locke's chair, put my head in my hands then laughed.

'He came, but there's nothing to warrant gossip. Actually, it was very awkward and uncomfortable. I shan't see him again, because of my sister, so it's for the best but – ' I stopped for breath – 'I'm disappointed.'

'I think that's a pity when he likes you so much. I suppose he's already left?'

'He's on his way to the station now.'

'Farringdon, you fool, go after him. Go to the station now and talk to him. You can sort out the business with your sister later.'

'But what shall I say?'

'Whatever you think of. Go on and catch him.' She pushed me towards the door, opened it. 'You're not a coward.'

No, never a coward.

Frank was on the platform. He looked at his watch and glanced along the railway tracks. The train wasn't due for ten or fifteen minutes. I wanted to speak to him, but I didn't know what to say so I walked off. I loathed myself. I said aloud that I was not a coward, turned on my heel, returned to the platform and then walked away for the second time. Why could he not have seen and come after me?

I lingered for some time. Small, hard lumps of rain fell. Frank put up his umbrella, lifted it over his head. I watched until the train puffed in with its whistle and shrieks, unable to go to him, unable to call out his name but not ready to leave.

Frank and I were to have so many goodbyes in the time we knew each other. I believe that's why I was paralysed that afternoon. I stood there at the platform's end and I slipped a little outside time, just fell out of it all. I saw all the many partings to come and the pain that we would go on to endure. I actually saw them, jagged flickerings of ourselves meeting and parting in light and dark. I was weighted with sadness and I was back in the picture gallery vestibule, watching but not having. Frank and I were connected but we would never be happy and I knew it, or thought it, as I stood and watched him under his umbrella. I should have spoken to him or gone away, not spied on his private moment but it was love, or the beginnings of love, so I exonerate myself. But it's nothing now. The memory is grey as rain.

I wonder what Frank would say of our secret meeting if he were alive to tell me. He would surely admit that he went to Wales that spring with the intention of seeing me, and that Wilfred was in on the plan. I think he would also acknowledge that he saw me watching from the end of the station platform. I've considered it over the years and I cannot see how he could not have known that I was there. Yes, he saw me seeing him and, I imagine, he was amused but shy. I think he would have been amused.

Now he comes to me at night, when the wind roars, and we have nowhere to shelter except the dank rooms in my mind. Frank, my love. I would tear off all my limbs and bleed for eternity if I could return to that afternoon at the station. If I could step forward onto the platform and say your name, what would happen to us?

No, I should not want to go back, for I would not be able to do better even after these decades of life in between that ought to have taught me something, and yet I want it. I am still greedy and I want it.

I wrote to tell him that I was going with my friends to climb in the Alps. He replied the next day and wished me the best of luck. Perhaps I hoped that I would descend from grassy foothills to find Frank in the garden of my hotel and that, as we had in Wales, we might walk together alongside a deep stretch of water and we would talk of wild places.

Frank, my love, kneels at my feet. We're in a sort of boat, you see. There is no sky. He shouts directions, instructions and warnings as the spray spatters his sou'wester and his ravaged, ungloved hands. Panic roughens the edges of his voice, but it's all right. It is all right. The bad nights are not here. They have melted into the sea, some of them, and the others have floated into oceans of boiling green. I know where I'm headed. I always know. This is how we get through the nights now, Frank and me. This is how we always – we always . . . Ah no. I thought . . . No, of course. But where did I . . . ? Oh, Catherine.

Chapter Twelve

Dear Catherine,

   If you ever come to London and think of visiting me,
do not imagine for one second that you will be welcome.
To stay away for fifteen years and never write a letter?
It is unforgivable. I always apologized to you – for
everything I ever did and more – but it is you who
should have said sorry. The newspapers wrote many
dreadful things and could you not have defended me?
Could you not have stayed with me when I most needed
you and ended up trapped in this vile house? And after
all the years that I tried to help and look after you. You
knew perfectly well that I was – am – innocent but you
were too cowardly to help me. Well, I tell you something,
dearest sister. You can stay in Scotland and mourn nasty
George for ever, as far as I am concerned. I don't care
what happens to you. We are not sisters.

   I hope Edinburgh is cold and damp.

   Yours,

         Grace

And that goes straight into the fire. Already I don't mean it. I am in the past with all the lights blazing, almost blinding me. Only when I reach the end will I know what I am supposed to say to Catherine, but I do want her to visit. I do.

Father died, just where I am sitting now, in 1911. Catherine found him on the hearth rug in front of his chair, as though he had stood one final time, stumbled forward to get somewhere and collapsed. After the funeral I stayed at home for a few weeks, miserable with Mother and Catherine. Without my father at the centre of every activity in the household, no one knew quite how to behave or what to do. I sometimes sat in his chair and read his books, trying to go a little way into his mind, continuing our arguments from his point of view, then mine, as though I might now be able to resolve them, not quite believing that my father and I would never quarrel again. Even now, so many years since he left us, I scarcely believe it.

Mother and Catherine assumed that I had left college for good and kept asking why my trunk had not arrived. When I told my mother that I had no intention of giving up my degree, she thought that grief had made me mad and threatened to call the doctor. She said she had seen me fumbling around the hall, clutching the hand compass and taking bearings as though I had lost my way. It was true that she had seen me with the Brunton but I was never lost. I simply liked to hold and read the thing, and it had belonged to Father so it gave me some comfort. Occasionally I went around the house and garden with it, but only as a mild distraction. When I returned to college, I took the Brunton with me and left my mourning clothes at home.

Catherine and I inherited a sum of money each, with a letter from Father telling us that it would be of help when we married. I read the letter twice to be sure that marriage wasn't a condition of the legacy – it was not – and I used most of it to pay my debts to Aunt Edith and to Parr. I put the remainder aside for my trip to Switzerland.

Locke, Hooper, Parr and I took rowing lessons on the Thames. We performed exercises in the college woodland, to the bewilderment of other students and, once or twice, we went out at night and practised hauling ourselves up trees with ropes. The trees were not particularly high and it bore no resemblance to rock climbing, but we did everything we could think of to stay strong and develop our coordination ready for the mountains. We attended our usual classes in the college gymnasium, where a lecturer led gentle exercises in balance and agility with Indian clubs and wands. We cycled, walked, swam and, when we were giddy with the whole thing – yet needed more – went skiing down the staircases of Main with a long tea tray under each foot. It never worked well but it started quite a fashion among the students, until someone crashed into Miss Hobson at the bottom of the stairs and the practice was banned.

Parr took us to a lantern lecture at the Ladies' Alpine Club headquarters in the Grand Central Hotel at Marylebone, and to talks at her mountaineering friends' homes. We sat in rooms with men and women who recounted their climbs in the Alps, the Himalayas, of treks through the jungle, across the Near and Middle East, into deepest South America. They told of deadly insect bites and fevers, encounters with wild animals, hostile tribes and friendly tribes. Corners of the world uncovered themselves to reveal vivid flora and fauna we had never known existed. I took careful notes and tried to ask informed, pertinent questions, but in my imagination I was already a thousand miles away.

After an enlightening discussion on the ill effects of sunburn, the Society made a trip to a mountaineering store near Piccadilly to buy goggles and sun masks.

'Teddy will appreciate it if I don't return as a berry.' With her skin already brown and freckled, I thought Hooper more egg-like, but not unattractive. I was more concerned that she would change her mind and decide not to come. She sometimes said that she was so afraid of the Alps that she lay awake all night worrying. When she did sleep, she had nightmares about the mountains, about Teddy hating her strange hobby.

'My lover couldn't care less,' Locke replied. She was probably talking about Horace, though there may have been a new beau by then. 'But sunburn sounds unpleasant.'

'And I need to stay pale so that my mother and sister don't guess where I've been.'

'Farringdon, you'll have to tell your family when we go to Switzerland. It would be irresponsible to keep it from them.'

'I can't tell them. They're in mourning weeds and think that I am too.'

Parr adopted what Locke called her ice-axe tone. All warmth and colour drained from her voice and what came out was a hard, clipped sound. 'Then you should stay at home. It's perfectly possible that you could be seriously injured or killed on the mountains. Have you even thought about that?'

'Of course I have.' But, no, I never thought that I would come to harm. In my imagination I was always surviving, rescuing weaker travellers, and returning weary but safe to cheering crowds, newspaper reporters and photographers. Perhaps this had come from my childhood fantasies of rescuing the three sailors in China but, whatever it was, I was not worried about dying.

The Ladies' Alpine Club held an exhibition of mountaineering equipment and we went together on a Saturday. I remember it as a heady, sweet day and, in my giddiness, I persuaded my friends that we must each purchase a green Tyrolean hat. We stood in a row before a mirror and put them on. We laughed at our reflections – even Parr – but, I must say, the hats were rather fetching. We did not stop but went off to examine a range of new, lightweight tents. The stall-keeper, a genial young man who did not laugh at us or even express surprise at the sight of four mountaineering women in identical green hats, explained the equipment. The Whymper tent slept four, but the Mummery, which slept two, could be folded small enough to go into a pocket. I asked him to demonstrate this and he did so, two or three times, pronouncing that we lived in extraordinary times with such advances in the manufacturing of expedition equipment.

Even Hooper delighted at the array of clothes, coats, nailed boots, silk sleeping bags, folding lanterns, pots, pans and miniature containers of soup and jam. If she still had doubts, then an article in the following day's *Mail* persuaded her that we were not betraying our sex. I took it to her room and read it to her.

'Listen. *I have never known a lady climber to be either mean, gossipy or hysterical. Lady climbers invariably make good wives, good mothers and excellent chums.* You see?'

'It's a relief to hear it from a newspaper. I knew it already, of course. Look, as long as you will all understand that I'll never be fast or especially good at it, I won't stay behind.'

'Bravo. And here is all you need to learn about climbing: *Be very careful about the feet. At the close of each day bathe them well in hot water, and, after plunging them in cold and drying them, a little brandy may be rubbed in. Mind your boots, and keep them well greased.*'

We went to Ambleside and Keswick, explored the Langdales, scrambled up Striding Edge and Jack's Rake, climbing one or two peaks each day. We rowed on Grasmere, forgot that this was exercise and pulled in the oars to lie and watch the clouds spill over the hills. In winter we returned to Wales for a few days to practise working on snow and ice. Parr gave me her spare ice axe as I had no money now to buy my own. The end was broken off so the handle was shorter than it should have been, but it was good enough. I learned how to stop a fall by throwing myself onto my front and sinking the axe into the snow. We screamed as we slid down our practice slope, axes over our shoulders, like strange warriors, ready to flip over and spear the ground. Hooper always came last, apologizing as she caught us up, but always doing her best. We applauded her pluck, until she told us that she did not need our applause and only felt a little insulted by it.

My mother did not disapprove of my excursions, thinking I was with a wealthy heiress and friends. She imagined country houses, parties with games, rich relatives, suitors, and all sorts of doors opening to a good future for me.

Scott was now on his second expedition and we followed his journey in the newspapers. Ernest had tried to raise funds for another trip to the Antarctic but failed, so Scott had beaten him to it, setting off on the *Terra Nova*. I studied, climbed, rowed, planned and sometimes stood in front of my mirror dressed in all my gear: boots, bloomers, coat, hat, gloves, sun mask and goggles. I would lift my axe as though to plunge it into a wall of ice. My reflection thrilled me. It was bigger than I, something not human, more than human. I was a mighty, terrifying creature.

Amundsen reached the Pole. There was no news yet from Scott and I felt a certain disappointment, as all British people did, that Amundsen had got there first. Shackleton had said: *The Pole is hard to get*, but for Amundsen it had seemed quite simple. I was not particularly upset that it was Amundsen, rather than Scott, or even Shackleton, who got the Pole, more that my own preposterous dream – that it would be Grace Farringdon – must die.

A month later, the *Titanic* sank and my mother's mood and health went down with it. She had nightmares of icebergs and freezing seas. She had stayed calm and composed immediately after Father's death, but Catherine said that she would not stop weeping about the *Titanic* and kept looking through photographs of Father in his uniform, letters he sent her from ports around the world. She wrote letters to the families of the drowned, sent them gifts and clothes, and she cried every day.

Parr had graduated but continued her involvement with the Ladies' Alpine Club. The remaining three members studied for our finals and imagined life after graduation. Locke completed *Turn Back the Clocks!* and the Drama Soc performed it in the picture gallery. She found work in the office of a London theatre run by her uncle and planned to continue writing in her free time. Hooper's fiancé decided, to her family's distress, not to qualify as a doctor after all but become a school teacher instead. Hooper was surprised to find that she was pleased. They might start a school together, which was rather exciting, and he had inherited a large house in Shropshire so they would be comfortable even on a smaller salary than she had anticipated.

Not long before my finals, I came out of the library one

afternoon and bumped straight into Miss Hobson lurking in the shadows of the South Tower.

'Miss Farringdon, I was waiting for you.'

Her face was dry and wrinkled as a currant, but it was impossible to discern any mood or emotion from the patterns in the lines.

'You haven't come to see me about your future plans. We'll walk to my study.' And she set off.

'I haven't quite made up my mind.' I scurried to catch up.

'You have come to university, excelled in your courses and yet you have given no thought to your future?' Miss Hobson peered at me.

'I have thought about it, but I don't know the answer yet.'

'A girls' boarding school near Bedford has a vacancy for a science teacher. You would be suitable and I have recommended you. Of course, you'll be expected to work hard and live up to the good reputation of Candlin College, but it is an excellent position and you will enjoy it.'

'Thank you.' I was pleased and flattered but had no intention of working in a boarding school. 'I'm very grateful but—'

'I beg your pardon?'

'Perhaps I'm not the best person for the position.'

'Nonsense. You'll do fine and I have already said so. Miss Doughty has told me that you are a very able dissector and have a gift for leadership. Have you ever been to Bedford?'

'No.'

'It's a pleasant town and there are plenty of good schools so you'll meet other educated women and be very fortunate.'

I was hardly paying attention. I only wanted to get to the Alps and, after that, go further. I followed Miss Hobson into her study and she motioned me to sit in her armchair. I sank, small and low among tall bookcases, furry plants and dusty pictures. Miss Hobson perched, upright, behind her desk, reached into a drawer and took out a letter. She fixed a monocle to her eye, squinted and read the letter. Her right forefinger drummed the desk.

'Yes, it's a very good situation indeed. But I detect reluctance, Miss Farringdon.' She looked up with, I think, disgust. 'Are you required at home?'

'No. Well, my father passed away as you know but—'

After the Alps, I would need a job and money to travel, but a boarding school would not do it. I could not stand all the responsibility of teaching, setting an example. I did not want to be a grown-up yet.

'It's a pity. I'll have to write to my esteemed friend in Bedford and disappoint her.'

'Perhaps in a year or two I would change my mind and want to teach.'

'Don't be foolish. Another student will be glad of this opportunity.'

And I felt foolish as I left her study, but certain that I had given the right answer. It was embarrassing and a little annoying that Miss Hobson had offered me to the school without my knowledge. My friends were surprised when I recounted the incident at dinner. Many hoped to find just such positions and could not understand why I showed so little gratitude.

Hester Morgan leaned across the dining table.

'Is it because of the man you met in the picture gallery? Have you made plans?'

'No, no. Not Mr Black. I forgot him a long time ago.'

This was not true. We had written a few times, though we had not met again, and I longed to see him, to see his paintings and to tell him about my plans to climb in Switzerland.

Father glared down from somewhere near the ceiling of my sitting room and mumbled at me. What did I think I was doing, so soon after his death when I should be making a show of mourning him? Worse, it was his money I'd spent. I wept silently on my bed. Wasn't it enough that I had worn a black dress for months? I looked around for something that belonged to him. The Brunton, of course. I shouted silently back and shook the compass at him: *Don't complain. You started it all and I'm taking you with me. It's your chance to travel again.* And I ducked, laughing through my tears, as an invisible salt pot whizzed past my head.

There are hours more till sunrise. I'll play the piano for a while. It takes me deeper into the night and, of course, Father likes it. Yes, the keys are stiff, but I can make them yield. La ta dum doo di. I like it too. I have finished with college now and got my honours degree. I am going to the Alps where the air will thin, it might snow a little, and I can be cold, properly cold, again.

Part Two

Chapter Thirteen

It was almost twilight. A dozen or so men waited around a tree on Bahnhofstrasse, lounging on stools or their packs, smoking and talking. When travellers passed, they called out in French, Italian and English, offering their services as *bergführer* and porters, but most visitors went on their way to the hotels around the square or further up the village. Ahead of us, the Matterhorn's snowy top shone, blue-white, a rocky changeling among the ethereal peaks of the Pennine Alps. A wiry, middle-aged couple passed us, stiff-gaited, leaning awkwardly on mud-splashed alpenstocks. The woman nodded and said good evening with a slight German accent, and followed her limping husband down the street. We smiled but dared not laugh, knowing that we might be as badly off, or worse, within a few days.

'A guide for tomorrow?' The voice came from a young Italian man who caught us up as we passed on our way to the Monte Rosa Hotel. I looked at him, curious, and saw that he was not young after all. He had the upright, muscular stature of a boy athlete but weathered skin and sunken, shadowed eyes. He looked as though he had tales to tell, if only we would stop and listen. He shrugged and turned away as Parr grabbed my arm and ushered me into the hotel lobby.

'We have a guide.' Parr pressed the shiny bell on the desk. 'We'll meet him soon enough.'

The lobby was warm, luxurious and a strange mixture of the Alps and England. At the desk were copies of English newspapers and a sign directing guests to the lounge. Photographs of mountaineers on summits decorated the walls. Parr had chosen this hotel because Edward Whymper himself had been a guest here, as had many other famous Alpinists. Even Theodore Roosevelt had stayed here when he climbed the Matterhorn as a young man. I thought of the money I was spending – my father's legacy – and how this was just the right thing to do with it. If he could see me now, would he not feel a little vicarious pleasure or excitement? Surely he would not begrudge such an adventure.

A cheerful hotel boy took our luggage and we went to our rooms to rest before dinner. My room, which I shared with Locke, was like any hotel room in England, but I stepped out onto the balcony and looked straight up at the Matterhorn. It seemed closer and larger now, as though playing its own game of Grandmother's Footsteps with me. I would climb it one day, surely. Not now, not when we were so unready, but I would climb it. I breathed the pine scent of Zermatt and stared at the mountain that seemed, in its very shape and size, to insist on the challenge.

Fine, then. This might be my Pole, a vertical path to my ambition, if I could have no other.

Later, in the rosy lamplight of the lounge, Parr unfolded her map and, using her little finger to point the way, showed us the peaks of the Breithorn, the Klein Matterhorn, the Monte Rosa, Castor and Pollux, the Gornergrat, the Zinal Rothorn. We discussed, as we had before, the routes we might take, depending on what we decided to climb.

'Of course, our guide will make the final decision.'

We persuaded Parr that we needed a gentle start and must be reasonable in our plans. Parr might find the terrain easy but there were four of us and we didn't know whether or not we were good enough to climb the higher peaks. At the end of the week, we should make a decision based on our abilities and the weather conditions. If we were to climb a high peak, then we would take the guide and a porter. Parr agreed to this.

'And who is our guide?'

'His name is Alberto. He's from Brueil and is the grandson and son of guides and chamois hunters. He knows every glacier and ridge. He's climbed the Matterhorn countless times.'

Parr was hungry to climb the Matterhorn one day, but I was too. Perhaps I would even do it before she did. I pushed the ignoble thought from my mind and questioned Parr further on Alberto, glaciers and the chamois.

*

I woke in the night to hear the bedroom door creak open. A figure slipped into the room, banged a foot on my bedpost and cursed. I lifted my head.

'Locke?'

'Sorry,' she whispered, pulling off her coat. Her pyjamas were underneath. 'Tried not to wake you. Ouch, my toe.'

'Where have you been?'

'Just along the street. I couldn't sleep.'

I raised myself onto my elbows, squinted at her. 'You've been outside? Alone?'

'I just wanted a few minutes by myself, to see the place. Come with me now. It's so peaceful.'

'What time is it?'

'It doesn't matter. Come on.' She pulled at my wrist.

I dressed and followed Locke along the landing and downstairs to the door. The night porter let us out. We went along a small street with pretty wooden houses. Some hotels had lights on but most buildings were dark. Around us, though we could hardly see them, was the sense of mountains, watching and listening.

'It's beautiful.' My voice sounded strange to me.

Locke nodded. 'I'm going to buy a house here one day.'

We reached the river, stood on the bridge and listened to the water chatter and tumble over stones.

'Will you live here?'

'No. I know I can't live anywhere except London, but I'll come here every summer to write my plays. I decided when I was walking by myself.'

'Then I can come and visit you.'

'But you should live here, Farringdon. You could have a house a bit higher up than mine – because you like to be up high – and marry a mountain guide. It would suit you perfectly and we can spend all our summers together.'

I laughed. She had planned my life so carefully. 'Let's choose houses tomorrow then, when we can see them all. I shall want good views, and a garden.'

We linked our arms together and walked back to the hotel.

'Of course,' I said, as we reached our room, 'Parr might be here too.'

Locke was quiet for a moment. 'No, by then she'll be in Bolivia or the Himalayas. We shan't have to worry about that.'

'I didn't mean—'

'I know.'

I curled up under my blankets and smiled to myself thinking of Locke's idea. I knew that I did not want to stop here, though. Zermatt was an adventure, the next stop after Wales and the Lake District, but it was just another point on the journey and not its end.

We climbed shady routes through forests of larch and rhododendrons. Paths opened out onto rocky green hillsides where marmots played, an ibex trotted by and sloped shyly away. Sometimes we stopped at a teahouse for bread and cheese, made conversation with other trampers.

Parr led us along moraine paths, steep ridges. We passed travellers on mule-back, and, on the Riffelalp, we even saw a man in a sedan chair. We walked long days and took in much ascent, stopping sometimes to catch our breath, wipe sweat from our hands and faces. After the first few days, our rests were shorter and our packs seemed lighter. We were growing used to it and, other than a little stiffness in the mornings and a blister here or there, suffered no ill-effects. From the Gornergrat we watched as clouds covered and uncovered the spiny top of the Monte Rosa, the Lyskamm's deadly white cornices, the long snowy ridge of the Breithorn. Glaciers poured down into the valley, where they joined and swelled into strange shapes. We ate chocolate, gulped water and did not speak but tried to take in everything we saw.

We climbed higher. Locke picked an edelweiss for her hat and Hooper chided her. *It's a protected species.* Locke apologized but kept the flower and wore it in her hat, since it was already picked. We learned how to cut steps with our axes, how to trudge along the ice in our nailed boots, walking with a wide gait so as not to spike our ankles or trip ourselves. A glacier was not always the jewelled floor of beauty I had imagined but something that moved from brown to grey, was harsh with pleats, whorls and ugly growths that looked like tongues and fingers. In places, it seemed solid and ancient. In others it rippled like a sparkling liquid. I learned that ice can be any colour of the rainbow. Sometimes, light in the head from the effects of altitude, I thought I was looking out on some giant machine, with knobs and levers to move the landscape around or open it up.

'Come on, Farringdon, you're slowing us. Chop chop,' called Parr when, once or twice, I paused to wonder at our progress or take in the changing views.

On longer days, we hired a porter to carry our equipment and food. His name was Ulrich and he was a quiet but friendly man from Zermatt, who helped when we needed him and stood back when we did not. When we stopped for lunch or tea he would unload food from his pack and tell us of his ascents, pointing out a peak or col with a piece of cheese or the wine flask. One day Locke begged him to tell us his most terrible mountain experience. We were sheltering from rain under overhanging rocks and Locke wanted a story to pass the time. Ulrich crossed himself and walked out into the rain muttering.

'What?' Locke mouthed at us.

'You shouldn't ask him that while we're actually on a mountain,' Parr whispered. 'It's awfully bad luck.'

We took a day's rest in Zermatt, wrote in our diaries, read a little and napped. That evening, after bathing our feet and wrapping them in cotton wool, we retired to the lounge and sat around our favourite table in the corner to discuss the final few days of our trip.

'Shall we meet Alberto tomorrow?' I asked Parr. I was impatient to climb higher.

'I have not hired him after all. We shan't need him.'

'Is that all, then?' Locke cried. An elderly couple at the fireplace turned and stared. We moved our chairs closer together. 'Are you saying that we have finished with climbing?'

'No, that is not what I'm saying.'

I could see that Parr had some clever plan. She seemed rather smug about it. 'Oh, God. You're not thinking of taking us up the Matterhorn? We're not ready for it. We don't have the skills.' I thought perhaps that the guide had refused and so Parr, certain that she knew better, had dismissed him.

'No, no, of course not. Don't be so foolish. I'm surprised at you, Farringdon. Now look here, I'll tell you the plan.' Parr placed her hands on the table, leaned in. 'I thought we would make a guideless ascent of the Breithorn. It's high but relatively easy from the south-west slope. We'll climb up to the Gandegg Hut tomorrow and sleep there to get an early start. If we're quick about it, we can perhaps also climb Pollux. It's very near.'

'You've climbed the Breithorn before?'

'Oh yes. We shan't have any problems. If you all like it, we could still do a guided ascent of another peak before we go home, perhaps the Bishorn or one of the Monte Rosa summits.'

I was ready to go and pack my rucksack, but Locke and Hooper looked miserable.

'It will not be so hard, really not much more than what we have already done,' Parr continued. 'We won't have Ulrich either, of course, so we'll have to carry everything ourselves.'

Locke rubbed a sore spot on her heel and winced. 'You shouldn't have decided without asking us. It isn't fair when we are all affected. I say we hire the guide.'

'It's too late, I'm afraid. He's taken an engagement with another client.'

'Parr—'

'I didn't want a lot of squabbling and discussion—'

Locke clapped her hand to her forehead. 'You are beyond belief.'

Parr looked at me for help. 'Well, I knew that I was right and I made the decision accordingly.'

'The question is,' I said, 'are we really able to do this on our own and, if we are, do we want to? And can't we at least have a porter?'

'No. I mean it to be just us.'

'Then we certainly don't want to do it. I've had enough,' said Hooper. She left the lounge and hurried down the corridor to her room. We all followed her and crowded in the doorway.

Hooper pressed the bell for service. 'Where's that boy? I'm going home.'

'Please don't.'

'I don't know what to do if something goes wrong. I shan't go without a guide.'

'But I'll be the guide,' said Parr. 'And you just have to do as I tell you. I can do as well as Alberto.'

'You are like some army captain, Parr,' said Locke. 'Why do you think we should all fall in behind you? You should know us better than that.'

I went to the window. My legs were heavy and the tips of my toes were numb from striking against the ends of my boots, but I knew I had more climbing in me. The sky was dark and thick with cloud.

'We can manage without the guide since we have Parr.' I opened the window and let the cold air touch my face. 'That's the point of the Society.' I turned to my friends. 'Isn't it?'

Locke nodded. 'All right. But Parr, you cannot do this to us again. You must not.'

The boy arrived at the door and waited as Hooper dithered and sighed. He stood in the corridor leaning on one foot and then the other, too shy to look at us directly. When Hooper went to him, he seemed to blush as though he knew that he had entered an awkward scene. She looked at each one of us but we said nothing. Then she smiled at the boy.

'Thank you but I don't need anything after all.' She came to join me at the window. 'I don't want to be the only one who doesn't climb.'

I took her hand, pressed her fingers. 'It's the right thing. It would be no good at all without you.'

It was no trivial thing to take all our supplies on our backs. How would we manage if we had insufficient food, or could not carry all our equipment? We laid our belongings out on the floor of the hotel room and chose only what we needed. There would be enough food and no more, just a small amount of fuel for fire, a metal box of matches. Guideless climbing was rare in those days, especially for women, but I did not know this. Hooper wrote a letter and placed it on her dressing table.

'You must all do the same. Don't look like that, Farringdon. If you die, it won't be a secret any longer.'

'We're not going to die, Hooper.'

'Even great mountaineers have accidents.'

Hooper's quiet voice and serious expression moved me. I wrote a letter to Catherine. There was so much I should have said to her. When I was a child and she gave recitals, I always sat on the front row and turned to scan the audience as she played, delighted and proud when I saw their smiles. I wanted to say this to her, and much more, but when I walked out and left her with Mother, I believed that I had given up my right to be loved by her. How could I begin to apologize for being in Switzerland and not telling her anything about it?

I scratched a few unsatisfactory sentences on my sheet, tucked it into the envelope, placed it on my dressing table. The letters informed our loved ones that we had died knowing all the risks we faced and that we loved them and were sorry for the pain we caused, but that we had done it for the greater good of womankind and it was better to have tried and failed than to have stayed at home embroidering tablecloths. Locke addressed her letter to her parents and Geoffrey, and Parr's was addressed to her aunt and uncle in Wales. She grumbled that this was unnecessary and would put a curse on the adventure. *And it's only the Breithorn,* she said, but she wrote her letter nevertheless and placed it on her bedside table.

Hooper remained the reluctant mountaineer.

'If any of us falls ill or if the weather looks bad, can we turn back? There's no shame in turning back, is there?'

'None at all,' said Locke.

'But don't speak as though you were already defeated,' said Parr. 'You'll pull us all back.'

We made an Alpine start from the hut, setting off at half past two in the morning, sleepy and stiff. Each step was heavy, clumsy, to begin with, and our breath was laboured and loud. Hooper held the lantern.

We slipped our skirts off – Hooper too – and buried them in a dry cave-like opening between rocks at the glacier's edge. They would be extra weight to carry and our knapsacks were heavy enough.

There was a little light in the sky as we climbed higher, but the world was still colourless. We crunched up the glacier towards the Breithorn and Klein Matterhorn. The sun rose and disappeared behind clouds. We met climbers coming from the Theodul Pass. A group of seven or eight young French-speaking men were working on different parts of the ice, practising their mountain skills. The place began to resemble an eerie mine or quarry. The men moved silently with ropes and axes, climbing an ice wall, lowering themselves into dips and crevasses.

As we climbed a steep slope of snow, the glacier fell

away from us, curving down beneath the black moraine. Above us, dark, vertical gashes in the snow seemed to jump around, stretch and shrink under our gaze.

A party of four British men was sometimes ahead of us and sometimes behind. We spoke to them, but we didn't want to join them and, though we welcomed their friendliness, they would keep trying to help. This had not happened when we had had the porter. We had to ensure that we were particularly efficient whenever they looked our way and, sometimes, look ahead or behind us as though just waiting for our guide to return or catch us up. Eventually we invented an imaginary guide. His name was Bernard and he was always just around a corner, a little further up or down the mountain, so that we could call out for him and assure the men that we were safe.

We had not climbed with such heavy packs before and our pace was slower than usual. I found that the weight of the rucksack pushed my shoulders forward and made it hard to draw deep breaths. We changed from one rope to two as we moved from glacier to rock. I was roped up with Hooper, and Locke with Parr. Parr and I led. In a careless moment, Locke slipped on loose rock but she leaned back quickly and did not fall. Parr shouted at her and after that we all placed our feet more firmly. Wind seared our cheeks and made tears run down our faces, but we kept a steady pace. It was hard to move quickly at this altitude and we paused sometimes to catch our breath. My panting was so desperate and loud that I sounded like a child with whooping cough. I counted my breaths in and out as I walked, trying to keep steady and relaxed as we began our slow ascent of the Breithorn.

The sun had risen without my noticing it and, as we approached the summit, we could see for miles. To our left, the mountain dropped sharply away. Far below were the rocks and glaciers we had seen from our viewing point at the Gornergrat. We reached the crest and stopped. Mist rolled over us then hung like a curtain. It would lift in one place to reveal shocking and beautiful views, then fall and rise somewhere else to whole new worlds. We could see far beyond the peaks of the Pennine Alps to Mont Blanc, the Dolomites.

Hooper complained of a headache. We looked at her but said nothing. She waited, perhaps hoping that one of us would suggest turning back but we did not. It seemed too soon to have a headache and no good reason to stop.

'Never mind. It will pass,' she said.

'It will get better when we go down.'

We were so high now. It had taken us longer than Parr had predicted and so we decided not to attempt to go on to Pollux but traverse further along the Breithorn. We marched at the same pace, though Parr was at the front and pulling to go faster. Clouds gathered and the wind blew harder. We dropped down a little from the ridge and clambered over rocks and snow. The wind tried to whip us off the mountainside and we leaned forwards, fighting to keep on. I watched one foot and then the other, heard the bright crunch as they sank into snow, and forced my legs to keep going.

We had been walking for hours and were tired. Sometimes my limbs seemed made of liquid and I could not see how I was controlling them. I began to imagine that I had no legs and that I was climbing only with my mind.

We reached the second summit but could not see as far now that the mist had lowered. The snow was softening and becoming slippery underfoot. Hooper crouched on the ground and wept. I put my hand on her shoulder.

'My head. I must go down now.'

'It's mountain sickness.' Parr kicked at the snow, irritated and impatient.

'I know. And I want to go down.'

'I used to get it when I was a girl,' said Parr. 'And you can't do anything but wait until you've adjusted to the altitude.'

I suggested descending immediately and returning to Zermatt rather than traverse further. If we left it too late, we would be sliding around on slush and might have to spend the night in a bivouac. Locke offered to go down with Hooper so that Parr and I could go on but it was a pointless suggestion. We only had one map and, if the weather or Hooper's condition worsened, they might be in danger.

'We had better all go down,' I said. 'We've done a good job, so let's get back safely.'

'Rot.' Parr blew her nose, stamped her feet to warm them. 'We've time to get further. We'll find a sheltered spot, have a rest and some water.'

There was a speckling of snow in the air and we proceeded slowly. Hooper's whole body twisted and swayed from the effort of each step. We found shelter under rocks and took time to melt snow for tea and eat some biscuits.

The snowfall thickened. Our footsteps were soon covered and I pulled out my compass to get a bearing.

'Farringdon, who is the leader here?' Parr sounded tired.

'We're losing visibility. I want to know the way so we can get down safely.'

Hooper shivered. The wind whipped her shoulders. She buckled, almost fell to the ground under the weight of her pack. Locke took Hooper's arm and led her around to keep her warm. I grabbed Hooper's knapsack, took some of her load for myself and she did not protest. We climbed and slipped over snow and rocks, trying to keep a reasonable pace but not wanting to leave Hooper struggling.

The sky now covered the tops of peaks, I was not at all sure which of the mountains around us was which and, before long, we could hardly make out the path we had taken. We were in a sort of dip or col but possibly not the one we had intended to come down. Parr insisted that she knew the way, though I could not see how.

My father had taught me that it was always a mistake to trust one's instinct rather than the points of the compass. But Parr was our leader. Men must not question the orders of the captain, so the captain has to be right when he is wrong. And Parr had never made a mistake with navigation. She was far more experienced than I. This was not the time for mutiny and I decided that I had misread the compass or there was some sort of disruption of the magnetic field. I was now roped up with Parr, and Locke with Hooper.

'Parr,' called Locke, 'if Farringdon has checked and thinks that this is wrong, why don't we check again?'

'No need to worry. Cheer up, everyone. We'll soon be back at the hotel and I'll treat us all to a good bottle of champagne.'

'Cheer up, indeed,' muttered Locke.

Parr turned to me, dug one heel into the snow to steady herself. 'See? Now they don't trust me.'

'Never mind,' I tried to say, but my face was tight with cold. I couldn't make the words come out. I patted my cheeks and lips with my gloves. I was thirsty and gulped down mouthfuls of snow. It hit my insides with a shock then made me burn and feel feverish but I scooped up more and more to quench my thirst.

I began to fear now that we would not get home safely and, though we were all tired and Hooper was sick, I tried to quicken our pace.

'It's all right, Farringdon. You don't need to be so scared. We've made a simple navigational error. I think we've come down at the wrong angle so we're rather off our path.'

Parr slipped then and tried to gain her balance by reaching out her right foot and planting it firmly on the snow. She misjudged. She was on a snow plug over a small crevasse and she fell right into it with an angry scream. I leaned back, struck my axe into the snow and dug my boots in. I tried to hold Parr's weight, but I had not expected her to be the one to fall and so had not been prepared. Pain tore through my thighs and back. My shoulders twisted and, though I needed to pull back to hold her weight, I could not move my feet or legs. The pressure of the rope on my ribs made it hard to breathe. Hooper and Locke grabbed the rope's end and pulled. I kept my eyes on the top of Parr's hat, the brim just visible to me, and somehow managed not to slip. Within seconds, the rope loosened. Parr had stuck her axe into the snow and found a foothold. I fell back and sat gasping for breath as she climbed up. She kneeled, clutching her ankle, face and eyes screwed up. A line of blood ran across her cheek, thickened and began to drip. Locke took a small piece of cloth from her pocket and pressed it to the wound.

Parr rose to her feet and, limping with her ice axe as a walking cane and with the bloody cloth stuck to her cheek, walked on. The rope tugged at me and I followed. Weak and confused, she didn't look like Cicely Parr any more.

But the snow fell faster and harder as we marched on. Eventually we found ourselves at the foot of another peak but could not see its summit or judge its size.

'Pollux?' I said. 'It must be.'

Parr shook her head. 'The Lyskamm.'

'Surely we have not come so far.'

'I don't know.'

'What are we going to do?'

'I think it's too late to go further now. We'll camp up

here and keep warm.' Parr's voice was as loud and clear as ever, but she looked bad. Her skin was off-colour and her eyes unfocused. The scrap of cloth on her cheek wavered in the wind. Anger and sympathy mixed up inside me.

'If you think it's safer to stay till morning, that's what we must do,' I said.

'Yes, but I can't – I don't know where. Anyway,' she gathered herself, 'I've slept on my back on snow with nothing more than a cloth over my face for protection. Let me think.'

'Parr, we should make decisions together. There'll be more snowfall in the night and we should get further down so Hooper can breathe better.'

'Not in this light. One of us will fall.'

We walked on and found a small cave. We built a wall of snow to make it bigger.

'Hooper and Locke, this is yours.'

'Can't we all stay together?'

'It isn't big enough. Farringdon and I will find another place but you'll be well protected here.'

Parr went further up the slope to a large overhanging rock and made it our shelter. She gave the others a couple of lumps of charcoal and some matches. Then she and I climbed into our den and settled. We put our feet into our knapsacks for warmth, tied our bootlaces to our axes so that we could not lose them. We lay on our axes and covered ourselves with our spare clothes and our rug. The wind screeched and the cold gnawed at our skin and bones. I worried about our fingers and toes, kept rubbing them together to be sure that I could feel them. I should have known that I would end up just like Father. I pulled the rug up to my chin, making sure that I was not taking any from Parr. I remembered then that we had left the other one at the hotel.

'They haven't got a blanket.'

Parr moaned. 'You can't go out there now.'

'I know but—'

'This is a blizzard, you fool. We just have to make it through the night, that's all, and hope the others do too.'

Parr turned on her side with her face near mine. Her breath brushed my eyelids.

The racket above was like the brass and percussion sections of an orchestra. Behind them rose the wail of a lone soprano. Snow fell and fell. At some point in the night, a ledge of snow collapsed onto my face. It took some time to manoeuvre my axe without disturbing Parr, but I managed it and pushed away the snowfall. Parr shivered in her sleep. Though I wanted to take our rug to Hooper, when I thought of Parr in her lonely slumber, exhausted and humiliated by her error of judgement, I could not steal it from her.

Yet I worried about Locke and Hooper in their ice cave. They might freeze in the night or suffocate. I put my head out, let my eyes adjust to the dark. Snow was heaped up just where they had made their camp. I pulled myself from the shelter, tied my bootlaces and stood.

The night was too big, too angry. I managed only a few paces. I called out their names but there was no reply. Silhouettes of mountain peaks grew grey in the moonlight and they began to haunt me, as though ghosts had entered and possessed them.

Ice cracked like gunshot. I turned, lost my footing and glissaded some fifteen feet down the mountainside, with no axe to halt my fall. I landed on a soft ledge and lay still until I was sure that I had not broken any bones. The drop was too steep for me to attempt to climb back up in the dark. I wanted to cry, but I shook my head and ordered myself to stay calm. This was how men gave up and died. I dug myself a ledge in the snow and tried to keep sheltered for what was left of the night. The wind raced over me, berating me for my stupidity. I was at the edge of the world and felt as though I could be blown up to the stars or into the centre of the Earth. All I could do, and all I had to do, was survive till daylight.

Voices muttered, nagged and wailed in my head all night, the voices of my family and friends and some I recognized but could not place. I had fitful rests, floating on water and occasionally dipping under its surface but never deep or for long. Sometimes the cold felt like a kind of fire, burning at my skin, my bones. When a thin light washed over me, I lifted my head to see the sky bubbling and grey, like a vast sea. A new voice called.

'Farringdon?'

Parr was somewhere above me. I pulled myself to my knees. My body was convulsed with cold and it took time to stand. I could see the tips of my hair and eyelashes, white with rime. I tried to call out but began to cough. It hurt my ribs and throat but I could not stop. Parr called out again and I saw her boots in the snow.

Parr's cheeks and nose were blotted with pink patches. Her lips were cracked and bled when she spoke. When I reached her she took my arm and led me to the white mound where Locke and Hooper lay.

'I don't want to see,' murmured Parr. I shoved her out of the way and began kicking at the snow.

They were curled up together in their white nest. Their faces had no colour. Locke's hand was balled into a fist against her cheek. I knelt beside her, my dearest friend with her lovers and her bright green dresses, her room of flowers and her funny, ridiculous play set in the future. I had brought her to my world, without even understanding it myself, and what for?

I dusted snow from her face.

'Leonora.'

Locke opened an eye, screwed up her face. She and Hooper were rigid with cold but they were alive. We helped them to their feet, hardly able to speak. Parr crouched in the shelter, made a fire from our last few bits of charcoal and some rhododendron twigs she had carried. We drank lukewarm tea made from melted snow and winced as the heat hit our fingers and lips. We gnawed on frozen bread and cheese. I rubbed my feet again and again, making sure that I could feel every bit of them. I let the tea fill my mouth and warm my throat and I watched Cicely Parr. She was staring into the fire, muttering something I could not hear.

The sky turned blue and the landscape that had confused us in the blizzard became clear and bright with mountain peaks piling up to the sky, like giant cakes of coconut and cream. We were a long way from our route and would have to cross a glacier pitted with deep crevasses. Our limbs and joints were stiff, at first, and we could not walk but sat rubbing our arms and legs to warm them. When we saw distant clouds forming, we gathered our things and set off, all on one rope.

The glacier was steep and each step sent pain through our thighs as we tried to dig in and keep our balance.

'Will you be all right, Hooper?' Locke asked.

She nodded. 'I think so. Don't go too fast. My head is very sore indeed.'

Hooper turned her back, crouched down and rested her cheek on her hand. I sighed. We wanted her to hurry so that we could get her safely to the hotel. She slumped forward onto her knees and threw up into the snow. She coughed and sobbed as we stood waiting, not looking now, not speaking. Locke and I fiddled with the rope and Parr pretended to examine a small stone as Hooper was sick again, this time with loud, painful retches. I wondered how we would manage if the only way to get her down was to carry her. It would not be possible, surely, but we would have to try.

Eventually her breathing calmed. She sighed, shivered and wiped her face with both hands.

'Much better now,' she whispered. 'Sorry about that.'

'No, no,' we said. 'You mustn't be sorry.'

She stood, stretched her legs a little, took some hearty breaths and we set off.

Locke and I went first. We spoke about the night and how frightened we had been. Locke was behind me and talked loudly so that I would not have to turn.

'I knew we'd be all right,' she called. 'But it was such a long night.'

'I thought it wouldn't end.'

'You were brave to try and find us by yourself.'

'Foolish, perhaps.'

'No. A good friend.'

It became impossible to make our way around the many crevasses and so we moved from the ice to an exposed area of rock where, though there was a steep drop, it would be easier to move. We decided that it would be safer to go in pairs. Locke and I roped up together. We didn't pay much attention to the others but we assumed that they were roped up too. Hooper was, after all, moving slowly and needed support; Parr was the best person to look after her and the most experienced with ropes. Even so, we could have looked back just once. It would have been the correct thing to do. Locke and I were making our way along the edge, a few feet ahead of Parr and Hooper. We could hear their boots and their breaths. We moved as quickly as we dared, desperate not to be here any more but trying to be careful with our steps. The rope was like an arm around my waist, tender and protective. Each time it tugged, I was warmed and comforted by the knowledge of Locke's presence, her weight as counterbalance.

But the other rope was still a floppy coil across Parr's shoulders, tied to nobody. When Hooper lost her balance and slipped, there was nothing to hold her. We heard a shriek and turned to see Hooper stumble backwards to the edge of the rocks, arms swivelling. The moment seemed to last as long as my whole life and yet there were not five seconds for me to run and save my friend. Locke was close to me. I felt the rope loosen. The sky seemed to grow wider, bluer. I remember Parr clutching her face with both hands, red-nosed, claw-fingered. I had one foot on a stone that rocked and wobbled, but I did not move because I was already too late. Hooper rolled off the edge and plummeted. I saw her knapsack as it turned in the air, smashed against rocks and bounced downhill out of sight.

The church bells rang and people crossed themselves in the street. A small party of guides set out from Zermatt to find Hooper because we had not been able to see where she had landed. The hotel boy stood alert and pale behind the desk. I remember him staring at all the people coming and going with news. He gave us a frightened smile as we passed and later brought us cups of golden génépi to calm us. I think he must have stood in the doorway for some time, wanting to help us but not knowing what to do. I have a memory of his shadow at the door, finally leaving. The Matterhorn, hidden the previous day but now bold and clear, resembled the head of an old man, puffing balls of cloud from his pipe as though nothing had happened. I pulled the shutters over my window and banged my head against them, shouting and pleading for Hooper to come back.

Chapter Fourteen

I took some bread and jam to my room, wrapped a blanket around my feet and sat at the writing desk. My pen hovered over the paper as I tried to think what I should say. A blob of jam fell on the first sheet so I screwed it up and tried another. I began to imagine all the letters I might write. *Dear Mr Shackleton*. No, but I was not interested in the Antarctic for now. I had been home for only a few days. I needed time to think about the South Pole and whether or not I still cared about it.

Another sheet. *Dear Parr*, but I heard Locke's voice from her bedroom at the Monte Rosa accusing Parr of causing the accident. Locke was flat on her bed, staring at the ceiling. She said that Parr had not wanted to rope up with Hooper. She knew that Hooper would slow her down or make her fall, so she never intended to use the rope. I told Locke that this was too harsh. There had been no time to think, nor for Parr to do any such thing. She had forgotten to use the rope. If anything, the fault was with Locke and me for setting off without checking that the others were ready, but Locke raged through the night and the next day, sobbing with her pillow over her face. I thought that Locke exaggerated Parr's guilt through grief – we must all share the blame – but her anger had affected me too and now I felt strangely towards Parr. I didn't write to her.

Dearest Locke . . . but what could I write to my friend? She thought that I was a fool and Parr a murderer.

Dear Miss Hobson, my pen wrote. Yes, Miss Hobson would surely help. A job must be first. At the funeral Miss Hobson had been sympathetic to us all and had not seemed upset by the inadvertent burst of publicity we had given Candlin College. I continued the letter and enquired as to whether or not the teaching position in Bedford had been filled. A boarding school in another part of the country seemed just the place for me now. I could spend the holidays with Catherine and Mother but find some other kind of life for myself away from home. Parents and teachers would have read about the accident, but I could work hard and make them forget it. I put my letter on the hall table for Sarah to post.

'Grace, is that you down there?'

'Yes,' I shouted up the stairs. 'What is it, Mother?'

'Would you come and make me comfortable?'

Mother was propped up on her pillows, like an old-lady doll in her lacy bonnet, sipping pale tea.

'The damp gets into my bones. It's miserable.' She clamped her lips together, sighed through her nose.

'Would you like more blankets?'

'They won't make any difference, just weigh me down.

At least I have you back now. I trust you're staying this time. Not that I even know who you are any more.' She looked at me with reproach and a touch of suspicion. 'That dreadful girl who took you all up the mountain. It goes over and over in my mind and I don't understand why you went with her. I always thought she was your friend and had a nice family who would be good to you, but she could have killed you as well. What a monstrous sort of person she must be. It's terrible to grow up an orphan, even a rich one, but her aunt and uncle might have shown her a better way.'

'They're climbers too. I've told you that it wasn't Parr's fault and I don't blame her. I'm staying with you now, yes, until I decide what to do next.'

'What do you mean, *do next*? Is your life a game of gin poker?'

My mother shifted her legs. Tea sloshed onto the eiderdown.

'No, but I must have something to do with myself.' I reached out. 'Let me dry that.'

'Never mind. It'll dry by itself but my pillows keep slipping down. Would you put them up again?'

She leaned forward and the knobbles of her spine showed through her nightdress. I plumped up her pillows and set them behind her. She wriggled and huffed.

'To be racing up mountains when we have been wearing black and remembering your father, and I have been so ill. It's extraordinary that we had no idea. You are certainly clever.'

Cleverness in our house was always an accusation, not a compliment.

The sky had cleared. Next door's three boys kicked a large ball along the street and their mother called out. *Don't come back inside till it starts raining again.*

'Despite everything, it's pleasant,' Mother said, eventually, 'to have you here.' She shut her eyes and sighed again. A loose eyelash quivered and fell to her cheek.

'You must have been lonely since Father died.'

'Listen.' Her whisper seemed to scrape the sides of her mouth. 'The house is so quiet. It's strange.' The garden sparrows made a faint descant to the voices of the boys playing. Mother shook her head, changed her tone. 'Did you see edelweiss on the mountains?'

'Yes, a few. And much prettier flowers too.'

'A lot of saxifrage, I expect, and gentians. I like those colours, purples and mauves. I always wanted to see the Alps, though not to climb them, of course.'

'You'd have to go up to see edelweiss. They don't grow on lower slopes.'

Hooper's family must have all her sketches now. I wished that I had just one of them to keep.

'No, well, you could have picked one for me then.'

I perched on the mattress edge. The room was beginning to look shabby. The wallpaper had once been the colour of bluebells but now it was faded and soot-stained, a clouding sky. At the ceiling, it peeled off and curled away, as though the house were still growing, and outgrowing everything my parents had put in it.

'It wasn't your fault, was it, Grace? You would have saved her if you could. You're a brave girl.'

'I hope I would have tried if it had been possible, but she was behind me when she slipped.'

And Hooper began to fall before my eyes, turning over and over, a tiny version no bigger than my fingertip, tumbling through the air of Mother's bedroom, past the mantelpiece and towards the empty grate, and when my fingers reached out, sunlight caught her and she vanished. I blinked.

'Mother, why don't your friends visit?'

'I don't invite them. The neighbours despise me for being a widow.' She twisted her neck and screwed up her face in pain. 'I despise myself.'

I took her hand and stroked her fingers with the tip of my thumb.

'But they must understand that misfortune is nothing to be ashamed of.'

'If my son – if Freddie had lived. Oh, it would all have been different. He'd be out working somewhere in London, bringing food to the table, making sure that we're all right.'

'But we *are* all right, aren't we?'

'Your father's investments haven't turned out well.'

'What do you mean?'

'A large sum of money has disappeared altogether. Mr Kenny always told him to invest in the railways and I thought he had, but it seems he didn't. We shan't starve but we shall have to be careful. Mrs Horton has gone so we just have Sarah now.'

'I'll find a job.'

'No, I don't think so. I'm ill, Grace. I need a daughter to look after me and Catherine won't do any more. I'm sorry about it but you'll see what she's like when you've been here longer. She just sleeps and sulks like a little girl. She's hopeless.'

'Perhaps she needs more interests outside the house.'

'Try if you like but she hasn't got any friends, as far as I can see. She has no ability to make any either.' Mother passed her teacup to me and I placed it on the bedside table.

'I thought I would go away, to teach.'

She shook her head, slid down in the bed and pulled the eiderdown up to her chin.

'You can't leave us now. You'll see how much we need you, and how lucky you are to have this safe, warm home and a forgiving family.' The bedsprings squawked as she rolled away from me and disappeared under the eiderdown.

Hooper's death had been in the newspapers, along with sensational and inaccurate accounts of the four foolish girls attempting to climb in the Alps and, inevitably, meeting disaster. I tried not to mind about the newspapers since what mattered was to give an account to Hooper's family and to Teddy, but it was painful to be criticized as though we had never seen a mountain or snow before. Our attempt to climb without a guide seemed to have sent the journalists apoplectic, as though they were all experts now. Women and men criticized us. They ignored the great climbs of Lily Bristow, Gertrude Bell, Annie Smith Peck, Fanny Bullock Workman, Mrs LeBlond, Lucy Walker and all the regular members of the Ladies' Alpine Club. One kind journalist pointed out that any mountaineer – even the most experienced of men – could be unfortunate enough to slip and fall and I was grateful to him. On the whole we were pitied, not blamed – it was the fault of universities and feminists for putting the idea into our heads, that such a thing might be done – but they were wrong in every way. We knew what we were doing but we were also, between us, to blame for Hooper's death.

The funeral was muted and confused, as though no one could understand how a quiet, feminine and sensible girl, who was embroidering pillowcases for her marriage, had ended up in a mountaineering accident. In my pew I dreamed up miraculous scenes where it was all a mistake and Hooper had not died. I remembered my argument with Parr about needing to rest but now I insisted that Hooper be allowed to stop, and so she survived. Locke, Parr and I stood together and sang 'Abide with Me' in feeble voices. We avoided each other before and afterwards. It was agony to be three when we should have been four.

I left Mother to sleep. Catherine was waiting on the stairs. Her nightgown hung absolutely still. She had been listening. She tucked a strand of hair behind her ear, followed me into the drawing room, shut the door and held the handle behind her with both hands.

'Grace, you mustn't think of leaving. I need you to stay here with me. Do you promise?'

'Well – I can't promise. I'll stay for a while, a few weeks, until I have a job, but then I shall probably leave.'

'But you can't find work if it means moving away. You see, I won't be here much longer so you will have to take my place.'

She knotted her hands together in front of herself, like a nervous child.

'What do you mean?'

Catherine rubbed her check with the heel of her hand. 'I can't tell you yet but I'm expecting to go away one day soon. You'll be Mother's nurse now, won't you?'

'But why can't you tell me? Have you met somebody?'

Catherine's eyes darted around the room. 'No, though I did see Frank Black a month or so ago.'

'Ah, Frank. And how is he?'

'I don't know. He was at his parents' house. I was visiting his mother for tea and he was there too. We didn't talk much but he was very pleasant, very amusing as he always is, you know.'

'But why will you be leaving? Has it something to do with Frank?'

'I can't tell you.'

She didn't seem to know what she was saying and I thought that it was something she had invented to keep me in the house.

'Catherine, it's only fair that you should do whatever you want and I should help, but Mother does not seem so ill to me, just weak from mourning and getting used to things. What if we help her get better, encourage her to see that there's plenty still to do and enjoy?'

'You're going to refuse me but you mustn't. We can't both be free, not while *she's* alive being ill, and I know that she's not even properly ill. That just makes it worse. She's decided to be ill until she dies but that won't be for years.' She turned and opened the door, stepped through into the hall and screwed up her eyes to glare at me. 'It's your turn to stay, Grace. This is your life now because it has been mine. Goodnight.' She scurried upstairs, tripping halfway and clutching for the banister.

Miss Hobson replied to my letter. The position was not available, she wrote, and she was not inclined to recommend me for another. She gave no explanation. Perhaps it was because of the accident or perhaps it was because I had rejected her attempt to help me at college. It made no difference. Without a reference from the college, it would be difficult to teach anywhere. I must think of something better. I sat on the stairs with the letter, rested my elbows on my knees. I pictured Frank with the four members of the Society behind the window of the hotel in Wales, chattering around a table with cups and scones and teapots everywhere. Rain spattered the glass and obscured our faces as we laughed and shared our stories. There were no voices, just the bluster and slap of the wet wind from the hills.

Five or six thick cobwebs dangled from the recesses of the ceiling, fluffy black scarves and beards. I looked down at the dark walls of the hall, dusty photographs of grumpy ancestors and pictures of unvisited, bucolic landscapes. A vase of yellow flowers made the hall table pretty but it was jetsam on a miserable ocean. The wind rattled the panes in the door. I thought of Catherine on her bed, crying and dreaming of the day that Frank Black would beat down the door and rescue her.

And what was I doing there, in the middle of it all, Father? Don't look at me as if the answers are all mine to give.

A key in the front door. A creak and shuffling feet. It is Mr Blunt. His umbrella rustles, slots into the stand in the corner of the hall. His overcoat and hat come off, land on the hooks behind the stairs. He works in a bank and goes somewhere most nights afterwards, but I have no idea where. There is a pause as though he has noticed light from behind the drawing-room door, heard the chatter of the flames and coal. He is wondering whether or not to greet me. It is late. It must be the middle of the night and I don't care where he has been. I don't call, *Evening*, as I sometimes might, and he says nothing either, but pads up the two flights of stairs to his room, straining not to be heard. Goodnight, Mr Blunt. Threads of cigar smoke creep under the door and taint the air.

Chapter Fifteen

Locke visited. Her anger had not waned. She wanted us to tell Hooper's family about Parr and the rope, about their daughter's mountain sickness, that we had let her down and we wanted to apologize, but that Parr was mostly to blame. Now Locke had heard that Parr was writing her own account of the tragedy for a mountaineering journal.

I poured tea and offered her a scone. She waved the plate away.

'It will be a tissue of lies, with no mention of the fact that she chose not to use the rope or that she drove Hooper to exhaustion. We have to tell everything before her story is accepted as truth.'

'I don't know about this, Locke. What do we have to tell and to whom?'

'Farringdon, don't stand up for her now. You simply cannot.'

Locke grasped the sugar tongs, dropped a lump into her tea and stirred it as though she were beating an egg.

'I'm just not clear what good—'

'I need to know that you will support me and that we

shall be united on this. Of course I do not say that we were blameless in the accident. We weren't.'

I nodded. 'Indeed. We should have listened when Hooper first mentioned her headache.'

'But the responsibility is Parr's and she must take it.'

We sipped our tea. I nibbled a bit of scone but I had no appetite. Catherine moved around upstairs, opening drawers and cupboards. Sarah was in the kitchen, splashing water and clinking cutlery. I wished that something would happen to make Locke go away. She wanted to worsen a situation that was already bad and would cause more pain for Hooper's family. It irritated me that she would not let it rest, let Hooper rest.

'Parr can tell her story,' I said. 'She'll give the truth as she remembers it. Only Parr knows why they didn't use the rope. It's cruel to think the worst, cruel to blame her when none of us could help Hooper.'

I choked on the last words. Locke's eyes filled and she looked away. We weren't able to comfort each other. Locke covered her face with her handkerchief and wept. I stared at a smear on the window pane.

'I remember saying that I would spend all my summers in Zermatt.' She sniffed. 'Ghastly place.'

'But that's it, Locke. You're angry with Parr because it's all so fresh and terrible. Wait a while—'

'Don't insult me.' She folded her handkerchief into a neat square and tucked it into her pocket. 'I'm going home. You may as well know, I've decided to write a play about the whole affair and then the truth will be public.'

'Why deepen the agony for Parr? Leave it alone, Locke. Hooper is gone. Please stop this.'

She stood and left the room without looking at me again. Sarah came to the hall, but Locke already had her hat and coat. I watched her from the window, pulling her arms into her sleeves as she hurried away, almost tumbled along the street, like an injured bird trying to take flight.

The argument upset me, so I curled up on the settee and lay in silence for the rest of the afternoon. I did not want Locke's friendship just now, if it had to be filled with anger and accusation, but I did not want to lose it either. She was my best friend and had sometimes seemed closer to me than Catherine. I decided to wait, perhaps for a few months, until we were all a little stronger.

Parr had been silent since the funeral, so I wrote to her and received a brief message in return.

> *I can't bear to be in Europe now, not after the accident.*
> *I'm making arrangements to go to South America and*
> *climb there for a few months, at least, perhaps a year*
> *or more. Come, if you can. We could even travel to the*
> *south of Argentina and look down towards Antarctica.*

I clutched her letter and went to the window. I gazed over the rooftops to the sky and at the faint glimmer of sun behind the clouds, feeling that I could jump to the grass below, run and run. South America. We might climb in Peru, follow in the footsteps of Annie Smith Peck, ascend the north summit of Huascarán and more. We could indeed visit Buenos Aires and travel down through Argentina towards – but – but I had no money for this sort of adventure and it was out of the question. And then, even if I could afford it, what of Hooper? Was it decent to climb again so soon? And what of Catherine and Mother? Yet it might shut up the naysayers in the newspapers, if we did it well and bagged new peaks.

'What shall I do, Hooper?' I had taken to addressing my dear friend from time to time since she always seemed to be nearby. 'Shall I go with Parr?'

There was no reply, of course, but I imagined an emphatic *No*. It was the right, sensible answer. Catherine needed my help with Mother and I had neglected my family for too long. If Catherine wanted to leave home, I must let her, though I did not believe she had anywhere to go. And, I reminded myself again, I could hardly afford a passage to South America.

Mother liked me to do my reading and sewing in the drawing room because it was directly beneath her bedroom. She could bang on the floor with Father's old walking stick when she needed me and didn't have to use her voice or press the servant bell, which was, she complained, stiff and put her finger out. The thud of the stick might disturb me at any time and I gave up trying to read. I played Patience or slept. Sometimes I shut my eyes and spoke a few silent words to Hooper, asked her if she was warm enough. When my mother called me upstairs for no reason, I cursed her and asked Hooper to give me strength. Mother was difficult to please, often angry and stubborn. One day she asked me for a book, did not like the one I chose, and threw it at my head. The urge to throw it directly back at her was strong but Hooper told me to resist, so I took the book and, quite calmly, left the room.

Dr Sowerby sometimes visited but Mother's illness remained mysterious. Pain moved from limb to limb. Sometimes she could not move her legs and, on other days, she walked around but her neck and back were sore, or her hands tingled.

'She has a touch of arthritis but her main complaint is probably nervous,' Dr Sowerby told me one day. 'Ensure that the house is always clean and quiet with plenty of fresh air circulating. Nothing must happen that might upset her routine and cause her anxiety or surprise.'

'Anything that causes surprise in this house now will be a surprise to me too.'

But I woke that night feeling strange. I could hear music and I realized that I had been listening to it in my sleep and that it had been playing for some time. Catherine was at the piano, working her way up and down a slow chromatic scale. I sat up to listen. She played three octaves then moved up a semitone and began again and again. I got out of bed and pulled back the drapes to let a little moonlight onto my clock. It was ten past three. She was banging confidently up and down the keyboard as though it were daylight. I went back to bed but by half past three she had moved onto arpeggios and then minor sevenths. Each exercise segued into the next as though there were some deeper compulsion pushing her on.

I tiptoed down to the drawing room and pushed the door. Catherine rocked slowly back and forth as she played. She looked like a ghost with her white nightgown and loosely plaited hair. Her eyes were wide but there was no expression on her face.

'Catherine? Are you all right?'

'What?' She looked up but her hands continued to play.

'Catherine, it's the middle of the night.'

'What?'

'I can't sleep.'

'I can't sleep and you can't sleep.' Her voice was sing-song. She paused. 'Oh dear.'

I wondered if she were sleep-walking. She didn't seem to be talking to me but to herself. She played to the end of her arpeggios and brought her hands together, then placed them in her lap, head bent.

I waited for the notes to fade. 'Catherine, if you've finished, why don't you go to bed?'

'If you've finished, why don't *you* go to bed?' She turned slowly to me, eyes flat and empty, like buttons.

'Why are you practising scales in the middle of the night?'

'Scales are very easy if you practise every day but you have to practise every single day. The middle of the day and the middle of the night. Where is he?'

'Who?'

She frowned.

And her fingers found the keys, meandered back into an uneven chromatic scale. I opened my mouth to persuade her again to go to bed but stopped. Her mind was somewhere in a dream and I could not reach her.

I looked into Mother's room before returning to my own. She was asleep. The moonlight bathed her white bedclothes blue. The piano was faint here so it was possible that Catherine often played in the night and Mother never knew. Her arms and legs splayed at gawky angles and her covers were sliding to the floor. She mumbled that she was cold. I tugged at her blankets, trying not to disturb her. I drew the bedspread gently to her chest and I watched her for a while. Some days, when she sat up and rapped her stick on the floorboards, I had wanted to shake or hit her but now I wished her sound sleep.

'I'm warm now,' she whispered.

I touched her brow and she rested her hand on my wrist, her powdery fingertips quivering on my skin.

The following day, Catherine called Mother and me into the drawing room to announce that she was going to get married and leave us. Mother collapsed into her armchair and Sarah brought the smelling salts.

'Catherine, who is he?' I whispered.

'Frank, of course.'

'Frank Black? You have been meeting him after all?'

'No. I have only seen him the once recently – I told you about it – but I know he likes me. I'm not lying so you needn't look at me like that. I couldn't have done anything before you came back because my responsibility was to *her*.'

'You mean nothing has happened. Aren't you hurrying a little, if you've only seen him once?'

'No. He loved me then and he still does. Now you're back and I'm free to do as I please.' She loosened her hair, ran her fingers through it, then held it up into a knot on top of her head, using the glass in Father's portrait as a mirror. She sucked in her cheeks and lifted her lips into a haughty smile.

'But Frank didn't propose?'

'No, but he will. You see, I have seen him pass by the window twice. He was looking at the house both times – really staring – so he must have hoped to see me.'

'Then he might have rung the doorbell.'

She pinned her hair back the way it had been, patted down the loose coils at her temples. 'He wouldn't want to disturb us while Mother is so ill and we're still mourning Father. He was always a gentleman. Well, you wouldn't remember but he was. I'm tired. I'm going to bed now. Goodnight.'

It was not yet evening but Catherine left us, yawning and rubbing her eyes.

Mother had recovered and was sitting up, holding a handkerchief across her forehead and shooing Sarah away.

'Oh, Grace. Whatever is she thinking? I swear your sister is touched. It's not only that she's lost all her manners, but she is more eccentric by the day. We should never have let her spend so much time at the piano. It's worse than a drug and I don't know how she'll ever get back to herself now.'

'I hadn't realized that she was so badly off.'

'And what did I hear her saying just now about Frank Black? Imagine. Who on earth would marry her now? What sort of a wife would she make? I shudder at the thought. Poor girl.'

Perhaps I had imagined, in my first year at college, that Frank might return to Catherine and fall in love with her again, but I knew better now. She was too far away from him and all of us. If Frank were really walking past our house and it was not a fantasy of Catherine's, then perhaps he was hoping to see me. I longed to see Frank again. I longed to talk about Switzerland, the accident, my three friends and all that had happened between us. He had met them all, Locke, Parr and Hooper.

Locke would be working in London now, a bachelor girl, perhaps lodging with other young women, or perhaps still at home with her family in Kensington. She had not replied to my last letter and I imagined her writing her play every evening, her version of the truth, commuting each day to the West End to work and, somewhere between, perhaps meeting a lover. He would be an actor or writer too and they would share heated conversations about the world and theatre. They would have free love and not care who knew. Parr would be preparing for her grand voyage to South America now, packing her ropes and boots for the next big climb.

I attempted a letter to Teddy. I jotted some memories of Hooper, found a photograph of her in the college woods, gave him my warmest regards. I looked at the picture, her soft face and surprised smile and felt that somebody was taunting me. I rubbed my eyes. Should I tell Teddy that Locke was writing a play about his fiancée's death? It was bound to portray her as a weak, sickly girl, dropped into the abyss by her selfish, scheming friend. I thought of Edward Whymper and the Taugwalders, survivors on the broken rope. As my father had told me, Peter Taugwalder could not have had time to cut the rope when the others were already falling. He would have been pulled before he knew what was happening. But, if he had done it, could he be blamed for it? He would have saved not only himself but his son and Edward Whymper when it was already too late for the others. I remembered the story of Parr's parents, the pair of them on one rope, slipping over the edge of a broken cornice to their deaths. What if Parr and Hooper had been roped up and both had gone? I imagined Parr packing her trunk for South America, off into self-imposed exile, unable to keep away from mountains no matter how much of her they destroyed.

Chapter Sixteen

'Mother,' I said the next morning, 'why don't we sell the house and move somewhere smaller? We need the money and there are too many rooms for the three of us. A fresh start would do us good, don't you think?'

'Great heavens. You are always trying to get from one place to another. This is our family home. Your father would be horrified to hear you say such a thing.'

'Change might be good for us. Catherine is losing herself here. Perhaps away from her childhood home—'

My mother nodded and clasped my hand.

'Catherine *is* a bit of a lump, but she would only get worse elsewhere. She's still mourning her father and needs to be close to his things and all her memories. Do you see? If we took her away, I'm afraid that she might not know where she was. This house gives her comfort and safety, puts some edges on her world that the piano took away. I've talked to Dr Sowerby and he says so too.'

'Perhaps, but we can't go on like this. I am not going to stay for ever and I can't leave you and Catherine alone here to fall apart.'

'Don't say that. You're too cruel.' Tears slipped from her eyes.

'Please don't cry about it. I'm trying to help all of us.'

She rested her head on my shoulder and tucked her fingers into my sleeve.

'It will be all right,' I whispered, stroking her hair. 'It will be all right.'

'I'm too tired for all this trouble. I don't like arguments and discussions. Read to me, Grace.' She patted my head. 'Read something soothing.'

I read a story from one of her journals and she listened with her eyes closed, occasionally asking me to repeat a passage or explain something.

When she was asleep, I tiptoed up to the attic room. It had once been a servant's room but was now a store for odds and ends: a desk and chair, a few hat boxes and some old blankets, nothing more. I had not intended to go up there but perhaps some reluctance either to go down to Catherine or to be alone in my own room had drawn me towards the top staircase.

The carpet smelled musty and the door creaked when I pushed it. I turned on the light and went to the chair. I sat on it and stared through the window. The clouds were piled thick and low in the sky, resembled hazy mountain peaks. I imagined that they were some fragile version of the Alps and sat for some time, blinking, sometimes almost slipping into sleep – perhaps I did sleep for a time – for what happened next was a kind of half-dream. I found myself sitting on the summit of a mountain, one I had never seen before, with Hooper at my side. She was on the same rock, one heel tucked into a ledge. Strands of her hair flicked and twisted in the wind. She scooped them away from her spectacle lenses with her fingertips. I asked her how she was and she told me that she was very well, thank you. She didn't seem angry, or sad. I missed her, I said, and promised that I would never stop thinking about her. She smiled, kept her eyes on some distant point. Of course, I knew she was not there. She was not a ghost and I was not mad. It was something I imagined because I could not help it and afterwards I felt better because of it.

In the following weeks, I began to go to the attic more frequently. I could still hear Mother, if she needed me, but it was nicer to be at the top of the house where nobody came. Sometimes I remembered old conversations with Hooper and I ran over them in my head. We were always side by side on our rock, though the views and the weather changed, and I spoke aloud to her, about the climb, our equipment, the plants and animals. Hooper never said much in return, but I knew she was listening. Sometimes, as I spoke, she grew sad. Then her body would fade into a girl-shaped cloud and she was gone.

Mother became suspicious that I was searching for another house, trying to sell ours, and interrogated me when I went to take her food or medicine.

'What are you doing all the time? You're up to something.'

'I'm thinking, writing letters. I'm looking for a job.'

'You can't sell this house, you know. Only I can do that.'

'I'm not thinking of selling the house. It was a suggestion, that was all.'

'It's in my name and I'm not dead yet.'

'I can see that. We'll all stay here then, but Catherine will get worse.'

'As long as she doesn't go out or meet people and bring shame, we'll manage. You need to make yourself more useful about the place. Never mind finding a job. You have work enough looking after us. Put the tragedy behind you and stop trying to change everything. There is nothing at all wrong with things being the same tomorrow as they were today.'

It was around this time that I paid a visit to Mrs Kenny. She was about the same age as Mother and we had known her for years. She was a witty, friendly woman who always made Mother more humorous. She had often popped over to share gossip or borrow some book or cooking utensil, but had rarely come since Mother shut herself away and refused calls. Her husband was in hospital and she invited me to drop by one afternoon and play cards, share some stories and cheer her up. It was a welcome diversion from my routine and I was glad to accept the invitation.

However, as I closed the front gate and twisted round to prevent my skirt catching in it, a movement in one of our upstairs windows caught my eye. I glanced up to see Mother settling into an armchair which was pulled right up to the pane, apparently so that she could watch me cross the road. Our eyes met and she glowered. It occurred to me that she was preparing to sit there, eyes fixed on the Kennys' house, until I emerged. Either she could not bear for me to have a few hours to myself or she did not trust me. I pulled a rose from a bush near the gate, crushed the yellow petals in my palm as I walked away, threw the broken bloom onto the pavement. It was a childish and pointless act which only pricked my hand and spoiled a fine rose, but it felt good to squash the life and beauty from it. A ruby of blood rose in my palm and I was satisfied.

I did not stay long with Mrs Kenny. I could feel my mother's eyes trained on the house even as I shuffled a pack of cards. We played one or two games of cribbage and I learned a little news about the neighbours. The Jacksons' daughter, whom I had known at school, had become a nurse and now worked at the hospital where Mr Kenny was being treated. Mrs Kenny lowered her eyes and said that she hoped Matilda Jackson was not treating Mr Kenny, for that would be most uncomfortable for all concerned. She did not tell me the nature of Mr Kenny's ailment or injury – suffice to say that homeopathy would not cure it – but blinked the subject away, flicked efficiently through her cards ready to make her next move. After playing it, she mentioned that a doctor's family, all Fabians, were to move into the big house at the end of the road and they were known to be very respectable and sociable, so that was pleasing. Then Mrs Kenny asked me if I knew of Frank Black from round the corner.

'A little. He's a family acquaintance but we haven't seen him for a long time.'

'Well, he has caused quite a scandal.' She smiled as though it were something delicious. 'Mind, it is only a rumour and may not be true so don't tell anyone but –'

I thought that she was about to announce his engagement or marriage and, God forbid, to Catherine.

' – he is said to be having an affair with Mrs Granger-Dawes.'

'Mrs Granger-Dawes?' I had heard of her, the wife of a wealthy industrialist, but I knew little except that she must be forty, at least. Somehow the news did not hit me very hard so much as it surprised me. 'Are you quite sure?'

'They met at an artist's party and he has been seen with her on several occasions. A couple of times someone saw her emerge from his flat in the morning. And I don't know but I heard that when it's warm she sleeps in the garden with her two babies because she believes that moonlight, or starlight – I'm not sure now – shines goodness on their souls. She stands on her head for half an hour every morning and I've even heard that she walks in front of her windows,' Mrs Kenny leaned forward, '*nude*.' She nodded for emphasis and a faint blush spread across her nose and cheeks. 'Her husband must rue the day that he met her.'

'Good heavens. And Frank Black?'

'Besotted, they say. And perhaps that is so, but I suspect he saw an easy opportunity and took it.'

'I thought – well, I thought better of him.'

'Grace, let me tell you something that your mother may not tell you. It's no bad thing for a man to have some experience when he marries. I'd go so far as to say that it is the best thing for both husband and wife, as long as it is all over before the engagement. Frank will want to marry within a year or two so I don't blame him. It's all to the benefit of his future wife. What to think about Mrs Granger-Dawes is another matter.'

I could hardly consider myself betrayed by Frank but somehow I did.

'Mrs Kenny, I am trying to remember Mrs Granger-Dawes but I can't picture her. What does she look like? Is she a beautiful woman?'

'Very handsome. She has fine bones and dark, deep-set eyes. Men fall for her charm but what always strikes me are her beautiful lips and teeth. She has a melodious laugh.'

I imagined Frank with this modern beauty and was curious. He was not, after all, the same person Catherine dreamed of marrying or, indeed, the man I had almost fallen for. He was now much more exciting.

Mother was still at her lookout when I returned. She spotted me and pressed her hands and face to the pane. I considered heading off in another direction but really had nowhere else to go. I laughed aloud. The sound was not melodious at all.

'Goodnight, Grace,' says a black and white vision of Catherine in the doorway.

I try to stop her. 'Don't leave yet. We'll have something to eat. Cherry cake? Pork chops from the butcher? A ginger nut? Boiled eggs and kippers? A tin of treacle with a large spoon, perhaps. And I have pictures to show you. The piano will be tuned and the tone will be so sweet, so – so just right that you can play all day and all night. We need never leave the house again. Mabel will do the shopping and suchlike. If you wanted to venture out, just sometimes, I would try to come with you.' I gaze at the window. 'Do you see how I need you?'

But she has gone. She was not there but in my head.

The front door opens, shuts. The quiet feet of Mr Blunt pad through the hall and reach my door, seem to stop as though he has just noticed that the light is on. I don't know where he has been at this time of night and I don't much care but—

Ah. No. We have had Mr Blunt. He went to the attic and has not come down again, unless he keeps a rope ladder up there and has used it. Somebody else is in the hall and it is surely not Miss Cankleton, who goes to bed at nine o'clock. I tread softly to the door and listen. I wait for several minutes. Nothing.

Chapter Seventeen

It was November or December 1912. I was sitting at Mother's window watching the children playing with a ball. It was a pleasing, bright red thing and bounced from one side of the street to the other, as three boys and a girl chased it along, taking it in turns to give it a kick. Mother was wheezing in her sleep and I had been in my position for half an hour, too bored to move. I had visited my old school in the hope of taking a little work but Miss Ladbroke had passed away and the new headmistress did not know me. There were no vacancies at present, she told me, but she would let me know if the situation changed. The ball came over our garden wall, as it often did, and then a pair of hands reached up to catch it. I leaned forward to see who was in our garden – we did not expect visitors – and it was Frank, right in the middle of the path. He tossed the ball back to the children then caught sight of me upstairs, squinted and shielded his eyes to see me better. He waved and raised his hat. I opened the window.

'Hello.'

'Good afternoon.' His face was fuller than when I had last seen him. He had put on a little weight and it made him seem more grown-up. He wore a grey morning suit with a pale silk cravat. A silver watch chain glinted from his waistcoat and he beamed at me.

I remained there with my head out of the window, conscious that my mother was stirring.

'Are you visiting us?' I asked stupidly.

'I'm in Dulwich for a few days, seeing the old family. Thought I'd drop by.' He took a step back to see me better, let his hands drop to his sides. I thought he seemed nervous but pleased to see me. 'Though you'll be the one to drop if you're not careful.'

I laughed. 'How lovely. But Catherine's at a church meeting.' I said this because I was not all sure which of us he had come to visit.

'Is she? It would be nice to see you both but—'

'Just a moment. I'll come downstairs. Ring the bell and the maid will let you in.'

My mother sat up with a snort. The bed springs twanged and pinged. 'What's all the noise? Why's the window open? You're frightening me.'

'It's nothing. Go back to sleep.'

I dashed into my room, powdered my face, saw that I had overdone it and wiped most of the powder onto my hands and then my skirt.

Frank stood at the drawing-room window. In his right hand he clasped his gloves, flicking them gently against the side of his leg.

I called his name. Father's portrait gazed down, neither approving nor disapproving.

'Grace.' Frank sighed. 'Oh, Grace.'

'Catherine mentioned that she saw you recently. But you don't live in Dulwich?'

'I did see Catherine a month or two ago. I had forgotten that. No, no. I have a flat in Russell Square, but I come to see my parents.' His voice lowered and he looked at me kindly. 'I heard about your terrible time in the Alps. I was very sorry to learn about poor Miss Hooper.'

Hooper and Catherine were clambering over each other in my mind, trying to catch my attention, and here was Frank, who had been there all along, just leaning against some post or pillar, biding his time.

'I suppose you read about it in the newspapers.'

'I saw one or two things. They were nonsense, entirely. I took no notice.'

I nodded my gratitude, stuck my fingernails into my palms so that I would not cry.

'Frank, what do you – I mean – do you still paint?'

'Oh, well. Work takes up most of my mind so there isn't much room for hobbies these days. I get the brushes and easel out from time to time, splash the paint about a bit. I want to make it into parliament in a few years' time, you see. You can imagine, it requires a certain amount of manoeuvring, not to mention sucking up to people.'

'And the ideals of your youth? You haven't lost them, I hope.'

If I sounded a little cynical it was because I remembered

his abandonment of Catherine when she lost her chance to be a concert pianist.

'Yes, well – no. I shall always have ideals, I hope. I mean, I'm a Liberal, you know, and always shall be. No, it's just that my ambitions these days are tempered with realism. I want to paint but not to the exclusion of everything else. And, you know, you're partly responsible for this change in me.'

'I am?' Mrs Granger-Dawes, with her pretty eyes and teeth, popped into my mind and tipped back her head to let out a melodious laugh. Two years or so had passed since I had seen Frank and I should not expect him to be the same person, nor to like me in the same way as before.

'I long to travel. I want adventures, like the ones you have, and for that I'll need, well, a certain income, a career.'

'True.'

Frank rested his eyes on me, assessing me, working me out. He tilted his head, half-smiled.

'The whole truth, Grace, is this. I'll never be good enough to make a living from painting. It was a schoolboy thing. I've spent time with artists and writers recently and I know that I'm not one of them. They have a fire, a certainty that nothing else matters, and I don't have it. I thought I did but it turns out that I don't.'

'Oh, I see.' To be polite I asked, 'Are you sure?'

'I am.'

'And does Mrs Granger-Dawes share your opinion?'

Frank reddened. 'Ah – you know her? I – I'm not sure.

She—' He seemed to flail, searching for words, an appropriate expression or gesture. 'I didn't realize that you knew her. Well, Mrs Granger-Dawes is a good friend and has been very encouraging but I made the decision myself.'

I regretted my boldness – I had only meant to tease him – and could think of no response. The clock ticked and Father watched us, now with mild interest. Mother's stick gave a series of firm raps and made the ceiling tremble. Frank glanced up, then over at me.

'Was that some Morse code message from upstairs?'

I nodded. 'But my mother expects all her messages to be understood as SOS. She doesn't trouble herself with anything less.'

'Oh dear. I'll get out of your way then. Will you be all right?'

'I'm much better already.' I called through the door, 'Mother, just a minute.'

Frank touched my hand. 'You've heard something about Mrs Granger-Dawes and me.'

'I'm sure it was nothing but gossip.'

'Well – it was only a little more than nothing, but people will talk. Perhaps we could go for a walk one afternoon, if – if you'd like to.'

'I don't know.' I chose my words carefully. 'Catherine and I don't go out together. It's best if one of us is always here.'

Frank seemed nonplussed for a moment, then nodded.

'Quite. Quite. I understand. So – so we can't do that then or one of you would be left out. Well, we could play a game one afternoon, for old time's sake. Shall I be Scott and you be Oates?'

I smiled but I felt sad. 'We don't know where they are now.'

'We can imagine.'

'I don't think – I can't imagine now. What if we stumbled upon the truth, and it was bad news?'

'It's a game, isn't it? If your sister were here to provide an accompaniment—'

The piano was heaped with wool and four or five of Catherine's dolls.

'I don't think so.'

'Doesn't look as though it gets much love now. Poor thing. How is Catherine these days?'

'She's – ' I regarded him closely. His concern for Catherine was born of politeness, I was sure, and he was embarrassed – as I was – by the memory of our doomed meeting in the college woods. 'She's very well.'

Frank left before Catherine returned and I did not mention his visit. I prepared bread and cheese for my mother, and did not stay to talk to her. Instead I went to the attic and I told Hooper about Frank.

'I wish we had been together for a long time, the way you and Teddy were. I thought it better to forget him and I tried, but he's back. It may not be too late, after all, as long as I am considerate of Catherine. I don't want to leave you behind, Hooper. I hope you don't think that I do.'

*

Mr Blunt is certainly in his room. He creaks about up there. His little sounds flit through the bricks in the walls and down the stairs like curls of falling leaves. If he hadn't come home, I might have gone up for a look at the room, but it would not be the same as when I used to find Hooper there. When Mr Blunt came to see the room, he had the choice of the attic or the one Miss Cankleton now has. I thought the attic was the lesser of the two. It is smaller and the fireplace is poky. I said to him that it had not been much lived in, except by servants. It was even considered to be haunted at one time. I explained this to Mr Blunt and his eyes rather seemed to feast on the picture. He liked the room all the better and was anxious to take it. I thought then that he was an odd one, but I let him have the attic as the other room would be easier to let. I don't know what he does up there or when he goes out late at night, but he's a very quiet man and this house has never tolerated much noise.

Once I wanted to be in a house full of life – the Lockes' home in Kensington was bliss to me with its lively, clever people and magical parties with champagne and lilies and charades – but I was not to have that for myself and now I think there is no greater human virtue than the tendency to be quiet. That makes Miss Cankleton a saint, of course, and I think she might be. She is about forty-five but has the extraordinary talent of being able to look seventy no matter what she wears. She works in the post office. I have seen her there, polished knob of grey hair atop her head, thick spectacles and the habit of leaning towards the customer because she is just a little deaf. I cannot be the only person in the queue who thinks that she resembles a silver teapot pouring forth. She'll be deep in sleep now, stamping envelopes, or climbing some secret Matterhorn of her own.

Chapter Eighteen

A letter from Locke. I sat beside Hooper in the attic and read it aloud. Locke wanted me to visit her at work so that she could show me around the theatre and catch up on old times. She was now active within the Actresses' Franchise League, like her mother, organizing public meetings and writing her sketches for performances around the country, sometimes acting in them herself. In the meantime, she did clerical work at her uncle's theatre in the West End. She also told me that Hester Morgan, our old friend from Candlin, was in prison for smashing shop windows.

> *Come and see me, Farringdon. These weeks have*
> *been terrible. I have been making myself busy,*
> *working, writing and campaigning, but the ache*
> *never dulls and you are the only person who will*
> *understand. I am so sorry that we argued. We*
> *mustn't lose each other because of this. I miss you!*

'I have missed her too, Hooper, but perhaps she is no longer angry and that's why she has written.'

Indeed, I was almost tearful with relief that I seemed to

have my dear old friend back again. We would meet in the afternoon, sit on the floor, and talk long into the evening, sometimes tipping a little more coal onto the fire. We would share old jokes about college people and perhaps even sort out our future lives.

Life flowed up Charing Cross Road, pumped in and out of buildings and the smaller streets. I dodged between carriages, buses and bicycles to cross the street and inhaled a mouthful of dust. I spluttered and wiped my face but I was enjoying it. At Cambridge Circus I stood for a few minutes to catch my breath and let the thundering chaos blast my senses. A weak sun shone through the trees and it felt as though it had always been sunny here while the clouds gathered over the house in Dulwich. I walked a little further, found the theatre and followed an alley to the stage door. A boy let me in and led me to Locke's office.

The staircase was shabby, high-ceilinged and turned several corners before we reached a small door on the landing. Locke opened it and pulled me inside with a shriek. She seemed to have grown much older in the months since I had seen her last. She wore a blue dress and her dark hair was fastened at the back of her head in its usual elegant roll but she looked careworn.

'I can't believe we've left it so long. Let me clear these papers so you can sit down.'

The room was poky with a sloping ceiling and small window. Piles of documents and letters covered the desk and part of the floor. There were two chairs, an aspidistra and several framed photographs of scenes from plays. The one nearest me, on the desk, showed a young man in a top hat strangling an older one with his bare hands. Both actors wore frenzied expressions, eyes bulging with ecstasy and pain.

'What play is it?'

'I've no idea. I just like their intense enjoyment of the murder, you know. When office work gets dull it cheers me up.'

'Dull?'

I peered out of the window at the busy street and wondered at Locke's good fortune in having this place to come to every day.

'I've missed our conversations so much, Farringdon. I wish we could see each other more.'

'So do I.'

We had talked about wanting to talk but neither of us could think what to say next. I fiddled with my gloves.

'It's a beautiful office. What do you do here?'

'Cut out the reviews and make sure that we're selling enough tickets, that sort of thing. It's mundane, but it means I can do my work for the AFL when nobody else is about. We're recruiting new members all the time. It has given me a reason to get on with things after – all the bother. It's just a matter of time before we get the vote.'

'And what about Morgan? Is she still in prison?'

'I think so but, even if they let her out, she'll be straight back in.'

'Do you remember having to waltz with her in the picture gallery? I can't imagine her jumping out of trees and running around to smash things. We should visit her next time.'

'She won't see anyone, not even her father. Too proud. She has to wear some coarse, horrible garb and probably has lice.'

Locke pushed a cigarette into a scratched black holder and lit it.

'Want one?'

'No thanks.'

'I keep having this idea,' said Locke. 'It's foolish but, look, imagine this. We get the climbing ropes from Parr and then we scale some building or tower, get ourselves in the news. With a newspaper or sign, *Votes for Women*. Like Fanny Bullock Workman did in the Karakoram, but we'd do it in the city instead.'

'And we could have Parr climbing up behind us with a sign saying: *No Votes for Women at All, Under any Circumstances. So Pull Yourselves Together*.'

Locke giggled. 'Do you think she's changed her position? I feel sure that she must have by now but she'd be too haughty to admit it.'

'I think she'll be sailing to South America soon. She's going to be a great mountaineer and nothing will get in her way.'

Locke blew a thin wire of smoke from her mouth. It curved away behind her ear.

'No. Nothing will stop her. It never does.'

'I meant—'

'Sometimes I forget that I can't just write a letter to Hooper. I kept some of her sketches, ones she did in Wales. I don't even know why I had them in the first place. I should probably return them to her family. Mosses, petals, leaves. Pretty things.'

'Her family must have plenty. I'm sure they wouldn't begrudge you a few sketches.'

She nodded. 'Will you climb again? I shan't but I hope you will.'

'I don't think so.'

I heard myself say this and did not like the way it sounded. It seemed sad and hopeless and made me want to change my mind, though I was not sure that I could.

'I'm not going to forgive her.'

'Parr? We can't blame her for everything.'

Locke gave a short, irritated sigh and adjusted a hairpin.

'You may think so. But I've started to write my play.'

Locke was annoyed with me, but her self-righteous manner and refusal to see any other point of view were tiresome and I wanted her to see that I was irritated too.

'Why do you think it will help people to know that Hooper was miserable and ill before she died? And that there may have been a mistake with the rope. Isn't it better left as it is?'

'No, because it isn't the truth. She need not have died.'

'But the truth won't do any good now.'

'Let's not argue again.'

Locke leaned on her elbow, rubbed her forehead and

said nothing. Feet clattered up and down the stairs and we heard the boy shouting at somebody then laughing.

'All right,' I said.

'Let's talk about something different,' she said eventually. 'Everything and anything except mountains.'

I knew one topic that always made Locke cheerful.

'Have you met any nice gentlemen recently? Do you still see Horace?'

'Ah, indeed. Guess what. Horace got married to a singing teacher so I don't see him any more, but I've been having an affair with my uncle's friend and it has been very helpful while there is so much grief about. He's separated from his wife but not divorced, so I really shouldn't, but I was lonely and he does make me feel nice.'

'I'm glad.'

'He doesn't want too much, so I can do my campaigning without worrying about him. It suits us both, for now. By the way, speaking of affairs, your friend, Mr Black, has been making himself rather well known, I hear.' She smiled and it was as though we were back in her college room again, judges and conspirators. 'The chap we met in Wales, that's him, isn't it? A certain Millicent Granger-Dawes fell in love with him – and the neighbours saw him coming and going over the back wall – but her husband got the gun out and put a stop to it all.'

'Good heavens. I'd heard some of it, but nothing quite so dramatic.'

'It's probably been exaggerated.'

'I've seen him and am inclined to think that it did not come to guns. He is still alive, at any rate.'

Locke's eyes roamed across my face and she drew so hard on her cigarette that I could see her struggling not to cough. I told her more of Frank's visit and she was impressed.

'I'm sure you're much better for him than Mrs Granger-Dawes. If I were you, I'd fall properly in love with him. It's what you need.'

'Perhaps.'

We talked a little more like this and then, soon, we had nothing to say. I wanted to get out of the theatre and back to my room in the attic with all my things. The business of Parr and the rope would always come between Locke and me. Every mouthful of air I took in that room was soured with it.

Locke saw me down to the street. It was still daylight. Cars, horses, buses and bicycles sped and trundled around us as we hugged and promised to meet again soon but did not mean it.

I could hear them from the street. Mother and Catherine were in an argument. Catherine had locked herself in her room and refused to come out when Mother called for her medicine. Mother heard Catherine dragging furniture about the room, the wardrobe doors banging. She rapped on the door but Catherine would not let her in, nor would she make tea or fetch the medicine. Mother's hair hung in grey-blonde strings down her back. Her nightgown was crumpled and coming unstitched down the sides. She pressed her cheek to the door and shouted, 'Dr Sowerby will put you in the asylum if you carry on like this. What are you doing in there? I don't know what this family's coming to. Grace, thank goodness you're back. Help me to my room. My legs are bad today and she doesn't care.'

I took Mother's arm and steered her away from Catherine's door.

'If you shout, she'll only stay in there. She's trying to escape from you.'

Mother put her hand to her neck and muttered, 'And now my throat hurts from shouting at her. Really, she is testing me. You can't go out for whole days any more, Grace. It's impossible for me to manage by myself. You'll have to stay indoors so I know where you are.'

'But I'll be finding a job soon. I won't be able to stay indoors and you must get used to it.'

'No. No, I don't want you to go out. I'm getting worse. I won't survive without you here.'

She burst into tears and limped to her room. I brought her medicine and sat with her. I hoped that we might discuss the sort of job I would take, but she rolled over and pretended to sleep.

Chapter Nineteen

'Grace, you must be Captain Scott.'

'I never liked him as much. Father was always Scott. Why can't I be Amundsen?'

'Because he is Norwegian and we are British. Anyway, he's not there any more and Scott is. Shhh. I'll be Evans.'

'I ought to find the map and dice.'

'But you're beautiful, Captain Scott. Come here. No, come on. Don't look worried, my dear. They won't hear anything from out there, or upstairs. There are no creaky floorboards at the South Pole. You're pretty in the firelight.'

'Ah, Evans. Your hands are cold.'

Oh, Frank.

We loved to fool around like this in the drawing room. His visits were weekly now. Our expeditions became more adventurous but we never left the space by the fireplace. It was our tent, or hut, cosy even when the fire was not lit. We kept our voices low so that no one but Sarah would know Frank was here. My relationship with him was now far beyond what Mother and Catherine could ever have approved of. We held each other, skimmed the ice and seas, crashed through mountain huts and ships' cabins, and we never left our safe place.

Sarah let him in through the kitchen door when Catherine was locked in her room. All I had to do was to tell Sarah that Frank and I were having private discussions in the drawing room and must not be disturbed. Sarah would nod, give me a clever, sympathetic look and close the door behind her.

'I love you, Grace.'

'Shhh.'

Frank squeezed my ankle, ran a finger along my calf.

'Your muscles. They're very tough, and smooth. You remind me of a seal, or what I imagine a seal might feel like.' He laughed at himself.

'They're not so bad, are they?'

'They're rather good. Did you knit these stockings yourself? They look as though you stole them from Captain Scott.'

I had taken to wearing my mountain stockings every day because the house was chilly and we were trying to use less coal.

'Anyway – ' I guided his hand away from the stocking and onto the floor.

'You must be hot now. Why don't I just remove—'

'Shh. Catherine might come out of her room.' I pushed him away – reluctantly, I admit – and lifted myself onto the settee.

Frank threw the die hard against the fireplace. It bounced then quivered to a stop on the hearth.

'I'm sorry for Catherine, but what can we do about it? How much longer do we have to hide ourselves?'

'We could go away.'

'Where?'

'I don't know.'

'You could come to my flat but people would talk. Everybody knew about Millicent when we thought it was a secret. I don't want to do that to you.'

'You didn't mind when it was her.'

'I regret the whole affair. All I wanted was to give her some happiness. She has a stupid, dull husband who does not show love or even seem to know her. I encouraged her to escape a bit and do some of the things you do.' He nodded and pointed his finger. 'And now she has taken up golf. She is just like you.'

'I don't play golf. I've never even thought of playing golf.' I loved Frank but sometimes he was a fool.

'It's the same sort of thing. And do you want to hear the truth?'

'I don't know.'

'I was always telling her about you.'

'Oh.'

'As an example of what she could do, if she were brave enough. And she pointed out that I seemed to be in love with you, which was true, of course, but no consolation to either of us.'

'I didn't know.'

'That was two months ago and we haven't seen each other since. It's you I want, Grace.'

'I thought that the incident with her husband's shotgun precipitated the end of your affair, not I.'

'It was you. The gun business – it has been much exaggerated.'

My nose tingled and I found myself blinking back tears. I pretended to cough.

'But if we want to be together and I can't come to your flat—'

'You don't want us to get married, do you? It's a prison for women. Millicent says—'

'I don't know about any of that. I just want not to be here.'

'We'll think of something, Grace. I do love you. Now, if I throw a six, can I make it to the opposite coast?'

'It's not your turn. And you have just thrown a three anyway. Frank, did you say that you love me?'

'Yes.' His face softened and he ran his hand over my hair, stroked the side of my neck. 'Of course I do. Look, one day we'll go to Switzerland and I'll climb an Alp or two with you. I'll don the garb and follow you to the top. If I turn out to be any good at it, why, we may attempt Everest together. They call it the Third Pole so I think we should. First I must sort out my work, though, get a secure income.'

I laughed. When Frank spoke of the mountains, they were not hostile or cruel, just places for a few larks and a bit of an adventure.

'We'll race against Cicely Parr to the most devilish peaks and we'll set up our own Antarctic expedition. Why not? I'll do it for you, Grace. We'll pay for a nurse – the best we can find – to look after your mother. If we hired an older woman, they might become friends. It would be much better for her than having you here, miserable and all cut off.'

I shook my head. 'She'd never agree.'

'She will.' He kissed me.

I tilted my head so that his cheek rested on mine. His hair smelled of cloves and tobacco. I buried my head in his neck to inhale the scent, kissed the soft skin.

'If you came into the wilds with me, you'd end up with a beard and whiskers, you know. Your skin would get as tough as old boots and your artist friends might find you a little – weather-worn.'

'But I'm willing to undergo all necessary hardship, you see.'

We lay on the rug for a while, arms entangled.

'If you won't live with me and don't think we should marry either, I'm not sure what you want for us.'

'Neither am I. I should not have complained. What we have now is extraordinary. Let's not hurry but see how things will go. When you think the time is right, you must talk to Catherine.'

Frank left, eventually, through the back gates, and Catherine walked in through the front door. I adjusted my stockings and went to greet her but she passed me, telling me about our neighbour's at-home and the dreary gossip of the day.

'They're only interested in flowers for their hats and who is having problems with the servants. I don't know why I went.'

'Why did you go?'

'Actually – ' Catherine's voice shifted, a note higher – 'I'd hoped that Mrs Black would be there. Frank's mother, you know. Sometimes I do see her at these things but not today. She wasn't there.'

'What a pity,' I said and hurried upstairs.

I returned from a walk in the park one day. Mother was waiting at the drawing-room window for me, crying because of a strange episode with Catherine.

'Not again. What is it?'

'Grace, she is not herself at all and has been making dolls all day. My legs ache and I'm too dizzy to do any more. I'm going to lie down. You have to deal with it and make her see sense.'

'Making dolls? She is always making dolls. It is the least of our worries.'

'You'll see what I mean. Gruesome. I'll have my tea in half an hour.'

Catherine was sitting on a chair in her room. The rest of the furniture had been pulled around so that the wardrobe was in front of the window and shut out the light. On the floor around her were pieces of fabric, all chopped up and tangled, and on her bed was a small army of unclothed rag dolls, the kind she made to sell at the church bazaars, but there were thirty or forty of them, all misshapen, strangely deformed with heads sewn onto their sides, stuffing falling out, limbs hanging off their bodies. I started at the sight of them. Catherine was snipping intently at a length of blue silk, tongue poking out at the corner of her mouth.

'Catherine?'

'What do you want?'

'You've made a lot of dolls.'

'Aren't you clever? Yes, I'm making their clothes now and then I'll find wool to give them hair.'

'You're making them very quickly.' I picked one up and turned it over. The seams were hardly stitched.

'Thank you.'

'Is there any need for such a hurry?'

'Oh, our mother says I never do anything so I'm making myself busy.' She dropped the scissors onto the carpet and picked up a reel of blue thread. 'The girls will all have blue silk dresses and go out to play.'

Most of the silk lay in strips around her feet and I took a strip in my hand.

'Catherine, this was my skirt. You've chopped up my skirt to make clothes for the dolls. You could have asked me.'

'You have others, and the dolls need clothes. Why don't you have a doll? Choose the one you like best. A gift from me.'

I looked at the mess of fabric and limbs. They were just cloth but they had a macabre quality that Catherine and I might once have laughed at together. I didn't understand why Catherine couldn't see it.

'Best to save them for the orphans.'

'I'm making more. Look, I've cut up Mother's old coats. Oh, don't pull that face. She doesn't go out any more. None of us does. The ladies from church will collect the dolls so I won't even need to take them myself. I'll see if I can make a hundred by bedtime.'

An idea went through my mind and I tried to dismiss it but it would not go. It occurred to me that Catherine was cutting up our clothes to stop us leaving the house. The debris of her doll-making lay around her and she looked like a little wren in a nest, pecking at the end of the thread to damp it for the needle.

I went up to the attic room, opened the window and put my head out to feel the wind and rain. I stayed for an hour, recounting to Hooper what was happening in the house. Then I went to the cellar, dragged all my mountaineering clothes and equipment upstairs and took them into the attic. I looked at the pieces one by one, turned them over in my hand. I found my little frying pan and cup. I sat on the floor with my things around me and I waited for Hooper to bring me an answer. She was near. The wind pulled through the room a rustling sound that might have been her skirts. I began to sing, one of the silly made-up ditties we'd sung together in Wales.

'Talk to me,' I said. 'See how warm this blanket is? Feel it. You shall have the blanket tonight and then tomorrow, when you're rested and warm, we'll go on.'

The sky darkened. I opened the window and pulled the curtains as far apart as they would go. I crawled into my silk sleeping bag and slept.

*

There is somebody in my kitchen. Water came from the tap, the pipes hissed and now the kettle is bubbling. Must be Mabel. Her mother did not need her in the end, or she forgot something. She does not want to disturb me. The clock says half past two, a strange time for Mabel to come home. Or it is Miss Cankleton after all. I don't remember hearing her today. She may have been out and come home late, some family emergency or late-blooming love affair I had never imagined. Burglars don't let themselves in with a key and go to put the kettle on so I shan't worry. But just in case my visitor has returned, I'll have the poker on my lap.

Chapter Twenty

It said in *The Times* that Shackleton was planning another expedition, this time to cross the whole of the Antarctic continent with his men. I remembered his glove, still in a drawer. I wished that he had something of mine so that it could travel with him, a handkerchief, perhaps, or my knife. There was still no word of Scott, and Amundsen wrote an account of his journey to the South Pole. He praised the work of Shackleton and said that if he had started at the Bay of Whales instead of McMurdo Sound, he would have reached the Pole himself. In a foolish moment, I wrote a letter to Shackleton and offered the three remaining members of the Society to his expedition. I didn't make it clear that we were women but I did not say that we were men. I signed the names of my friends, above my own, certain that they would come if he asked them to. He would never accept, but I sealed the letter in an envelope and, as I did so, I heard my father's voice.

You see what I meant about that charlatan? His brother is accused of stealing the crown jewels of Ireland. Do you put the honour of the nation and empire in the hands of such a man? Pray God that you never get the right to vote.

I didn't post the letter. I hid it away with the glove and I never mentioned it to Locke or Parr.

Frank and I met one night when all of Dulwich was asleep. I crept out of the front door, bundled up and hidden in a dark shawl, and ran to the end of the street where Frank was hunched on a garden wall, shivering. Without speaking we hurried past gardens, the station and shops, heads bowed, scared and edgy in the quiet city.

A grand house with giant chimney stacks, balconies and long, winding gardens stood at the corner of a small street, near the park. Frank led me to a gap between the fence and the wall. 'I used to play here as a boy with my friends. It's like a forest. No one ever saw us.' He crawled through then held out his hand. I tried to see his face in the dark but could only make out the vast hollows of his eyes, a glint from his mouth. I grabbed his fingers and let him lead me. He pulled me through the leafy corridor, tripping sometimes, on roots and weeds. When we slowed to catch our breath, a tree trunk, knotty and complicated, caught us and I slid my hand around the back of his neck, through his damp hair. He pulled me closer, placed his knee between my legs.

'I can't see your face.' His voice was thick. But I saw his, clearly now. Then, like a blind man, he ran his fingertips over my face, my neck, the loose strands of hair under my shawl. 'Are you too cold? We can go back.'

I rubbed my nose against his. 'I'm not cold enough,' I said.

*

Ah, the cold. Frank, I remember your fingertips, the soft skin between the knuckle and the nail, the way you kneaded my spine. I had forgotten but your hands were often speckled with oil paint, green, mauve and blue. I liked to rub at it with my fingernail.

Scott and his men were dead. It was on the front of every newspaper. I spread the pages out on the dining-room table and read them all thoroughly, though the information was more or less the same in each. It happened just as I had imagined it, as Frank and I had played it by the fire. Three of them, including Captain Scott, stayed in the tent and died there. Titus Oates had left them and died outside in the blizzard. They had fought for the Pole, found that they had lost it, then lost their lives. They had been dead for months. I sat in the garden for an hour, let the cold breeze nibble at my skin. Oates's death made me think of Hooper, weakened and lonely. I never cared much for Scott, out of some sense that he belonged to my father whereas I had Shackleton, but now I cried for him.

I thought again of my night on the mountain when I had become separated from the others and fell. I remembered the strange feeling of being alone with the whole universe, somewhere before birth and after death, and yet alive. It was distant, now, and strange to me, as I had come to think of the whole journey as a prelude to Hooper's death, but it was not like that at the time and need not have ended as it did. I thought of Parr and her

odd way of being our captain. I wondered how Scott and
his men had spoken to each other in the final hours, if they
had spoken. As I asked myself these questions, Hooper fell
and fell, turning, falling further, shrinking up so tiny that
she never had to stop.

'More rest, Mrs Farringdon, and if you feel strong enough
a stroll in the garden once a day but no more. I'll give you a
stronger dose for the pain.'

I was outside my mother's room. The door was an inch or
two ajar and I could see Dr Sowerby standing over the bed,
waving his long, black-sleeved arms around.

'There's something else. I'm worried that my daughter
has lost her mind. She no longer takes proper care of me
and seems to live in a dream. There has been much tragedy,
of course, losing her father and so on, but she is behaving in
a very odd manner. And now I worry that she's going to try
and sell the house with me in it.'

I stepped back a little so that they could not see me.
I had thought that she meant Catherine, of course, until
she mentioned the house. Surely Catherine had not also
thought of selling.

'I'm sure she could not do that.'

'And there are rumours about her – *behaviour*. The
servants were gossiping over the garden fence and I heard
it all. It was shocking. She seems to be meeting somebody
in secret, a man I presume.'

'I had better examine her.'

'I don't want to frighten her, but I worry about the future. If the servants and neighbours are going to talk and what with all the discussion in the newspapers and everybody knowing that she was mountaineering without my knowledge . . . You must be able to prescribe something that would quieten her a little, knock the edges off.'

'If she is suffering a mental disorder, then there are treatments that we might consider but she must see a specialist. A good spell in hospital would certainly be in order. I must say, she struck me as being rather agitated when I last spoke to her.'

'Oh, I hope it will not mean a sanatorium, not for long. I need someone to look after me and we've only got one servant now, but I fear I have lost her anyway.'

'Is your daughter here?'

'I expect she is in the attic being strange. She takes food up there and I hear her bleating away. She was very disturbed after the mountaineering accident and that in itself was a sign that she was already . . . I mean, she is mad, isn't she?'

'I couldn't say without a full examination.'

'No, but now that I think of it, she has been going to pieces for years. Her sister is not much better, but she is a quiet girl who will always find things to do in the home and take flowers to the family graves, so I put up with her. Grace is altogether more alarming. She has a look sometimes, as though she resents me, wants to hurt me, but I'm her mother. It's distressing. It must come from her father's side. His sister was never quite right. I wanted Grace to stay here and help me but if she's determined not to do it, I think it might be better if . . .'

Dr Sowerby came towards the door so I swung back into the alcove on the landing.

'Your older daughter is quiet but has always been so, hasn't she? A docile girl. She is probably affected by her over-excited sister returning with all her demons. I'll come tomorrow morning, so be sure that Grace is here.'

He shuffled downstairs with his bag in his hand, and did not notice me. I packed a few clothes into a suitcase, then added my mountaineering clothes and tent. Parr's broken axe was too long to go in so I wrapped it in a cloth and fixed it to the side of the case with a leather strap. I hurried to the station.

But there is somebody in the kitchen and he – I do not know why but I am sure it is a *he* – has been quiet for some half an hour.

Hello out there. Hello?

Nothing but the drip of the kitchen tap. Yet, if I listen closely, perhaps I can hear something more, a rustle and swish, like somebody turning the pages of a newspaper. If it is the man who jumped over the fence, I could speak to him without telling him anything. I could trust myself to do that, I think. I wonder if I dare ask for a little company in this lonely night.

Chapter Twenty-One

'Grace, this is not the answer.' Frank passed me a towel and called for his housekeeper to bring me tea. My clothes were damp from the rain and I moved closer to the fire. The room was small, packed tight with overflowing bookcases, and smelled of wet sheep. The smell, I realized, came from my woollen shawl. I let it drop to the floor and kicked it under the chair.

'I had no choice.'

'You've the rest of your life to consider. I won't be responsible for ruining you.'

'Ruining me?' As soon as Frank had opened the door, I knew it was a mistake to have come. He had looked down the hall and stairs before letting me into his flat, as though it would be shameful for his neighbours to see me.

'You can stay here tonight, for a few nights if you like, but . . . Have your family discovered the nature of our relationship?'

'No, no. At least, they don't know that it's you.' I ran the corner of the towel between my fingers. I was tired, wet and had to think of something to make him my Frank again. 'I thought we would go away together. You said . . .' I tried to kick my suitcase away from him so he would not see that I had brought the ice axe.

'My dear.' He managed a tight smile, still standing before me. 'One day we shall go away together but I can hardly drop everything and go tomorrow, can I? I'm just beginning my career. I have no money yet. Look how small my rooms are. Look around you.'

His flat was small but very clean and cosy with books and furniture that gave it the mood of an old library. I would have loved such a place.

'No, of course not. I didn't expect that you could leave immediately but—'

'And I didn't expect you to come here. Really, Grace, not when you can be safe at your mamma's house.'

I said nothing.

'You really think she'd let the doctors put you in an asylum? I can't believe it. You must have misheard, or she spoke in a moment of haste. You just have to tell the doctor that you are perfectly well and there is no need for any treatment. He will say that he's glad to hear it and that will be the end of the matter. Grace, I do love you and we'll think of something but, for now, please go home. They don't know you're here, do they?'

I shook my head. 'It was a little hasty, I know, but if you had heard him—'

'So it's going to be the devil of a mess. Perhaps we'll get married one day, but these are not the circumstances in which to make that decision. And, to be honest, I'm rather alarmed by you myself.'

'I wasn't thinking of marriage, just that I could stay here for a while until – I don't know.'

'You haven't given it any thought. How will it look that you just ran off? How will I look? You're giving them grounds for saying that you're mad. Do you understand? You must see reason and go home now, my Grace. If you don't, you may prove that they were right.'

'Of course.' I tried to smile. 'I'm sorry I troubled you.' I blinked back tears and the overwhelming knowledge that Frank did not want me here.

'Look, I have something for you.' He went to his bookcase and took a volume from the top shelf. 'I saw this in the shop and thought of you immediately. I was going to bring it the next time I came to your house but you may as well have it now.'

I took the book. I just had time to imagine what it could have been, the tales, maps, poems, stories that Frank might have thought the perfect gift for me.

It was a textbook for learning Pitman's shorthand.

'I thought that you could study it on your own. You're not going to teach but you need to work and this will give you your way in. Then you can stay with your family but have some routine and a little income and you'll soon be back on the right path.'

I flicked through the pages, a blur of strange symbols and half-written words. Was I supposed to thank him for this?

'I must go,' I said. With the book still in my hand I rushed to the front door.

He offered me his umbrella but I refused it, which was foolish. The rain was harder now. It beat down on Russell Square and the plants in the garden bent and buckled under the weight. I pulled the brim of my hat over my ears as I stood on Frank's doorstep and sobbed. Nobody would hear my pathetic convulsions above the rain and traffic so I wept with abandon.

Locke would be at her parents' beautiful house in Kensington now, or perhaps at the theatre. I blew my nose and wiped my face. Locke would surely let me stay with her but then what? The lights in the houses around the square burned happily away and spoke of cosy evenings, of friends and families around fire. I had no place in London any more and I was no longer sure of my friendship with Locke. If Frank would not travel with me, it was no matter. I had my things for the mountains and I would use them.

Parr lifted a jigsaw piece between her finger and thumb, held it to her eye, then snapped it into place in the puzzle on her table. The picture on the box was something commonplace, a thatched cottage with pink and blue flowers around the door. Her hair hung loose down her back, thick and crimped. Her face seemed a little fatter, more relaxed. There was a faint scent of violets in the room.

When she had done two more pieces, she set the puzzle aside to talk to me.

'I have to place a certain number of pieces before I can allow distractions. It's just the way I've always worked. What's wrong? You're a wreck, Farringdon. Sit down and we'll get you a drink.'

'Parr, let me come with you to South America.' I pulled off my shawl as I sat down. 'I can't pay for the passage yet, but I'll find the money somehow before we leave or, if you could lend me some, I promise I would repay you. It's urgent. I absolutely have to get out of London immediately.'

I explained my predicament and she listened, with quick, impatient nods.

'I'm awfully sorry for you, but I don't see what I can do. I'm leaving next week and everything's arranged. I suppose you could join me there later, if you're desperate to escape, but how will it help? It's just a trip and you'll have to come back afterwards.'

'It will take me away, give me time to decide what to do next.'

'You're too impetuous. You need to find a job, a room to rent, then earn money and establish a life for yourself.'

'But you invited me.'

The doorbell rang and the maid announced a woman's name. Parr excused herself. 'It's the neighbour and she's like a runaway steam engine when she starts talking. I'll keep her in the other room so you don't get trapped with her. Oh, here is my article about our trip. You must read it. I hope it will put paid to the idea that we were naive and inexperienced.'

Parr passed me the journal. A lace bookmark drooped

from the middle. I slipped my finger between the bookmark and the page as Parr stepped into the hall.

The piece started well enough but, as I read further, I became uneasy. Parr's account of our adventure was not at all the way I remembered it and some details were much exaggerated. Her description of the ascent and our night in the storm was barely true. She made it sound as though it was all a disaster with her three helpless companions, and it was she who kept us alive and safe. There was no mention of her fall, of our dispute regarding navigation, or the early signs of Hooper's illness. The final sentences shocked me.

> *Dear Winifred was a truly stoical woman and a*
> *fine climber. I admired her strength and good spirits,*
> *which never failed to cheer us all when the path*
> *was tough. When the accident happened, Hooper*
> *and I were side by side, talking and singing some*
> *Alpine ditty. I tried to pull her to safety but there*
> *was not time and so we lost our dear friend. It is a*
> *small comfort to know that Winifred loved the Alps,*
> *climbed them with passion and delight, and passed*
> *away where she was happiest.*

I let the journal fall to my lap. I swallowed and swallowed and I thought I might be sick. The sweet violet smell was intense now and I put my handkerchief over my nose and mouth to breathe. Parr's account was nonsense. Hooper had been ill and Parr had known it. How could Hooper have sung and talked when she could barely see or hear? Parr had dragged her on and on. We all had. There had been no singing. It was ludicrous. I read the article again and could only think that Parr's intention was to protect Hooper's family, somehow. By suggesting that their daughter's final moments before the accident were jolly and fine, ecstatic even, she might have given them some dry crust of comfort. I blew my nose, rested my head in my hands. Well, it was probably much better for them than the truth. Locke's version would be far worse. Perhaps it was the right thing to have done.

But Parr also seemed to say that she had made some sort of attempt to save Hooper and this was not true. Neither was there any mention of the rope. The night before the accident, Parr had not even wanted to give up the blanket for Hooper. I replaced the bookmark and pressed the journal to my face. I thought it through. Parr had been ill too, that night, and needed warmth. Giving the rug to Hooper would have made no difference in the end.

Parr returned looking pleased with herself.

'Did you like it?'

'This – this is not quite how I remember it.'

'I have lived the moment again and again.'

'But—'

'You were in front. You didn't see.'

'I know but Locke said—'

'*Locke*.' Parr spat out the name like a bad almond and glared at the wall. 'What did she say? It was always you two against me, wasn't it? Your hours of giggling and sniping at my expense, silly girls in your bedrooms with your cocoa and stories. But she's a damned coward if she needs someone to blame for an accident. Let Locke write her own account. She doesn't understand the mountains and she never did. It was something for her to show off about to her theatre friends.'

I nodded. 'I rather wish nobody would write anything at all. It haunts me, Parr. Does it not haunt you? Please let me come to South America so that I can have somewhere to go.'

'Farringdon, you seem very agitated and it's concerning me.'

'I'm not ill. I find myself in a difficult situation this evening and now this—'

'Your hands are shaking. You look – you don't look right.'

'I'm cold and wet.' I clasped my hands together. I could not tell whether or not they were shaking, but my whole body pulsed and I craved fresh air. 'I'll leave. I'm sorry to have disturbed you.'

'If the doctor wants to examine you, you must let him. A stay in hospital might seem frightening but, if the point of it is to treat you and make you better, it is a good thing.'

'I'm leaving.'

'Your family don't know you're here, do they? Have they got a telephone?'

Her voice was cold, malicious, as though she thought she knew best for me when she could not know anything. I took my case and stumbled for the door.

'No, they haven't. And don't you dare, Parr. Don't you dare try to have me locked up. I came here for help.'

Parr followed me outside. She stood on the doorstep,

arms akimbo, and shook her head as though bemused by my strange behaviour.

'You threw yourself at this man who clearly only wanted one thing and now you're running through the streets of London, trying to escape to South America. You really must get a grip. If you can't, then you must get help. And if you can write a better account of our climb, then you are free to do so but this – ' she waved the journal in front of my face – 'this is the truth and it is what the public and Hooper's family want to know.'

'Thank you for all you did for me. I'll manage by myself.' I remembered the axe and unbuckled it from my case. 'I'd like to return this to you.'

'Keep it.'

'I don't want it.'

'I won't take it. You're not being reasonable.'

I struck the axe against the wall of the house, not particularly hard, but a loose piece of brick fell and hit the doorstep. Parr jumped back with a shriek.

'Did you come here to kill me?' She pulled the door to her face, peered through the gap. 'I should call the police. Get away from me.'

I dropped the axe, bewildered.

'Parr? I wasn't going to touch you.'

I play solitaire with Father's old marble set. It was under the settee and I had forgotten about it. A layer of dust has turned it grey. There were mouse droppings in the hollows.

I tipped them onto the floor and kicked them into the grate. The poker is by my feet, but the sounds from the kitchen don't worry me now. Somebody is getting on with his business and it is a comfort to hear. It must have been Mr Blunt after all – perhaps I lost sight of time and he came in once not twice – and is having a little bread and butter before bed. It can be nothing else and I find that I am almost disappointed that there is, really, little possibility of anything worse than my lodger. I make the marbles jump quickly, easily, soon plucking out the jumped ones, filling the ridge around the edge of the board. I remember all the moves from childhood. It is too easy. And there, the last one is out and I have won.

Chapter Twenty-Two

The waiting room at Paddington was almost empty. I sat in a corner with my suitcase and my ticket for the night train to North Wales. Trains screeched and hissed, guards whistled and bellowed as though the world were coming to the end. I felt as though the asylum had already come for me and screaming inmates were attacking me. I pulled my hat down over my ears and kept my head bowed in case they were following me. Dr Sowerby, Parr, Frank, nurses from the asylum, even my mother could be waiting in the shadow of a pillar.

Around me families talked of journeys, friends and luggage. A young man and his sweetheart whispered tense and serious words, but when the girl leaned over to fiddle with the lock of her case, he tried to catch my eye. I pretended not to notice. My dress and suitcase were rather smart and I looked quite ladylike, I was sure, despite my damp hair and shawl. People must think that my chaperone was just around the corner somewhere. Yet I had in my case a knife, a tent and a strong pair of nailed boots. I ached for the mountains and the rough air, nothing else, not even Frank.

I slept well on the train, was woken in the early hours by the guard knocking on compartment doors, shouting that we had arrived in Shrewsbury. I made my request to stop at Ruabon, where I would change for my next train. Shrewsbury was far from home yet still too close. The land wrinkled into thick green hills. Time slowed as the wheels clacked on, and the train curved upwards through fields and forests.

I emerged into a mild, damp day. The edges of the sky blurred the mountains with soft fog. I drew deep breaths as I looked in each direction and wondered where I should go. A few herring gulls stalked the street around the station entrance. I left my suitcase in the station hotel, giving a date for my return but not being at all sure about it. I sent a postcard to Catherine and Mother telling them that I was well and would come home soon. With my knapsack on my back and wearing a long skirt over my mountain clothes, I headed for the hills and the sea.

Was it possible that I was truly alone and could go anywhere I wished? It didn't take long to reach the wilderness. I walked and scrambled all afternoon, slipping sometimes with carelessness but not minding as I became muddy and ragged. I went quickly, as though running to save my life. My breaths were fast and shallow, and seemed to come from somewhere outside me. Sometimes I had to stop still to reassure myself that nobody was running after me.

When the sun began to drop and the rocks and grass lost

their edges, I found a spot with a clear view of the coastline, the mountains, of Anglesey. With the land spread beneath like a map, I was in no danger of getting lost and it didn't matter if I did. I pitched my tent in a sheltered spot and I sat on a flat rock, rough with lichens of white and green. Sheep wailed from each direction, and I watched the world slip down into darkness.

I have never been sure but I think I spent a little more than a week in the mountains. I pitched my tent away from the beaten track and met few people on my way. I listened to the bubbling call of curlews, watched ravens play in the sky, sat on stones with sheep around me and I probably talked to them. When, occasionally, I passed other hikers, I nodded and walked quickly on so that they would not stop to talk or wonder what I was doing out there alone. I had biscuits, small pots of jam, and ate these sparingly. I picked wynberries and chewed them as I walked. I boiled up water for tea. If thoughts of Frank, Catherine or my mother entered my head, I sang to myself until I had banished them.

On the second or third morning, camped up on Y Garn, behind the Devil's Kitchen, I saw a party of boy scouts, winding round the mountainside directly towards my tent. By the time I spotted them, it was too late to move or hide so I gave them a cautious wave as they passed. They regarded me with a certain curiosity but continued on their way. I crawled into my tent to put on more clothes as it was a cold morning, and soon heard childish voices outside. I stuck my head out. Two boys had left the pack and were coming towards me.

'May we see inside your tent?'

'Have you seen Mr Lloyd George? He comes walking round here, we heard, but we haven't seen him.'

They were thin, cheerful boys, both freckled and smiling under their wide-brimmed hats.

I couldn't find my voice at first so my answers came out jumbled and perhaps did not make much sense, but I climbed out and allowed them to crawl in and investigate.

'Do you ever go into the village to have a hot bath?'

'What do you eat in winter?'

I shook my head and laughed. 'I don't live here. No, I live in London, but I just came to think about things and decide what to do for the best.'

'You're on the run, aren't you? Have you killed your husband?'

The boy's eyes glittered and I was tempted to say yes, to satisfy him.

'If you have killed someone,' said his friend, 'we won't tell anyone. We could help you live as a runaway and bring you food and things.'

'No. I haven't killed anybody. It's much duller than that. You see . . . Well, isn't it marvellous here?'

'You could shoot birds and cook them, if you can't go back home.'

'Or sheep.'

'Or boy scouts,' I said.

They soon ran off back to their pack, impressed. I realized

how much I had enjoyed their company and that being alone was to inhabit an entirely different sort of world, one with no edges and no ripples.

It was that evening, a particularly cold night, that I began to hallucinate. I took my veronal, drifted off to sleep and when I woke I thought that I was outside the tent, trying to get in. I went round and round the tent, pulling at it, searching for the opening. When I managed to get inside, I expected to see myself in my sleeping bag but the tent was bigger and it was not mine. There were three men lying in different positions in this large, cold tent. As I stepped closer I saw that their fingers were black, their beards and whiskers were twists of ice.

All the next day I was certain that I had visited the Antarctic during the night. Somehow I had transported myself there and I persuaded myself that this was the power of the mountains. There were moments of clarity, when I laughed at myself for thinking this way and, in these moments, I thought it perhaps best if I did not stay here much longer. Then something would catch my eye – a raven turning upside down in flight or a mountain ash twisted by the wind – and my mind flicked back into its strange state. The following night the vision came again, but there was more detail in it. I could reach out and touch the men, their stiff clothes, frozen books, a torch, a cup. I walked among them, breathed gently onto their faces and tried to coax them back to life. I wanted to talk to them, you see. I wanted it badly. I asked them if they had seen Hooper anywhere because I could not find her. Their skin softened and warmed. The men began to breathe but they did not wake up.

During the days I continued to cross miles of grass and moss, scramble over rocks and along ridges, all the time trying to keep my head clear of home, Frank and my family. At night, the mountains of the Ogwen Valley and beyond became a sort of sea I had to cross in my boat – the tent – to reach the mysterious places where real explorers journeyed and to which I always returned, rocking and cowering in the wind. Daybreak brought me to land at the end of my rough journeys and someone was always there to help me to my feet and embrace me. Sometimes it was Catherine and sometimes it was Locke, Frank, or even Parr. I thought that one night I would use up the whole bottle of medicine in one go – it might be enough to take me on the full journey – but I never reached that night.

Then, one morning, I woke shivering in pale sunshine and knew that I must leave. I didn't know where I was, but I had a clear view over fields of rooftops and a chapel. I had no food left and I didn't want to travel alone any more.

As I rose to my feet to head for the village, and then whatever station was nearest, I began to form a plan. By the time I had retrieved my suitcase and boarded the train to Paddington, I knew what to do. It was a simple plan and it was not exciting but when I thought of the house in Dulwich, the three of us stuck there, miserable and half insane, I knew it would work.

*

A human being has just snored in my kitchen. I'm certain of it. I tiptoe into the hall, past the stairs and push open the kitchen door. A small, plump man is asleep with his head on the table. He snores again, a rumbling that ends with some chewing and a smack of his lips. Dribble trails from his mouth to his wrist. A half-full teacup stands on a pile of papers. He has grey hair and wears a suit and dark overcoat. Beside his polished black shoes is a small, brown suitcase. I watch as his back rises and falls. The air between us wobbles.

I watch him for a moment, wondering whether to fetch Mr Blunt or the poker. The snoring settles into a low purr, and I find that I want to lean forward and stroke my visitor's neck. He seems so tired. I shan't wake him yet but I must find out who he is. I step into the kitchen, reach for his suitcase but it is heavy. He catches the movement. His head lifts, turns, and he squints at me. I draw back.

'Miss Farringdon?' He is hoarse. He swigs the cold tea and clears his throat. 'Please – please don't call the police.'

He has a foreign accent – German, perhaps, or Dutch. I don't know how to tell.

'What . . . ? Who . . . ?' I'm not sure which question to ask first, so I stop and wait for him.

'I'm terribly sorry. I'll – I'll take my things and leave immediately.'

'I'd like to know who you are first.'

'Of course.' He stands, flustered, and gives a light bow. 'My name is Peter Nussbaum. I would have introduced myself this morning if your maid hadn't been so protective of you.'

'You had jolly well better get off my property now, Peter Nussbaum. I know your sort and I don't want you here.'

'Please. I'm not here to hurt you. I would have gone to a hotel, but I couldn't take myself away once I had seen you at the window, and then it was dark and I didn't know my way. It was so very cold sleeping in the garden, so – so – I didn't break any doors or windows to get in. I knocked a few times but you didn't seem to hear and there were no open windows, so I looked around the front garden and found the key under the geranium pot.'

He looks at me with hope and a certain friendliness.

'What do you want?'

The man regards me as though he knows me, indeed, as though he is very fond of me and I am supposed to know it. I squint hard as though this will pull him right into my eyes. A name shapes itself on my tongue.

'Heinrich?' I tilt my head. 'Is it you?'

He smiles, shakes his head. 'Heinrich? No. I'm not he.'

The fire is dying. He brought the cold with him.

'Well, I don't know what to do about this. You can't have the spare bed, I'm afraid. I don't know you and it would be foolish.'

'I wouldn't dream of—'

'It's chilly.' I think for a moment. 'If you want to be useful, you had better fetch more coal and then perhaps we'll sit together a while.'

The request surprises but pleases him. 'Of course. Where is it?'

'Outside the back door.'

'You're very kind. And then may we talk?' He picks up the scuttle and swings it slightly, a playful, uncertain gesture that is almost flirtatious.

'We'll see. I thought you wanted to sleep.'

'But I had hoped to talk to you about Cicely Parr. It's the anniversary of her death.'

'Not yet. Tomorrow is the day.'

He checks his watch. 'It has been tomorrow for more than three hours.' He glances at me but I do not respond. 'The coal.'

Off he goes. Now is my chance. I could wake the house, rouse the neighbours and scream for help. At the very least, I can lock the doors and keep him out. Unless – unless he is my friend. Is it possible that we have met before, that I know him from somewhere? Bring in the coal, Peter Nussbaum, and let me see your face again.

Chapter Twenty-Three

Frank thought that I had thrown myself in the Thames out of love for him. Poor Frank. A few days after our meeting he was kind enough to visit my house in order to reassure himself that I was not in locked up in Bedlam. On finding that I had disappeared, he stood before my mother and confessed to our relationship and final meeting. Catherine lurked behind the kitchen door and listened.

'Is she – in a bad situation?' my mother hissed.

'No.' Frank stopped to think. He reddened and began to stammer. 'At least I – no – I'm sure. I don't know but – I'm – no. No, it can't be that.'

'But why would she have disappeared so suddenly if not? Is it her madness?'

Frank explained that I had overheard her conversation with the doctor and had been frightened.

'But I just wanted some medicine to help her get better. She is ill, as we are all ill in this house. The hospital could have saved her from herself. Great God, I didn't mean to harm her. Dr Sowerby is a good man.'

Fortunately my postcard had arrived the previous day so,

though they did not know my exact location, they knew that I was not at the bottom of the Thames and now they sent Frank packing. Catherine called him a heartless toad and chased him out of the house with a broken umbrella. When she told me this later, it made me smile.

'If you were both in love, why couldn't you have got married?' I knew Mother's next question before she even asked it. 'Was it because of me that you didn't?'

'Or me?' asked Catherine. She seemed puzzled by the whole event and completely cured of her love for Frank, perhaps because she had seen him again and the reality did not match her imagined version, a man who sat beside her on the duet stool and played music all day and night, not some cad who addressed her as though he barely remembered her.

'In the end,' I said, 'Frank did not want it and I don't think I did either.'

'Still, at least he could have hailed you a cab on a dark rainy night like that. It does not reflect well on him that he had to come round here to find out whether he'd left you dead or alive.' Mother fell quiet for a few minutes. 'And I understand, from his response to a question of mine, that he – he took advantage of you on at least one occasion.'

'No. That is not what he did.' I would let her misunderstand me.

'Oh. Then I am greatly relieved to hear it. We shan't speak of it again. And what were you doing in Wales?'

I explained that I had spent a few days alone but did not mention the tent or the outdoors. Even thinking that

I had stayed in a hotel, Mother's case for contacting the asylum was stronger now than ever, but I did not feel ill and nor did I believe that any doctor could make me regret my unexpected trip. Thankfully, Parr had not written to them, so they knew nothing of my attempt to get to South America, nothing of the incident with the axe. None of it mattered now because Mother had finally decided to get better.

'We are a family and we must make the best of things. When you were gone, Grace, I was so worried that we might not see you again. I was very sorry that I had asked so much of you, things I could have done myself.'

We sat around the fire and I put my plan to them. At first Mother thought it unpleasant, unworkable and somewhat disappointing, considering I had announced it with such triumph.

'Lodgers?' she kept saying. 'Sharing our house with strangers to make money?'

'We need the money and it will bring new life into the house. It's a beginning.'

'No, well, I see that we can't go on as we are. At this rate we shall all three end in the asylum or workhouse.' Mother put her feet out to warm them, leaned back in her chair and kicked her slippers off. 'We used to be a happy family. Do you remember the beautiful evenings we shared in this room?'

Catherine jabbed her chin into her hand, rested her elbow on the arm of her chair.

'I don't care if we do it or don't do it,' she said. 'So we may as well. What do we have to do?'

'You'll arrange it all, Grace, but don't give your approval to anybody until I've interviewed them myself. I don't want fallen women or suffragettes here, just quiet and respectable ladies, like us.'

Mrs Delaney and her niece, Miss Porter, moved in a few weeks later. They were the first in a long succession of temporary residents. I like to think of them as forebears of Mr Blunt and Miss Cankleton. Mrs Delaney was a widow in her sixties who knew the neighbourhood well and was already involved with one of the local churches and its various voluntary groups. She visited the library several times a week and had piles of books in her room. She would sit in the bay window with her feet up on the cushion, and read novels for hours a day. Mother liked Mrs Delaney and they often sat together and talked about some item in the newspaper or gossip from the shops. Sometimes they played cards, long games of rummy that lasted until late in the evening.

Miss Porter was a quiet, closed-up woman of twenty-eight. She illustrated story books and was, according to her aunt, very talented. She worked at the desk in her room and sometimes went to meetings in Bloomsbury. Miss Porter's parents lived in the north of England, so it suited her to stay close to her aunt. I tried to befriend her but she was shy and rarely stopped to talk.

With their rent, we managed to pay the bills.

'Everything's going bad in Europe,' said Mrs Delaney one

evening as I took towels to her room. She had a newspaper open on her writing desk. 'It says that there might be war. Then what will happen? Thank God I have a niece, not a nephew. Have you got a young man, Miss Farringdon?'

'No. No I haven't.'

'Neither has my niece, I'm glad to say. Much for the better. But I don't suppose it will be as bad as all that, if it happens at all. Do you see how that window pane rattles when the breeze blows? Do you think you could have it fixed for me, dearie?'

The news didn't seem to have much to do with us any more. Our house was a new landscape now and we explored it with pleasure and curiosity. Mother was cheerful and hardly referred to her illness, beyond a nagging ache or spot of dizziness. Catherine sleepwalked to the piano once or twice and sometimes shut herself away for a few days at a time, but, on the whole, she seemed much happier than before. She often walked in the park or went to visit the family graves, and occasionally came with me to see Mrs Kenny. At home Catherine was quiet but joined us in conversation and sometimes asked Miss Porter about her illustrations. She did not mention Frank any more.

In July or August we left Sarah in charge of the house and took the train to Margate. It was a hot, blue day so we hired a bathing machine and rolled out into the sea, laughing and squealing because we had not done this for years. Catherine and I dangled our legs in the water – it was bracing – then plunged in and swam. Even Mother donned a costume and took a brief dip, in the hope, she said, that it would do her joints and circulation good. This must have been a few weeks before the outbreak of war, but when I try to recall the moment I learned that we were at war, all I see is a very clear picture of the red spotted handkerchief Mother tied around her hair, the white parasols dotted on the sands, and hot, shining people leaning back into striped chairs. All I hear are Catherine's happy giggles and squawks as she waded into the chilly sea. I feel the warm sun on the side of my face and the salty breeze across my back.

We are in the den together, Mr Nussbaum and I. He tips coal into the fireplace. My eyes travel from the top of his head to his feet and I am disappointed to see what was obvious.

'No, you're not Heinrich. Heinrich was tall. He was handsome. Who are you?'

He sits in the armchair, rubs his eyes as though he is as surprised to find himself here.

'Just someone, like you, who has an interest in mountaineering. I own a hotel near Chamonix and I write little articles for newspapers and journals, mostly about the scenery and the weather.'

'A journalist, then.'

He flaps his hand and shakes his head to gesture that I am flattering him. 'A hotelier with a hobby for writing. Just now I'm working on something about – well – about you, and so I decided, quite on a whim, to come and find you.'

'And you broke into my house.'

'I apologize.' He shakes his head, gives me a crinkled smile. 'It is unforgivable, I know. But you are always welcome to come to my hotel and stay as my guest and friend. I invite you.'

'Thank you, but no.'

I wonder if he is real, if I have conjured him from the night with all my memories and nobody to tell. I gesture to the teacups. 'Wouldn't you like something stronger? I once had a bottle of génépi in the cupboard but I expect it has evaporated by now. There is always brandy.'

'Do you still go to the Alps?' His face is strange. There is a smile about his lips even when he doesn't appear to be smiling.

'No, no. I don't go anywhere.'

'It must be boring. You were an adventurer once, a young woman of the mountains. How can you bear to be shut away like this?'

His eyes search my face in a way that feels warm, kind. It is as though he is appraising a long-lost friend or relative.

'It is never dull. Sometimes the walk from here to the kitchen is as fraught as a lightning storm on a mountain peak. I can get as far as the post office down the street but that's my adventure nowadays. I'm not the person I used to be. I've changed. It's just – I am often nervous.'

He nods, full of respect.

'Of course. I understand that. Still, it's a pity to waste time, isn't it? You are hardly old and if there is war—'

'My housemaid is always saying so.'

And I do feel a kind of unrest when I read the newspapers, the sense of distant fires growing and spreading outwards, of cruelty on the march. I have felt it much recently but have not thought to act upon it.

'Winifred Hooper. I wanted to talk about her death first, before Parr's.'

It is a shock to hear Hooper's name. The scene plays again, brighter, worse than I have remembered it for years. Locke, Parr and I are tumbling into the hotel. The soft, smooth boy is at the desk, beside the bell. Then all kinds of people surround us with questions and shouting. We are trapped in noise and nobody is looking for Hooper.

'I shall have brandy,' I say, 'even if you won't. Would you get it from the pantry? I have some sort of paralysis just now and you seem to have found your way around.'

'Certainly.' He trots away for the second time. 'Brandy. I'll fetch it. We don't have to talk about the past if it's painful. I'll just sit quietly with you until sunrise.'

No, no. This familiarity, it is his trick. He is some low reporter pretending to like me, or else he is the sort of murderer who slips into your house and makes a friend of you before he bludgeons you to death.

Part Three

Chapter Twenty-Four

During the first few months of war, we were busy inside the house and I did not pay much attention to the outside. One could not ignore the shops being emptied of food, but we had plenty in the pantry and did not worry too much. I remember a point when the war was all around us but I hadn't seen it arrive. One day there were queues of men at the town hall, the post office. The toy-shop window had filled with dolls in nurses' uniforms, soldiers, guns. Photographs of the king and queen hung in the greengrocer's and butcher's shops. Gradually the streets seemed to empty of the young men I was used to seeing and uniformed soldiers took their places. Mother would scour the casualty lists and read out names she thought we might know or that struck her as being interesting or unusual.

'Here is a Struton in Bristol. Your great-grandmother on your father's side was a Struton and they were somewhere down there. I wonder if we're related. He was shelled, poor man.'

'Frank Black has enlisted,' Catherine told us one day. 'Mrs Black told Mrs Hunt and she said so at the greengrocer's, but I don't know any more than that. He can make a man of himself, if he wants to.'

'I doubt it's true,' I said. 'I don't think Frank is a militarist.'

'That's hardly the point,' Catherine sneered. 'Even a coward like him wants to be a hero now.'

Mother affected not to hear this. 'We must just keep the home fires burning. That's all we can do.'

We knitted socks and helmets for soldiers. The three of us would sit around the fire, working quickly, barely watching our needles or glancing at our handiwork but taking some comfort from the rhythm of the click-clicking. One evening I found that I was absently unravelling the stockings Catherine had just finished. When Catherine realized this, she and I laughed ourselves silly. We giggled and snorted till our sides hurt and Mother smiled uncomfortably as though she could not quite find the joke. Then we began again and settled quietly into the hypnotic work. I tried not to think any more of Frank.

The Ladies' Alpine Club gave up its axes to be melted down into knitting needles and its ropes to be made into bandages. They moved out of their club rooms at the hotel. All the climbers were down from the slopes and mountaineering was over for now. Frank did not write to me and I tried to be glad. I scanned the casualty lists and sometimes forced myself to walk past his parents' house to look for signs of them, some signal that perhaps he was home on leave. I never saw his parents or even a servant about the place. I heard nothing from Parr and did not expect anything. I guessed that she had returned to London, but she might just as easily be tramping across some glaciated peak in Peru.

I remember the hurried note I received from Locke in 1916. She had left the theatre to train as a VAD, but never told me which hospital. She said that Geoffrey and Horace had both enlisted and gone to France. I don't remember writing anything to Locke at this time though I thought of her every day. I'm sure I intended to reply, but I was waiting to learn her new address. I imagined her small, elegant frame weaving between hospital beds, mopping floors, tending to stinking wounds and whispering comfort to frightened men.

Mother and I ran the house together with the help of Sarah and a new cook. Every Thursday Mother went to Father's study with a notebook and a large money box and counted money in and out.

'It is pleasant,' she said to me one Thursday evening, 'to have the house bustling. It has never really bustled before, even when the two of you were children. Or perhaps it did and I've forgotten.'

Miss Porter had put away her illustrations and begun working as a tram conductor. I thought this a wonderful job and so did Mother. Miss Porter arrived home each evening with tired feet and shining eyes. I suggested to Mother that I might look for something similar but she pointed out that I had my work, looking after her and the house.

'You're doing plenty,' she said, 'though you could find more time to improve your knitting. Your attempts at hosiery are not going to win the war for us.'

We grew used to our routine and I cannot say that I was unhappy. I wrote to Locke once or twice at her parents' address but, if she replied, her letters never reached me. I guessed that her parents had moved. In her note she had told me that she would volunteer to work in Belgium. I meant to try harder to contact her parents and find out whether or not she had gone, but I never did it.

Zeppelin attacks destroyed homes, opened them up like twisted dolls' houses, left family belongings shivering and exposed to the neighbourhood. When we passed such houses in London and imagined our own home as a broken carapace, Catherine and I prepared ourselves for losing it. We moved from room to room, memorizing each space, the shapes thrown across the floor by the light, the number of paces from the door to the window, what the fireplace looked like from the door and the window from the fireplace. We reminded ourselves which floorboards creaked when we stepped on them and which snagged our stockings.

'Grace, do you think we should put Father's portrait in the cellar, lest anything should happen to it?'

'But he didn't like it. We shouldn't try too hard to save it.'

'But if he didn't like it, should we ever have left it on the wall in the first place? Should we not have hidden it?'

'I don't know. But then would we be putting it in the cellar to save or to hide it?'

'I suppose we could leave it there. There's not much space in the cellar.'

'Mother thinks that he is keeping us safe.'

We left the portrait in its place.

All our neighbours had lost a son or friend and sometimes it was too painful for them to tell anyone so they put notes through the door. My first big loss did not come until 1917. I received a letter from Mrs Locke telling me that Leonora had caught an infection and died in hospital in London. I fell to the floor with my arms crossed over my ribs, as though a heavy trunk had been dropped onto my chest. It took minutes to remember how to breathe and, even then, I could do little for days. I could not eat nor move about. I could whisper but I could not speak. I went alone to the funeral. Only Hester Morgan and Edith Foot were there from our college days. There was no mention of any play that Locke had been writing, or of our Alpine disaster. She had, apparently, devoted herself to her voluntary work and intended to qualify as a nurse and make it her career after the war. Morgan told me that when Locke first helped to save a man's life she felt redeemed in some way, released from her guilt. The memory that came to me most was of our first meeting, in the corridor on our first day at university, when she called out my name and smiled. I was sick every night for a week but I was unable to cry.

*

The next one came soon after. Frank died in a hospital in France of trench fever. Catherine heard it from his parents, who never knew about Frank and me. An explosion resounded in my ears when Catherine told me and did not die down, like a fire that roared and roared. We didn't find out exactly where or when he'd died. I could have read the newspaper but I did not want to know.

'But he came home a few months ago on leave,' Catherine said. 'He was at his parents' house so they were glad at least that they had seen him. That's what they told me. They seemed utterly destroyed so I can't believe it gave them as much comfort as all that. I suppose it might in time. I had no idea he was here a few months ago, just round the corner from us.'

'Catherine, shut up.'

Catherine played the piano deep into the evening and through most of the night. All I had from Frank was the Pitman's shorthand book. It had somehow survived my week on the mountains in Wales and was in my room, unread. I wanted to burn it – what an inappropriate token of our passion – but could not.

In the midst of this, or somewhere behind it, Shackleton and his men were missing. By the end of that year they had not returned and there was no word of the *Endurance*. I looked out for news in the papers, but it didn't matter to me as it would have mattered a year earlier. It was as though the explorers had fallen out of life, come too late to do their job, and history had simply pushed them down and buried them before they had quite finished. It didn't seem likely that they could come back now. Where would they fit?

Oh, what have you seen, Father, with eyes that search and always find us? Did you know that I would never leave, that I will probably die here in this room? Do the years fall out in order for you or do you see and hear it all at once? Perhaps Catherine is playing for you now and I am in the cosy corner seat and then Mrs Horton comes in with cocoa. Perhaps, for you, it is in layers, or all present in one moment, say the moment you died getting out of this chair and you are getting out of it to die, even now. Can it be true that Frank and I made love right here, under your shiny oil-paint eyes, with my mother upstairs and my sister nearby? And yet I do remember it. I giggle, cover my mouth so that my visitor does not hear.

Chapter Twenty-Five

I received an invitation to a talk at the home of a Mrs Gertrude Belcher by the renowned lady mountaineer, Cicely Parr – 'Peru Calling: One Woman's Journey into the Andes'. The Ladies' Alpine Club no longer had official premises but, it seemed, members had unofficial at-home gatherings with speakers. The invitation must have come from Parr as I did not know any other members. I took the card into the garden, read it several times. I was curious to know about Parr's adventures, but I wondered if I dared go.

Mrs Belcher's drawing room was vast, with seats for twenty or thirty people. I positioned myself to one side, near the door. Parr noticed me, just as she took her place to speak, and she gave a cautious nod and smile. She spoke very well, with a lightness and warmth I would not have expected. She even laughed several times, without any obvious effort. She made an amusing comment about the state of her bloomers after losing her footing and sliding down a wet, muddy hill. She showed us the mark on her hand where she had lanced and cut out an infection with her knife. She told us how the Peruvian expedition had almost ended in disaster as most of the climbers' equipment shot away down a smooth slope of ice. I watched, astonished, as Parr enjoyed the attention, the admiring smiles.

'It might as well have been a precipice, such were our chances of getting anything back. And it was partly my fault.'

She had changed indeed.

'But I managed to save the hypsometer from a fall and so we were able to measure the height, even if we then had to hurry down as we had little to eat and little to protect us from the wind. The Indian porters were camped on the foothills and helped us set up camp. Fortunately they had looked after our gear well and stolen nothing – I had been warned to expect otherwise, you know – and we were all delighted with ourselves.'

As she was leaving, I caught up with her. It was beginning to rain outside and was turning dark. We put on our coats and hats, set off together along the pavement.

'Farringdon, I trust you're not going to run at me with an axe, or perhaps you've come to suggest that I forged the details of my own expedition. No doubt you were there with me and helped me to the summit while I wasn't paying attention.'

'No. You're a brave climber and a good speaker. I wanted to ask if we could forget all the other business, if you would forgive me for upsetting you.'

'Thank you. Yes, thank you.' She nodded, solemn and

understanding. 'You seem more yourself than before, I must say. I wasn't sure whether or not to invite you but, then, I thought that if you were still mad, you wouldn't have come anyway, would you?'

'But I wasn't mad.' I tried to make my voice light, as though the question of my madness were a silly joke.

'Remember how unstable you were the last time I saw you? I really thought you'd cracked up and lost yourself for ever.'

'But I hadn't.'

'You and Locke always wanted to blame me, as if I had made Hooper fall on purpose. Hardly surprising that you went mad. Did you have treatment?'

'Parr, stop it. I did not go mad and I never shared Locke's opinions.'

'You came at me with my axe, remember? Struck the house with it. I was terrified.'

'I tapped it against your badly built wall, that's all. You know it.'

We reached the stop where Parr would catch her tram. I waited with her and we talked about Locke, about the war and when it might be over. The tram rattled in, spattered dirty rain on our skirts. A few soldiers jumped off and hurried away through the gloom. One bumped into Parr and apologized. She pushed past him and hopped on board.

'It's dark so early these days, isn't it? Goodbye then.'

She moved further into the tram and did not look back.

I wondered why she had bothered to invite me to her

talk. Locke would say it was because Parr wanted to boast about her success and see me envy her. If this was true, she had succeeded in some respects. I watched the tram drive off and felt the usual muddle of fear and awe, and had the strong sense that, despite everything, I would not want to be her.

I used to go to the stations and watch people arrive and leave all day. Waterloo, Victoria, Paddington. I'd find a seat and listen to the trains and the voices. I liked to see couples who might have been Frank and me. I'd follow them sometimes towards the platforms and try to catch their conversations. I'd walk home late in the evening, exhausted, and I'd think about what I would say to Locke about it all. Sometimes I saw people I recognized but I never spoke to them. I made vague plans for after the war, but mostly I felt that if it were ever to end, I would just rest. I would want to sleep. We would all want to sleep, I thought. Until then, I would continue in a state that was somehow both frantic and numb. Even at the stations, I did not wander aimlessly. I would make lists of the kinds of people I had seen, the soldiers, Girl Guides, schoolchildren, men with flat caps and women with fur stoles. I listed and categorized the outfits they wore. I counted the tickets as the clippies punched them. I thought that I would, one day, find the courage to ask for a job like this myself. Knitting and housekeeping did not keep me busy all the time, but I had lost my nerve.

I would go home and help the cook with dinner. I would

watch Catherine knitting, unable to concentrate on work of my own. The lodgers moved around the house, sometimes closing a door or scuttling over floorboards. I took Father's maps from their box and I imagined journeys through France, Belgium, Turkey, Germany. I sat by the globe and let it spin and spin. I measured distances with the nail of my middle finger (half an inch) and spent the evenings adding up measurements and comparing them, for no reason at all except to keep my head full.

Peter appears with two glasses of brandy, presents one to me. He slips into the hall and returns with his little suitcase. The brandy is good. I used to rub it into my feet to soothe them. Now it warms my throat and I think it will help me with Peter, with conversation. He settles under the lamp, takes a pile of papers from his case and sorts through them. It is some sort of typed manuscript and he shuffles the leaves, stacks them neatly with a certain fuss, as though they make him proud.

His eyes flick around the walls of my room. He makes a few notes on a slip of paper.

'You hide in your dark, dusty house. I can understand it. I left my village three days ago and already I'm homesick. I don't like the city at all. I would have been very lonely in a hotel tonight.'

Peter puts on his spectacles and studies his documents. I don't feel afraid. In fact, I like him being there but I won't hurry. I have papers of my own.

Chapter Twenty-Six

Dear Catherine,

    I was sorry to learn George had passed away. Please
accept my deepest sympathy. I have missed you very much
and was excited to hear that you are planning a trip to
London soon. I should so like to see you. Wouldn't you like
to visit me here in Dulwich and see the house again?
I have kept it just as it was when you left, but it has
always seemed incomplete without you. If you don't like it,
we can make any changes that suit you.

    I am sure that you know this already but I want to
tell you again. The scandalous stuff in the newspapers was
all untrue. It was based on gossip and a misunderstanding.
I realize that it was difficult for you because of the attention
from the newspapers and having to worry about George's
public reputation, but those people hardly bother me now
and they certainly would not trouble you. I think I am
largely forgotten so there is no need to be concerned about
all that. I am rather reclusive these days. I am sure that
few people know I am here.

    Write soon and tell me what you think.

      Your loving sister, Grace

It might do the job. I have written so many times I can no longer guess what will work best.

Just after Armistice Day, Mother caught influenza and was in her bed for a week. Dr Sowerby spoke to Catherine, for I refused to see him, and warned her that young, healthy people were vulnerable to this virus and that we must be careful. We took no notice, sat with her every day and we were fine. It was very different from the last time Mother was ill. *I hope I get better. I was enjoying myself,* she said in a small voice. *I'd just started to live again.* Then she seemed to recover a little, was able to come downstairs and sit with us for an hour or two one evening. She complained about the dreary colours of her bedroom so Catherine and I went to the shops the following day for curtain material. For some reason Mother decided to go into the garden while we were gone, perhaps to see if she was well enough for a stroll and some fresh air. Mrs Delaney looked out of her window to see Mother slumped on the garden seat, her neck uncomfortably twisted. The neighbours' cat perched on the arm of the bench, put its head forward to sniff at her face and she did not move. Rheumatic fever had weakened her just when her spirit was strong again. Catherine and I slept in Mother's bed that night top-to-toe and, in the hours when we could not sleep, we whispered memories and held each other for comfort.

We buried our mother in the churchyard, with Father

and Freddie, and spent the next days sitting in the garden because we could not stand to be in the house.

Catherine and I continued to take care of the lodgers and, after a year or so, I began to teach the odd class at my old school. Our schoolfriends were beginning to travel again, going to tea dances, cutting their hair short and throwing their corsets to the wind. We did not do these things. We had no part in this new London but stayed in the safety of our home. Routine had got us through the war and routine would keep us going. For a while we wanted nothing more. We took an extra lodger and gave the cook her notice. Sarah came every day and we employed a new girl, Mabel, to help on laundry day.

Frank came to my bed most nights. I would lie with my back to him until I felt the mattress tilt and then I waited for him to wriggle a little and get comfortable. His feet were always freezing and I would say, *Don't touch me with those feet until you've kicked the ice off.* He would laugh and put his arm around me, let his hand rest on my hip. I would tell him what I had done that day, the little incidents at school or at home. He listened and smiled. I would check his fingers for flecks of colour, to see that he had been painting. Then he would tell me about his life and this would coincide with my medicine having its effect and so his stories would be strange and wild. I would fall asleep no longer thinking of him but heading off for a distant, stormy slumber. With Frank at night, there were no questions. During the day I asked myself why he did not write to me.

I thought that Catherine and I would live like this for the rest of our lives, and consider ourselves fortunate. Four years passed where nothing much happened and then I discovered that Catherine was paying visits to Dr Sowerby. I saw her enter his surgery one morning when I was walking to school. Later, when I asked about her day, she said that she had not left the house. I began to watch her and saw that she was seeing him once a week or more. I feared that she was gravely ill and looked around the house for medicines or some clue. I searched the bathroom and her bedroom, even looked under the piano lid and inside the stool, but found nothing.

'Are you all right, Catherine?'

'Yes, why not?'

'You're not injured in any way?'

'No.'

'Or ill?'

'Why? Are you going down with something? I thought you seemed pale.'

The following afternoon, Catherine announced her engagement to Dr Sowerby. I was in the dining room planning meals for the following week.

'I know you're surprised and you don't really like him, but he wants me to be his wife.'

I gazed at her and this time I knew that it was true.

'Do you love him? He's rather old, isn't he?' Dr Sowerby's nasty, cold voice murmured near my ear. I saw his heavy black suit, his plodding gait as he trundled up and down our path. I could not imagine how they had come together, had any sort of conversation that could have led to a proposal.

'Don't envy me, Grace. He's a husband.'

'If it's what you want, then of course I'm glad but—'

'He'll look after me and you can have the house to yourself. I just want not to be in it any more. I'm so thirsty for something different—'

Dr Sowerby had known Catherine and me since we were children, but his Catherine was a mild and demure knitter and pianist, not the wild, confused girl we knew in private. Catherine was much better nowadays, since Mother's death, but she was not properly connected with herself or things around her. She was capable of sitting on the front-door step for three hours or more, looking into the sky, then denying that she had ever been there. She looked after the lodgers but never found work outside the house because she was not able to keep time or talk much to strangers.

'As long as this isn't some trick of his to have you locked away in some dark institution, I'm happy for you.' I took her hands and squeezed them. 'At least you'll be nearby.'

'He says he never wanted to lock you away, just help you get better from your illness. No, but we're going to live in Edinburgh in a year or two. Is that – is that all right? He's retiring and wants to live there near his brother. He says it's beautiful. I want to go so much.'

'Of course you must go. You don't have to ask me.'

I continued with my list. Asparagus, sausages, sugar,

ham, biscuits, mustard, stout. I must ask Sarah to finish clean-
ing Mother's room and move her things up to the attic.
We also needed soap and salt and vinegar. I scribbled the
words onto the paper as panic rose in my throat. Edinburgh?
Catherine had hardly been outside London. And to go so
far with such a man?

A lodger banged a door upstairs and a crackle ran down
through the walls. Sarah was cooking and the place smelled
of cabbage. Everything was rotten and I was still here.

'Grace?'

I turned. Catherine leaned against the door, wrapped her
fingers around the doorknob. She seemed so young, not a
woman of thirty-seven but a girl of eighteen or twenty. Our
lives had gone back to front. I had given up on doing much
with life, whereas Catherine was still waiting for it to begin.

'Will you be all right?' I asked.

She nodded.

'You've been steadier since Mother went, happier. What
if such a change has a bad effect?'

'It just – just seems as though I might as well. I think
I could be better in a different house with new things
around me.'

'I suppose you can only find out by doing it. Then we
must celebrate.'

We dined that night on oysters in aspic and sirloin steak.
We discussed Dr Sowerby. Catherine would not agree that
there was something sinister about him but did not claim
to love him either. Nonetheless, we had a glass of sparkling
wine and toasted the news.

'Such good fortune.' She made a pile of salt at the side
of her plate and swirled a pattern in it with the prongs of
her fork. 'I want it to be a beautiful house with gardens and
flowers. I want views of the city from the bedroom windows
and space for me to have lots of gowns and hats.'

'And George?'

'He'll play golf and go walking in the hills. We'll get
along.'

Catherine lay on the settee reading a serialized story about
a young woman and her romance with a cheerful, whistling
Tommy. She had a bag of peppermint lumps on her lap
and ate them one after another. I sat in Father's chair and
opened the newspaper. My eyes fell on a familiar name that
immediately made me think of Father.

'Good lord,' I said. 'The younger Peter Taugwalder is
dead.'

'Who?'

'From the Whymper expedition. The son of the older
Peter Taugwalder, who was also there. He climbed the
Matterhorn a hundred and twenty-six times in the end,
according to this. And I never did it once.'

'Do it now then. Why don't you write to Cicely Parr
and go together?'

'No, no.' I smiled. 'You have no idea. It's much too
difficult for me. I've had no practice.'

'Being married and living in Edinburgh is difficult and
distant but I'm going to do it.'

'Even the easy mountains seem distant now.'

'In that case, climb the easier mountains, but do it. Go to the Alps again.'

Parr's reply arrived a few days later. She would come with me and it would be a delightful way to remember dear old Locke and Hooper. I showed the letter to Catherine at breakfast.

'Look. I wish I hadn't had the idea now. I haven't spent time with her for years. I can't imagine how we'll get on. We still haven't quite sorted out that business of her wall and the ice axe.'

Catherine buttered her toast neatly, licked the knife.

'If she's unbearable you can always push her off the top. No one ever need know. Doesn't that sort of thing go on all the time on expeditions? Everyone must hate each other after a few days, even if they didn't to begin with. I say it's best to be with someone you dislike in the first place. You have less to lose. Would you pass the treacle?'

I tightened the lid, turned the tin onto its side and rolled it along the table to Catherine.

'Good shot.' She caught it without a blink, opened it and dropped a large pool of treacle onto her toast. 'We're orphans, so we can make our own adventures and nobody can stop us.'

Catherine replaced the lid and sent the tin rolling back to me. She rested her elbows on the table and, from somewhere, my mother's voice came to me.

'What's on the table gets carved, Catherine,' I said.

Catherine laughed. 'But I'm going to be Mrs Sowerby, the doctor's wife. You can't tell me anything.'

Peter leans towards me. 'When I read through my notes and look at you now – I – well, all I can say is that it's a huge honour to be sitting here with you. Of course, one can easily see why the trauma has affected you this way.'

'I expect one can.'

'To be involved in two Alpine deaths. Tragic.'

'An awful coincidence, when you look at it that way.'

'Too much misfortune for one climber.'

'I have always felt that.'

'Unless, of course, there was a connection between the two.'

'I have explained so many times why that is nonsense. One accident and then another, separate accident. Among mountaineers, it's not such a strange thing, as well you must know.'

He takes a clean sheet of paper from the bottom of the manuscript and notes down our conversation in scratchy pencil. An image flashes up and replaces him for less than a second, but it is vivid. It is the boy from the Monte Rosa Hotel, writing something at the desk in the lobby. The same forehead, eyes, mouth.

'You should learn Pitman's shorthand,' I tell him. 'Peter, have we met before?'

He lifts his head and his glasses do a little bounce on his nose. 'Do you think it is possible?'

'Perhaps you have always been in the hotel business?'

He raises an eyebrow. 'You mean—'

'The Monte Rosa Hotel in Zermatt. You were the young boy who comforted us when Hooper was dead, but we never knew your name.' I am excited now and my voice sounds loud and high. 'You were always in the lobby when we came and went. I know it.'

'Yes.' And he could be lying but I'm sure he is not. 'Yes, you're quite right. Well done. I worked there and I've never forgotten the tragedy, as you can imagine.'

'Why didn't you say so?'

'I never expected you to remember me and, if you did, I thought you wouldn't believe me.' He blushes to the roots of his hair. 'And – this will seem strange to you since I let myself into your house without invitation – I'm rather shy.'

'You were shy then, too.'

Oh, this is good. It is good to have Peter here with me.

'Such old, old memories. Now, Miss Farringdon, I want to know more about Winifred Hooper. Do you have any photographs of her?'

I pass him the box of pictures I have been saving for tonight. Winifred is at the top.

Winifred Hooper. Your body was half-covered in snow when they found it. The men who carried you down were weeping tears through streams of sweat. You were all wrapped up in a blanket, the roundness of your head, like the end of a ninepin, not you now and that was what I couldn't understand. The sky lowered and pressed me into a bubble that bounced and floated silently while, in a different world, people screamed. The horror is fresh. I thought I would never climb again or even see another mountain but, of course, in the end, one has no choice.

Chapter Twenty-Seven

The Ladies' Alpine Club had moved back to its premises at the Grand Central Hotel after the war. In 1922 the Club had hosted a dinner in honour of the first British Everest expedition and all the members of the expedition attended. Parr said that there were speeches of knights in the Age of Chivalry and it was a most convivial, romantic evening. Everyone hoped and believed that the party would triumph but they did not. Mallory was to make his third attempt the following year.

We sat at a cosy table beneath paintings of mountains and carefully hung ice axes. It seemed wonderful to be a member of the club, to be able to walk in and out as a proper mountaineer, to greet people you knew from expeditions and to make great plans. A portrait of Queen Margherita of Italy, the club's honorary president, hung on the wall and I glanced at her every now and again, as though I could somehow make her aware of me, earn her respect.

Parr's face was sunburnt. Her skin was red and in places beginning to peel and detach itself, like a carpet coming up at the edges. Her hair, now cut into a sharp bob, made her younger, somehow brighter.

'How are you?' she asked.

'I have been well. And you?'

'Yes, the same.'

The waitress placed the tea strainer over my cup and poured. Parr rubbed the skin under her right eye and tiny peelings balled on her cheek.

I smiled. 'You've been climbing recently.'

'Mont Blanc. I was in the Alps just weeks ago and the weather was good so we decided to do it. I have a new guide, recommended to me by friends. He's called Heinrich and we get along so well I wouldn't consider anyone else now.' She turned to the waitress, pushed her cup aside. 'It's too strong. Could you tip this away and bring me another? And we'll have some cake. Now what do you want to do, Farringdon? What was your idea when you wrote to me?'

'I'm not sure. You see, I may have been indoors too long to be any good now but—'

'You've certainly put on some weight.'

'I know. And yet I do want to climb again.' I leaned towards her. 'I want to do it for Locke and for Hooper and my friend Frank. Well, for all of us.' My voice cracked and my nose felt hot. I grabbed my teacup, took a gulp but it all went wrong and I was coughing and crying at the same time.

'Farringdon, what on earth is happening to you?'

I pointed at my throat and reached for my napkin.

'Are you all right?'

I nodded, caught my breath and wiped away the tears.

'Farringdon, I want to say something. I'm awfully sorry about that business with Hooper and my article.' She leaned forward and her hair swung about her chin, shrinking her face. She looked directly into my eyes. I felt embarrassed. 'I apologize for writing about it so badly.'

'I'm afraid that you did but, I must say, it's a relief to hear you say so.'

I found myself gazing at the nose of someone in the doorway. It seemed familiar but then it blurred.

She nodded to herself. 'I remember telling you once, I'm not good at knowing the best things to say sometimes but I've learned a bit. I was trying too hard to make a name for myself and needed to dispel the idea that we were naive schoolgirls, so when the journal asked me to write something—'

'Never mind.'

'But you hope to climb again and that's good because I have a great plan.'

'I just want to go back to the Alps and say goodbye to Hooper, make my peace with the mountains.'

'Yes, yes, but you won't say that when you get to the Alps. I'm not thinking of Mont Blanc, of course.'

'Good, I was thinking of a quick visit to Zermatt and then head for Italy and perhaps the Dolomites—'

I said this because Parr had taken over. I had not actually given much thought to specific peaks. Indeed, the mountains I had in mind belonged to some fantasy range based vaguely on what I had seen and climbed before.

'If we have time, I suppose, but that's not why we're going.'

'But I particularly hoped to climb in Italy. I've read that the scenery is beautiful and I've always wanted to visit Italy.' I meant to stand up for myself.

'No, no. I have something much better.' Parr clapped her hands together in front of her mouth. 'We're going to climb the Matterhorn.'

I was so surprised that for a moment I could not make any sense of the word. *Matterhorn*.

'We always planned to do it, didn't we? Heinrich and I have been talking about it for some time and when your letter came, it was perfect.'

'Oh no, Parr. You overestimate my ability. You go up with Heinrich.'

'But Heinrich won't come with us to the summit. Plenty of women have climbed and traversed the Matterhorn but there has never been a manless ascent, so he'll be our porter as far as the ridge. He'll bivouac with us the night before and then you and I shall make the ascent by ourselves. Heinrich will watch us through his binoculars, if he can. It's a very small piece of mountaineering history, the sort I thought you wanted.'

'I did, but—'

'It's more than fifty years since Lucy Walker reached the summit and that was only six years after Whymper. Everyone has been going to the Alps since the war ended and they're taking bigger risks than ever before. There'll be nothing new for us to do soon. Even Everest is about to be taken. Start preparing now and we'll go in June or July. We'll have a few weeks there so you can take in some lower ascents first, find your feet.' Parr tilted her head, scratched her nose and cleared her throat. 'I'm trying to make amends. Do you see?'

'I do and I'm more relieved than I can tell you.'

I had an income now from my teaching, as well as the money from the lodgers. It wasn't much, but there was also the possibility of selling the house and moving somewhere smaller when Catherine married.

'Dig out your equipment, Farringdon, and go walking every day. Up and down the stairs with bricks in your knapsack. Grease your boots and wear them around the place so you don't get blisters.'

'Parr, wait . . . I might not be ready for Zermatt. The memories—'

'This tea is much better. I can drink boiled string on the mountains, but in the club it's really another matter. You still have your things?'

'I do.' I decided to purchase a new axe so that we would not have to mention the old one.

My eye wandered again to the woman in the corner. The sight of her rigid black jacket and graceful posture pulled me back to the corridors at Candlin College, the murmur of young women's voices and sweet floor-polish smell. I took in her silhouette, the sharp nose and drooping eyes.

'I say, Parr, isn't that Hobson?'

Parr craned her neck, gasped and turned back. 'I think it is. And those are the Dalton sisters, who are going to climb in the Dolomites this summer. I've met them. Well, that does it. You can't think of going to Italy now. She might be going with them.'

'We'd never bump into her.'

'Of course we would. We'd be crossing a glacier and she'd pop up out of a crevasse in her black coat. She'd have us processing up the mountain in a line behind her, ringing a bell and saying grace before cocoa.'

I laughed and bowed my head lest Miss Hobson should see us. 'I'm still scared of talking to her. Who knew that she was a mountaineer?'

Miss Hobson left without noticing us and Parr waved to the Dalton sisters, Anna and Elizabeth, who were aged between twenty-five and thirty and reminded me a little of Catherine and myself. They resembled each other in appearance – dark hair, long fine-boned faces – but the older one had a distant, mystical quality, as if she might walk off into the broom cupboard and not notice, were her sister not there to watch her. They came and spoke to us for a few minutes and Parr told them our plans. They shook my hand and wished me the best of luck.

I marched up and down the stairs that evening, with a knapsack of coal on my back and my old boots on my feet. Catherine played Telemann fantasias and the music followed me up and down until I was dizzy.

Some mountaineers are peak-baggers and some are wanderers. The great mountaineers fall out, get on each other's nerves, send unsatisfactory companions packing or storm off home themselves. They sometimes give accounts that their fellow climbers will dispute. The truth, like bones in a glacier, may fall out one day or in hundreds of years, or never. Parr and I had no reasons to argue any more. We knew what we wanted and with us we carried the young ambitions of our two friends. Precisely because we knew already what it was to hate each other, we understood that we would be good climbing partners.

Peter sorts the pictures into piles and begins referencing and cross-referencing in a small notebook. He is absorbed in this work that seems to focus on Winifred Hooper. I don't know why he cares so much. What is there to lose if I trust him? I am already a recluse and people who know anything about me assume the worst. I could use him to clear my name. As I watch him write, I wonder why I did not see it sooner. Under the papery layers of the adult Peter, there is the brown-haired boy, around him the gentle glow of the Monte Rosa Hotel lobby.

'Did you work at the hotel for many years?'

'No. I left a year or two after the accident and went to work in a bank in Geneva. I saved up enough money to buy a small hotel in the countryside, but I didn't want to return to Zermatt so I moved to France. Accidents happen everywhere, of course, and I have lost guests to the mountains around Chamonix. It's always terrible but, as an adult, I can accept that it is inevitable. I was too young when the first tragedy occurred and it haunts me in a strange way. It has a heaviness that has never lifted.'

Peter writes and writes, sometimes stopping to suck the top of his pen, scratch an arm or leg. I have slept for an hour or so and am refreshed. No dreams about the Matterhorn tonight.

I take a candle from the mantelpiece and light it for Cicely Parr. I place it just beside the globe.

'What's that for?'

'Nothing. Just a candle.'

When Catherine comes, I'll make sure that everything is just right so that she will want to stay the night. I'll put silver candlesticks on the piano top and pour glasses of wine, dark as black vanilla orchids. Once we are squiffy, we shall begin to forget the years.

Dear Catherine

I can't wait until you are here! Everything is so much better than I thought it would be. I am recovering from the past and I long, yes, long, to tell you all about it.

Hurry up! We shall have fun.

Your Grace

Chapter Twenty-Eight

We got along well in Zermatt. That is not to say that we spoke very much to each other beyond simple conversations about what we needed to do, but that we walked together without much need for words. We had a comfortable familiarity and required nothing more. We stayed at the Riffelalp Hotel, in pine forests high above the village, so were away from the Monte Rosa Hotel and people who might remember us. When we went into Zermatt and had to pass the old hotel, we fell quiet or found some interesting new topic to distract us. The Breithorn was visible on clear days, but the sight was not as painful as I had feared it would be. The peak was white and pretty. I could imagine Hooper wandering up there by herself, listening for ice cracking in the night and descending to lower ground where forests might keep her warm and safe.

We walked and climbed with pleasure. It was hard work for my legs, at the beginning, and I often stopped, halfway up a hill, to lean against a tree and catch my breath. On the lower slopes, tiny purple butterflies like parma violets danced around us. We saw ibex, nutcrackers and all kinds of pink and lilac flowers. I noticed dark purple, almost black flowers that I did not remember from before and Parr told me that they were black vanilla orchids. I picked one to press and take for my mother's grave.

Heinrich met us on the second or third day and took us on the higher ascents. I was concerned that I was not fit enough for these, but I pretended otherwise and simply continued to put one foot in front of the other, no matter how sore or heavy they felt, and I progressed. We traversed the Monte Rosa and I smiled almost all the way. A proper mountain, with several peaks, and the second highest in the Alps. I could now call myself an Alpinist, surely. My arms and legs had not forgotten how to do it. Indeed, it seemed as though the memory was held entirely within my limbs and I was stronger than ever. Each time the sun came out or a fresh gust of breeze caught me, I wanted to laugh. I ached, of course, after the first few days, but it passed or I stopped noticing.

Heinrich was a calm, quiet man of twenty-seven from Zermatt. He was quite tall, slim with sandy hair and freckles. His leather hat would slip over his eye as he walked and he would flick it up with his thumb and forefinger. He had a cheerful, joking manner, especially at the beginnings and ends of the day when he was garrulous with plans and observations. During the middle part of the day, he liked to walk quietly and speak only when instruction was needed. He had climbed all over the Alps and in North and South America. He claimed that he was descended from famous guides, many of whom had made historic ascents and some who had died on the mountains. He and Parr walked side by side as we set out each day and returned, sharing Alpine gossip, sometimes teasing each other. No, I am wrong. Parr did not know how to tease. Heinrich teased Parr, and she enjoyed it, is what I should say.

'Miss Parr does not smile when she climbs. It uses muscular energy and is terribly inefficient.'

She laughed despite herself.

'Aha. The smile makes her blush and the blush warms up her face. It is a heating system. Now I understand.'

Parr shook her head, still smiling, and walked on.

Heinrich let Parr lead some of the climbs so that we would be confident on our own. He watched closely as she cut steps, tied on and off the rope, navigated on treacherous terrain, all of which she could do well. Parr demonstrated her skills with patience, never showing the irritation of her younger self. I had much still to learn but I worked hard and kept a good pace. Parr was pleased and we would both remark on what a good team we were, just the two of us with our guide.

'What do you think, Heinrich?' I asked at the end of our second week. 'The Matterhorn is not appearing any smaller, or less deathly, no matter how much I practise.'

Heinrich wrinkled his face and gazed at the sky. 'Just depends on the weather now. Don't worry, the peak looks steeper from down here.'

'Not so much so, I hope. I want it to be difficult after all.'

'It will be hard, but not impossible. We need to spend

more time on your rock-climbing skills and then you should rest for a day or two.'

Heinrich planned to be the first to scale the Matterhorn's north face. It looked to me like certain death, a dark wall of rock and snow rising from the Zmutt Valley, but Heinrich would go out in all weathers to study the shape and angle on each part of the ascent, possible routes, the way it looked in every kind of weather.

'It's the last Alpine problem,' he told me. 'And when we solve it, there'll be another last Alpine problem. And my grandchildren and great-grandchildren will be worrying about another yet Alpine problem.'

I liked to sit by a window in the hotel and draw the outline of the Matterhorn from memory, then turn my head to compare. It was easy enough to sketch an outline that was recognizable, immediately, as the Matterhorn, but I never got the proportions right so that my version was always too thin, too wide or too steep at the top.

I knew that Frank would be proud. Frank would have loved the Alps and would have wanted to climb high. We would have bivouacked in a Mummery tent and curled into each other for warmth. On a high, flat rock, we would dangle our legs, share bread and see the clouds change shape and colour.

Come down, O maid, from yonder mountain height, whispered Frank, and I smiled.

Still, I was here with Parr and this was quite a different

experience. We made our plan and discussed it with Heinrich. Parr and I would climb to the hut, spend the night there and start our ascent in the earliest hours before, we hoped, most other climbers. We wanted the mountain to be ours that day and told Heinrich not to oversleep but to get up soon after us and have his binoculars ready. We would wave our hats when we reached the summit so that he would be sure to see us. The weather forecast was good.

The incident was in all the newspapers, of course. They compared it with the Whymper tragedy, though it was not the same at all, and they recounted both in detail. It was of particular interest that I had now been involved in two fatal accidents on the Alps. I began to separate from my name as I saw Grace Farringdon became a heroic, tragic character, pictured in all her garb with the mountains behind her – rather striking and beautiful, I might say – and I stayed mostly indoors. It took weeks to locate Cicely Parr's body. They found her in the shadow of a rock, badly ripped and torn, a doll thrown from a window. Her skull was smashed to pieces.

The inquest declared her death an accident. There was no evidence to suggest otherwise. But rumours crept about the place as rumours will. Anonymous members of the Alpine Club and Ladies' Alpine Club suggested that perhaps there was more to this business than I had claimed. The rumour must have originated with Heinrich, who had been declaring his love for the enigmatic Cicely Parr in bars and hotels throughout Switzerland.

Then Parr's maid found a diary in which our arguments were detailed: Parr's inaccurate journal article, the deaths of Locke and Frank and my fragile state of mind, the silly incident with the ice axe, even her resentment towards Locke and me when we were foolish students and she knew that we laughed behind her back. It was published in some low-level newspaper.

> *I am in love with Heinrich. He is the person I have*
> *always been searching for but never realized it. I have*
> *felt so solitary all my life – but no longer! He will see*
> *me reach the summit first. I shall show him.*

Letters came, called me a self-serving mad mountaineer, a coward and a murderer. I burned the lot, shut the curtains and stayed indoors. I wrote to Heinrich. *Please speak up and defend my innocence or make a public accusation that I can answer.* I heard that he was rather vocal around Zermatt. He had been watching through his binoculars and, although he could not be sure, there was certainly physical contact between Parr and me just before she fell. Anyone from the various mountaineering clubs of Europe would have understood his insinuations. I kicked my mountaineering equipment into the cellar, bolted the trapdoor. Catherine had married and moved out. She and George were living above his surgery, preparing for his retirement and their move to Edinburgh.

Then one day I let a man into the house. I thought he

wanted to rent a room and I told him too much about myself. He was a reporter, of course, and all of it – my father, my sister with her piano and her dolls, even our unfortunate neighbour Margaret Mott, though she had nothing to do with anything – came out of me and went into print. Dr Sowerby could not bear the scandal, or my influence on Catherine, so retired early and took Catherine straight to Scotland. Their parting gift to me was money.

'This will pay for Mabel to come for as long as you want her. I know she'll look after you. Keep the house, Grace. It's yours to sell or keep. I don't want to know how Parr died. If you did kill her, I can't say that I would blame you, but it's very difficult for George.'

'Catherine—'

'He feels some guilt because he had the opportunity to get treatment for you all those years ago. He thinks he should have insisted when you came back. He's very sorry.'

She put on her hat, fixed a pin firmly into the side, and left. The front door gave a whisper of a sigh as it shut and I lay on the floor with a cushion over my head for the rest of the day.

I am very drowsy. Why did Catherine cut herself off from me because of an accident? Of all people, she should have stayed. It must have been something else, but what? Even allowing for George and his pig-headed stupidity, she has been cruel.

*

I am near the summit and can see it. One mitten has come off and I have lost it. My hand is numb, fingers bent like talons. I stagger and slide over rocks and ice, sometimes turning on my ankle, catching my foot between stones, falling flat onto my hands. The pain sears my skin. I must find help.

We left the hut, lit the lantern and set off along the Hörnli ridge. The peak glistened with crisp snow and the air smelled of pine and salt and the dirty, fertile scent of night. We did not speak until we reached the point where the mountain curves upwards and the climb steepens. Then we talked about our previous trip, Locke, Hooper and the accident. I asked Parr whether or not she ever felt guilty.

Parr seemed surprised. 'Do you imagine that, after losing my own parents in a mountaineering accident, I would have put our lives at risk?'

'But we were too hard on her.'

'What else could we have done? We were on our descent. If we had stopped for long, she would have got frostbite. I never understood why Locke became so angry with me.'

I nodded. 'You didn't use a rope. You had it but you took it off – or never put it on – and then Hooper fell.'

Parr said nothing for some time. We climbed over rocks and more rocks, some of which were rotten and crumbled to the touch, sent stone showers down the slope. 'I chose not to use the rope.'

'It might have saved her.'

'Or killed us both.'

'I understand that what happened to your parents –'

' – had nothing to do with my decision.'

I did not like Parr's tone, kept my own voice steady. 'You were stronger and a more experienced mountaineer. Or what is the point of carrying ropes?'

'Some people want to fail. Ropes are a safeguard but when a person wants to fail – even if he doesn't realize it – he is bound to fail whatever you do.'

'I don't understand you.'

'Hooper saw herself as a sweet, harmless girl and she delighted in being weak. She always said that she didn't want to come with us and then insisted on coming. I expected her to change, but she never did. We always had to stop for her, the little child. By the time we were coming down, I couldn't stand it.'

'She had mountain sickness. It was real.' I saw Hooper on her knees vomiting into the snow. 'But you weren't prepared to take any kind of risk.'

'She just set off, stumbling along, without waiting for me to uncoil the rope. I could have stopped her but I just thought, if she is going to be so stupid and expect me to take responsibility, let her see what will happen. I wanted to make her fend for herself. I didn't really expect her to fall, but I must say,' muttered Parr, 'I wasn't altogether unsatisfied when she did.'

And out there, in the blue sky above the Breithorn, Hooper's spirit roamed, lonely, wronged and unavenged.

'As you like, Parr.'

We climbed further and higher, moving to steep, rocky ground, using our hands, feet, knees as we went. The sky was clear and other peaks began to seem smaller as new mountains rose in the far distance.

Parr reached high for a hold in the rock. She shrieked as part of it gave way and pulled more rocks with it. They tumbled towards us, bigger than cricket balls. I ducked but one struck me above the eye and bounced off. We threw ourselves into the snow and put our hands over our heads until the torrent subsided.

Parr hauled herself to her feet. 'Someone is angry with us.'

Yes. Hooper was angry. Locke was angry. I touched my face with my unmittened hand. I was bleeding.

'Farringdon, you'll not mind if I'm the first on the summit.'

First on the summit. She had brought me to the mountains as a student and I would be for ever in her debt. I had not thought of getting there first or, for that matter, second. The point was that we were making the first manless, guideless ascent together. No, for me the point was not even that. *I* was climbing the mountain and it was my first ascent of the Matterhorn no matter how we made it, but how dare she assume the right to be first? Locke had used words to describe Parr – callous, treacherous – and I had always denied it. I had insisted, again and again, that there was more to Parr, but Locke was right. Parr did not care. There was nothing more to her at all. The mystery of Parr was quite the opposite.

There was something missing. She had no conscience, no heart.

'Perhaps I do mind.' I put my handkerchief to my forehead and blood soaked through to my fingers. The wound pulsed and ached.

'We might get there together but the first foot must be mine. Don't pull too tight. I'm going to do this quickly. What's wrong? It's just a bash on the forehead. You're not upset about Hooper again, are you? Teddy might have died in the war and left her a miserable widow, for all we know. I let her fall. So what?'

When asked to give evidence, Heinrich said that he saw us both through his binoculars, working up quickly and with ease. Then we stopped for some reason and Parr – Heinrich could not believe that this had happened – just tumbled off. In the controversy that followed, there was a suggestion that I had cut the rope and pushed Parr out of the way so that I might reach the summit alone and claim the first female solo ascent. An insulting, outrageous accusation. I don't know what happened to the rope. It must have been cut by rocks. I never reached the summit. I never did. Parr fell and, once it had happened, I turned back. I never reached my own Pole. I was very close – oh, *so* close indeed – and I could have done it but I did not. I went for help instead.

*

Peter stands over me with the brandy bottle, tops up my glass, pours another for himself.

'I thought you were working, Peter. You made me jump.'

I swish the brandy very slowly around the bottom of the glass. It glows and sends filaments of heat up to my eyes. It is beautiful.

'So did you push Cicely Parr?' Peter steps back, sits down with his drink, stretches out his legs and crosses one ankle over the other. 'You can tell me the truth.'

'Goodness, it was a long time ago.'

'People think you did.'

'I don't believe the truth will ever be known.'

'But you must know.'

'For which publication are you writing, Peter?'

'I'm writing a book.' He leans back, rests his elbows on the chair arms, then enunciates carefully, '*Bodies in the Ice: Mysterious Mountain Deaths*. It all began with a tragedy, you see. A friend of mine disappeared into mist on the Jungfrau and never came back but, though we searched for days, we couldn't find his body. I decided to write about it and, when I mentioned this to the mountain guides, they came and told me every manner of story. You know, broken ropes, ghosts, wild animals and chewed-up bodies. Some true, some clearly invented, and others where one really could not be sure.'

'Oh dear.'

'More and more I found myself thinking of Cicely Parr. Miss Farringdon, I cannot leave here without knowing the truth.'

'Do you know the mountain guides in Zermatt?'

Peter pauses, smiles. 'I knew some of them, when I worked there. It's a small place.'

'Heinrich. Is he still alive?'

'Yes, still guiding people up and over the Matterhorn. He has climbed it some hundreds of times now.'

'He must have courage.'

'He knows nothing else. All he can do is climb the Matterhorn, and sometimes the other peaks nearby. It would take courage for him to get on a train and spend a day or two in Geneva. I have interviewed him, of course.'

I recall the attitude of the newspapers.

'What annoyed me –' I wag my finger at him – 'was the suggestion that I kept going, even after she fell. I could have got to the summit if I'd wanted to by then, but I didn't. I really didn't. And Heinrich saw through his binoculars that I didn't. He never spoke up for me.'

'A couple of women did reach the summit without any men or guides a few years ago. 1932, I think.'

'It took that long? And the South Pole? Have they got there?'

'None, that I know of.'

'Ah, well it won't be me now.'

'My commiserations. Let's return to Cicely Parr. Heinrich didn't see how she could have fallen so far from the position she was in. Even if she had slipped, she would have landed just a foot or two below but she did not. She swung right out before falling down.'

I agreed. 'To have gone right off the edge like that, she must have been pushed.'

'But nobody else was there.'

'No.'

'You were the first climbers up that morning.'

'That's the funny thing.' I sip my brandy.

'Who pushed her?'

'Not I. I've always thought it was Locke or Hooper. It could have been both.'

'They were dead.'

'Yes, that's why they did it, you see.' It is confusing to me as well but I can't find a way to explain. 'All I can say is that I never felt like a murderer.'

'And yet a murderer is what I think you are.' There are tears in his eyes. He does not want this to be true.

I shake my head. 'No.'

He scrawls words and words into his little notebook, blinking and grimacing. When the page is full, he looks at me.

'I have to write the truth.'

'Write what you want. It's your book. Now that I look at you clearly, I'm not even sure that you're the hotel boy. I think you fooled me. Well, you have no evidence for anything I'm saying, not that I would bother to sue you.'

'I shall take that risk.'

I wake again and he has gone. It takes me a few seconds to decide that he must have been a dream, some projection from my own mind, a few seconds more to see that he was not. There are two glasses on the table, a radium glow of brandy at the bottom of each. Is it possible that I poured myself two glasses of brandy? There are my neat piles of photographs and letters, nothing of his. Even if he was real, was he the boy from the Monte Rosa Hotel or some London hack putting on a German accent to fool me into talking? Tucked beneath one glass is a yellowing postcard and I don't think it is mine. There is a picture of a pretty mountain chalet. On the back it says, *White Mountain Hotel, Chamonix* and gives an address. There is no message.

It is an invitation, perhaps, but I shall never return to the Alps.

Parr is still in Zermatt, in the cold earth of the cemetery, one notch in the rows of fallen mountaineers.

CICELY PARR

AUGUST 3RD 1923

PASSED INTO FULLER LIFE
FROM THE MATTERHORN
AT DAWN

It is enough.

Chapter Twenty-Nine

'Miss Farringdon, your post.' Mabel pushes the letter under my nose. She pads away to the scullery and I hear the sink filling up for washing. Three days have passed and I have had no contact from Peter or from Catherine.

'Is this all?' A couple of bills and an invitation to a neighbour's music evening. I put them in the fire. 'Is there nothing from Catherine?'

'It could be her mind has gone. She was already a bit that way.'

'Yes, yes.'

And. But. I want to see her but am rejected. It hurts in my chest. I am quite winded. I sit for a while, watch the sparrows peck at the crumbs in the garden. Catherine is not coming. She has had my letter by now but she is not coming. I am here alone and she will not come. Mabel sloshes and splashes for half an hour or more. When she has finished with the washing, she is off to the shops and still I cannot move.

Voices curl in from the street, two women – Mabel is one of them – making a sweet, excited music. Mrs Tickell,

I expect, has a new recipe for coconut rocks or has found a piece of lace that matches her bonnet perfectly and the world is overjoyed.

'Miss Farringdon, you have visitors.'

'Tell them to go away.'

'Come and see.'

Catherine is on the doorstep. It is Catherine as a girl of about fifteen, auburn hair pulled back into a wiry plait, swaying shyly in a Girl Guide uniform. She smiles. How strange. I grab the door frame and stare at this creature. And there's an older woman behind her. I am confused for a moment and then everything switches around and I see clearly. Catherine is inside the body of the older woman, snugly covered by layers of fat and skin. The girl is an entirely new person, a daughter, I presume. Catherine's face is weighed down by plump cheeks that hang over the edge of her jaw bone like icing sliding off a cake. Seams of grey run through her neatly set hair. She wears a cream pullover and a tweed skirt, brown lace-up shoes. She smiles, nervously, as though she is a little afraid of me. A muscle beneath her right eye twitches.

'We got your letter,' she says. 'You haven't changed.'

'Neither have you.'

'Well.' We laugh and embrace.

The girl is squinting up at me from under her hair, as though she knows it's not polite to stare but can't help it.

'Georgina, this is your Aunt Grace.'

I shake the girl's hand. 'Hello, Georgina.'

'How d'you do.' The girl seems less like Catherine now

that they are both properly in focus. She has a summer's dusting of freckles over an upturned nose. She is a sweet, pretty piglet of a girl.

'I never knew,' I say to Catherine. I'm not sure if it's an accusation or an apology. I want to laugh. Something good came out of Dr Sowerby.

'The mountain business. Cicely Parr. George thought it best. We both did. But when I got your letter I realized that I'd made a terrible mistake.' She touches her hair, pulls a strand of it over her ear and tugs nervously. 'And here we are.'

I nod. Catherine's face is wet with tears, and mine is too.

'We're at a hotel in town, just for a couple of days.' She sniffs, laughs at herself. 'I wasn't sure if you had a telephone—'

'I don't. You must come in. I've – I've had the piano tuned.'

Catherine shakes her head, puts up a hand. 'I won't go in that house again, thank you, but we'd love you to come to our hotel for lunch. We have tickets for a concert at the Royal Albert Hall this evening, if you'd like to join us. I bought one extra, just in case, but you don't have to decide now . . .' Her voice trails.

'Thank you. Catherine – ?'

'Yes?'

'I did kill Cicely Parr, you know.'

Peter will be typing, slowly, in a room in his hotel in Chamonix. The truth is out, and I do not care. I will stay in touch with him, whatever he chooses to write. He is my only connection to the Alps now and that is something strong, enough to last until one of us dies.

Catherine squints up at the sky, shields her eyes with her hand.

'I'm sure you had your reasons. Isn't it a pleasant day? Georgie loves London, don't you, Georgie?'

We both look to the place where Georgie was standing but she is not there. No, of course she is not. I would have known if Catherine had a daughter. Georgie cannot be, but Catherine is here at least.

'Catherine. Will you stay in London?'

'Oh, no.' She frowns at me. 'I live in Edinburgh. I wouldn't dream of staying here.'

And she has gone too. I am in my chair once again. I have been almost asleep, half-dreaming, I think, and yet they seemed real to me just now, Catherine and her funny daughter.

'Mabel? Are you out there?'

She calls from the hall. 'What is it?'

'Who was here just now?'

Mabel bustles into the room, half-in and half-out of her coat.

'Nobody that I saw. I was just talking to the Tickells and then I brought the shopping in. I've got my WI meeting now but I'll be back later to do your tea.'

She gets both sleeves on and tugs the coat across her chest.

'Mabel, does Catherine have a daughter? You would have heard from your sister, wouldn't you?'

Her lips press together, turn down at the corners. 'I never heard of any daughter.'

'You don't think that Catherine might be dead?'

The question surprises her. 'Goodness. Well, I think they ought to have told you if she was.'

I nod. 'That's true.'

'What are you thinking, Miss Farringdon?'

'Mabel, I want you to go down into the cellar and find my old mountain boots, my ropes. Bring them upstairs. My axe. I want that first.'

'You are not being sensible. What would you want with an axe?'

'I want to see it again. I need to grip it for a while, have it in my hands. I need it now.'

Mabel shakes her head, puts up a hand as though to stop me jumping at her when, in fact, I am sitting here calm as can be.

'It's my afternoon off. I'll have a look this evening, if you're still in this funny mood. Or you could go down there yourself.' She tosses the suggestion over her shoulder, leaves.

'Yes, Mabel. You are quite right. I shall go down there myself.' She is setting me a test, I'm sure.

Chapter Thirty

The light bulb still works. There's a smell of old books and tea chests and a tang of damp dog. Spiders have made a mesh of the ceiling and blurred the walls almost out of existence. All those years ago I locked the trapdoor, buried my things in the cold vault. I stole away and curled up in my den. There is the axe. It really is, the new one that I bought. It leans against the wall, furry with dust, heavy, but – yes – its edge is still sharp. I could cut a good step or two with this. And there, my beautiful boots, and my compass. My insides loosen as my old friends crowd into the room with me. I sit on the stool, pull on the boots. I sneeze three times and cough. The boots are big but with thick socks they'll be right. They need a good clean. Here in the drawer is Shackleton's glove. It's in fine condition, even if he is long buried in South Georgia. I'll take it too.

Shackleton wrote of the fourth presence, some invisible force or being that followed him on his long march with Worsley and Crean across mountain and glacier in South Georgia to rescue at the whaling station. I once imagined that it was Hooper's spirit, following them, continuing the Society's work. She became our fourth presence, after all. Then it seemed to be me, the ghost, the last of the four. Now I think that it was all of us, all who once dreamed it and knew that we must be there too, in some important but un-physical way.

An old blanket catches my eye from the chest in the corner, a pouch of grey and black bulging from under the lid. I drag it to me and drape it over my knees, hold my breath until the dust settles. My sister is not coming.

Hours have passed and I am shivering. I could sit down here until I freeze, let frost be my skin and let icicles hang from my chin, let glaciers creep through London and crush my house. It is how I have lived these fifteen years. I could pull down the trapdoor and wait.

I rub the frayed edge of the blanket. I don't think it belongs to me. I think it might have been Parr's and I must have carried it home. But the blanket makes me remember a night on a mountain, when I fell and thought that I was dying, a night so cold it seemed to burn.

And I survived it.

I stand, take a step in my old boots, and then another. I lean on my axe. I can smell fresh snow. Catherine may be dead or alive but I won't find out by staying here. I shall go to Edinburgh. Then, with my sister or alone, I'll head for the Highlands and climb. One day, after that, I shall think about Peter and the hotel near Chamonix. It is all fresh, uncharted territory.

Mind your boots, said somebody who liked to give

advice, and keep them well greased. I am for the mountains again.

Slowly up the mucky steps to the hall, I leave the chill of the cellar. It is warm up here. I spit on the compass, rub it over my cardigan sleeve, get myself pointing north. Here is the way to my sister and the future. Mabel has gone to her meeting, Miss Cankleton is at the post office and Mr Blunt is at the bank. I have the house to myself. I leave my things at the front door, keeping the boots on, and enter the drawing room.

There is something I must do before I leave.

I light a fire of all my papers and photographs, just in front of the hearth on the carpet. They catch quickly and make a cheerful blaze. With the fire tongs, I spread the burning items around the room and on the mantelpiece.

They will not be enough so I reach for a scrolled map that is burning at one end and I make it my torch. It may be the Antarctic for all I know, or the whole of Europe. I hold it high above my head as I clamber over the settee to the window, jump to the floor. These legs have spring in them still. I catch the bottom of the curtains with my flame. I fall to my knees, coughing. I am shivering with heat and sweating with cold.

Whips of black and yellow flay the window pane. The pelmet tilts, crashes to the floor. It lights the rug, crackles and spits. I push the globe into the burning silks and wood so that the whole world may be ablaze, and I rise to my feet.

Great God, this is an awful place indeed. I back into the doorway, gaze through dark smoke to the portrait over the mantelpiece, but I can no longer see his face. Soon the frame will start to burn. Goodbye, Father. I am going out. I may be some . . . No.

I shall not return.

Acknowledgements

Thanks to Bill Hamilton at A. M. Heath, Maria Rejt, Sophie Orme and all at Mantle; to Veena, Phil and Ingrid Hudson, Sean Benz, Judy Jones and Madeleine Cary. Thanks also to my family and friends, especially Esther, Ben and Dan Jones, Ian Robertson, Selena Class and Helen Grime. I am grateful to the staff at the Royal Holloway University of London archives, the Alpine Club archives and the Royal Geographical Society Library.

I am indebted to various works of non-fiction. These include: Mrs Aubrey LeBlond, *Adventures on the Roof of the World* (Unwin, 1904); David Mazel (ed.), *Mountaineering Women: Stories by Early Climbers* (Texas A&M University Free Press, 1994); Claire Eliane Engel, *A History of Mountaineering in the Alps* (Unwin, 1948); Frank Smythe, *The Adventures of a Mountaineer* (Dent, 1940); Sir William Martin Conway, *The Alps from End to End* (Nelson, 1921); Cicely Williams, *Women on the Rope: The Feminine Share in Mountain Adventure* (Allen & Unwin, 1973); Mike C. Parsons and Mary B. Rose, *Invisible on Everest: Innovation and the Gear Makers* (Northern Liberties Press, 2003).

picador.com

blog
videos
interviews
extracts